SIPS ABOUT TO GO DOWN

AUDREY VAUGHN

Book Cover by Mayhem Cover Creations

Created with Vellum

CHAPTER ONE

ROSE

I started my day getting chased out of my parents' tiny rental property by a raccoon, wearing nothing but a satin bonnet, a big t-shirt, and panties so matronly that my grandmother would judge me for it.

I'd say the day can't get any worse, but I'm already on a Slip N' Slide to rock bottom. My ex already dumped me and wrecked my career, forcing me to move back to my small hometown. I'm not going to tempt fate by being too hopeful.

"Just ask Mr. Stryker if Waylon's spare room is still available for rent," my dad says as we pull up in front of the Copper Moon, the bar where I'll be meeting with my new bosses. "If not, we'll sort it out, okay? Maybe you could stay on the air mattress while Natasha takes the couch."

My cousin, Natasha, is staying on my parents' couch so she can easily commute to summer classes at Crescent Hill University, which is thirty minutes away from town. As much as I love her, living inches away from her for months would drive us insane.

But I don't want to shoot Dad down, so I just nod.

"Okay," I say. "Maybe the commute to work will be even better from Waylon's spare room."

"Maybe." Dad shrugs. "That would make the job even better, wouldn't it?"

Fine, I'll tempt fate a little – I'm thankful my dad was able to hook me up with a job after my life went sideways. He's a sales executive for Stryker Liquors, the biggest employer in our town, Jepsen, Tennessee, so he put in a good word for me for this gig with the company.

And I hope this room he heard about works out. Out of the four sons in the Stryker family, Waylon is the nicest. John David, the oldest, and Ash, the second oldest, were a few years ahead of me in school, so I don't know them well. But Wes, Waylon's twin?

The worst. We've been competing since we were babies — literally. He won Jepsen's annual baby pageant and I came in second. In kindergarten, I won the grade-wide art competition and he got second. Science fairs, grades, art classes? All chances for him to try to one-up me, and I can't back down. I just can't.

Because if he wins, he runs his mouth and gives me a smug little smirk, his ink-dark eyes twinkling. And that drives me insane every single time. Throw in the fact that he can get away with pretty much all the BS he gets into because of his family name...

My patience with life is about as thin as a line of atoms, and living with Wes Stryker would be the thing that finally breaks me.

"I'll text you once I know," I say as I get out of the car.

"Good luck, Rosie," Dad says before pulling away,

leaving me standing outside of the bar, which the Stryker family also owns.

The Copper Moon has been around for twenty or so years, but I never set foot inside. It's a far cry from the bourgie bars where I made craft cocktails back in Brooklyn. Not that it's run-down or anything — it's just more rustic. It has huge windows, revealing a wood floor, wood-paneling on the walls, and a bunch of old photos and knickknacks decorating floating shelves. I take a deep breath and step inside.

I spot my new bosses, John David and Mr. Stryker — also named John David, but Mr. Stryker is the kind of guy who needs to be called Mr. Stryker — at the end of the bar. John David stands and nods in my direction. He's always been serious, but in the nearly ten years since I've been gone, he's become a little intimidating. Tall, broad, and bearded.

"Rose." Mr. Stryker nods at me in an eerie echo of his son. His full head of black hair has gone silver, and he's just as intimidating as I remember from the brief moments we've interacted in the past.

"Hi." I smile. A chunky chocolate lab lifts his head from under the table and wags his tail when he spots me. Even in my frazzled state, I can't help but smile. "Oh, cute. Hi, buddy."

"That's Big Bubba," John David says.

"Like the bourbon," I say, reaching down to pet him. Big Bubba Bourbon is one of the sub-brands under Stryker Liquors.

"Right. He's the brand ambassador," Mr. Stryker says, dead serious. I know labradors are supposed to be smart, but Big Bubba looks like he hasn't had a coherent thought in his life, much less have the brain power to be a brand ambassador. "Do you like bourbon?"

"I do." I've never had Big Bubba Bourbon, but Stryker Moonshine, their flagship product, has a good reputation. I'm sure the bourbon is decent.

"Good." Mr. Stryker sits back in his seat and checks his phone, frowning even deeper. John David does as well, but he excuses himself and steps away. "But anyway, thank you for coming and accepting the job. We've needed someone with your expertise, so your father's recommendation came at just the right time."

"Thank you for hiring me." I resist the urge to smile when Bubba rests his head on my foot. "I'm excited to hear about the role."

All I was told was that Stryker Liquors needs someone for their drink development and marketing, two things that are the perfect next steps in my career. I want to develop cocktails for high-end bars and eventually create my own brand. Sure, it's not the cocktail-focused TV show I was supposed to be on with my ex, Erik, but it's a path toward my goals. A slower one, but still, I'm going somewhere.

"We'll be able to get started in a second. Still waiting on someone," Mr. Stryker says with a heavy sigh.

"Of course," I say. "Actually, while we wait, can I ask something?"

"Go ahead."

"I was supposed to move into my parents' guest house, but unfortunately there's been some damage to it and I can't move in." A total understatement – a racoon Kool-Aid Man'd through the wall when I was half-asleep and wrecked the place. "My dad mentioned that Waylon had a room for rent.

I wouldn't normally ask, but they downsized after I moved out and my cousin is staying on the couch."

"Oh, Waylon doesn't. Wes does." His brows somehow furrow even more. "But it's a duplex, so Waylon lives on the other side."

Fuck. "Oh."

"But it would be perfect since you two will be working together in here." He drums his fingers on the table. "And the rent is cheap."

"I'll be working with Wes?" I can't keep the horror out of my voice.

So I *did* tempt fate. Living with Wes Stryker is my idea of a nightmare, but what else am I supposed to do? Live in the messed up tiny home with busted pipes, a huge hole in the wall, and something inside that's a magnet for raccoons?

"That a problem?" Mr. Stryker asks, an eyebrow lifting.

"No!" Oh god, *yes*, but I can't be prissy about this. "I'm just surprised. I didn't know that he worked in this division of the company."

"He's the assistant manager of the bar and he's decent at making cocktails," he says. What a ringing endorsement. "He pitched the idea. To be perfectly honest, we hired you on because Wes isn't exactly known for his follow-through. We need a steadying force to keep us organized. He doesn't know I've brought you on yet."

Well, shit. Does he know about our competitive dynamic? Wes can follow through, especially if it's something that'll drive me to the edge of my sanity. But I *need* this job and the room. Knowing Erik, he dragged my name through the mud in our circles back in New York, so this is my best shot at kickstarting my career in the direction I need it to go in again.

I can't be picky. I'm an adult. I worked with Erik's pretentious ass friends without snapping, so I can handle Wes Stryker.

I think.

"Okay, that sounds good." My forced smile will probably make me look like a crazy person, so I just fold my hands in my lap.

Mr. Stryker glances at the door. "Wes isn't the most reliable, as you can see by his lateness."

Yikes. Mr. Stryker isn't a nice guy, but dumping on his son feels like a bit much. I don't know what to say to this. The silence is killing me though, so I clear my throat.

"I'm sure we'll figure out a way to work together well regardless," I finally say.

"Good, because the business needs this," he says, leveling me with a gaze so serious that my throat clenches with anxiety. "We need to diversify our revenue streams and bounce back from several down quarters."

So a huge project is sitting on the shoulders of me and the one guy who drives me insane. Great.

Moments later, the door swings open and a sweet, dopey-looking Pitbull mix comes trotting in, followed by John David, then Wes.

The friends I have who are still in town aren't close with Wes, so I haven't even seen him in an Instagram photo. Back in high school he had girls all over him, and seeing him now, I doubt that's changed. His body has evolved from lanky teenage boy into delicious, built man — muscular, but not too bulky, with shoulders that make me physically angry at their perfection and aroused in equal measure.

His dark, loosely curly hair is tousled just right, and his stubble makes him look like he rolled out of bed and just happened to look this perfect.

The fact that I still feel a pulse of attraction to him even though he drives me absolutely insane is a testament to just how good looking he is. If someone erased our past and I met him, I'd definitely flirt with him. The way he carries himself has big-dick-and-knows-how-to-use-it energy, which unfortunately I'm drawn to like a moth to a flame.

Yeah, I've thought about what it would be like to sleep with him once or twice (or okay, three or more times). Someone would have to torture that information out of me, though.

At least he gives me that crooked smile of his that never fails to annoy me — the impish one that screams trouble – and I snap out of it.

"Look who's back in Jepsen," Wes says to me, that smile growing.

"Hi, Wes," I say, forcing as much cheer into my voice as I possibly can. I know I've failed at sounding normal – his grin just widens like he's caught me.

"Hey." He slides into the seat across from me. His legs are so long that his knees brush mine.

Mr. Stryker checks his phone before answering it. John David's dark eyebrows go up in question, his hand resting on the back of his seat.

"Excuse us for a moment," Mr. Stryker says, motioning for John David to follow him. "Get reacquainted while we handle some business."

I wait for Mr. Stryker and JD to get out of earshot before I drop the stiff fake smile on my face and sigh. Wes laughs – actually *laughs* – at me.

"Was your face hurting from smiling at me for half a second?" he asks, his smile lingering on his face.

"Yep."

"I never thought you'd show up here again, smiling or not," he says, resting his muscled forearms on the table.

"Things change," I say. Wes's dog sniffs my knee and I pet his blocky head. "Is that a problem?"

"Nope, just surprised." He holds his hands up. "It's been ten seconds — you can put the claws away."

"You think my claws are out already?" This time I genuinely smile. "You've gotten soft if you think they are. I've basically only glared at you."

"Nah, I figured *you'd* softened in the past ten years, especially if you decided to grace Jepsen with your presence."

That jab connects and my smile falters. I swore up and down in high school that I wasn't going to be one of those people who stuck around in Jepsen. Now I'm back here, a hot mess.

But then I remember he has no idea we have to work together. My grin returns. He's going to be shocked and annoyed.

"What's that smile for?" Wes asks, raising an eyebrow.

"Oh, nothing," I say, all innocence.

Before Wes can needle me about it more, Mr. Stryker and JD return.

"Y'all got reacquainted?" Mr. Stryker asks, grunting as he eases himself into his chair.

"Yes, we did," I say, putting on my polite mask again.

"Pretty much," Wes adds.

"Good. Rose is your new partner for the drink project," Mr. Stryker says, like he's just telling him the weather.

The smirk melts right off Wes's face and is quickly replaced with the same horror I felt when I heard the news. His expression almost makes up for the fact that we're stuck together for however long this'll take.

Almost.

CHAPTER TWO

WES

"Wait, *what?*" I blurt. "Partner for what?"

Dad looks at me like I've just spoken Portuguese. "For what I just said. For that drink project that you've been harpin' on."

I sit back in my seat and try to get my expression to stay neutral despite the irritation pushing against my lungs. I started working at the bar six years ago, and for the past three or four years, I've been trying to move up past assistant manager.

But even though John David is now Dad's right-hand man, he refuses to step down as manager. Does it matter that I do all the shit the manager is supposed to do? No. They can't see that I'm not a dumbass twenty-year-old anymore. John David swoops in every once in a while like an asshole, then disappears back to the office.

So, a month ago, I pitched an idea for a canned moonshine mixed drink since liquor sales were down. If I can't be manager for no fucking reason, I can try to get out of the assistant manager pit another way. When Dad said he'd entertain the idea in a meeting today, I thought I'd have to convince him. Not that he was down with the idea and had already brought Rose in to be my partner.

But of course, he'd only say yes if someone else was on board. I was dumb as hell if I thought he'd trust me with something like this. Dad's probably half the reason why JD is still manager. The idea of handing the bar over to me entirely — a bar that brings in a shitton of money we need — is probably unbearable to him.

Then again, it's not like I've done anything big enough to make up for all the hell I put my family through. Especially after the incident that led to me dropping out of college.

My eyes flick to Rose again and I find her staring back at me.

In high school, I thought Rose was pretty cute, at least as far as girls who found me as irritating as a gnat went. But now she's undeniably hot. She's grown into herself a bit, her curves a little softer and thicker in a way that I'm already fond of. Her delicate features are more mature too, her rich brown skin glowing even in the shitty lights of the bar. A little golden hoop is in her nose, and her hair is in braids that are so long they pool in her lap.

But those eyes. They haven't changed a bit — they're dark, framed by equally dark lashes, and so damn observant. My stomach does a weird flip-flop, up into my chest, then back to where it's supposed to be. How long has it been since a woman's looked at me like this? Like she can see straight through me and she doesn't care that I know she's doing it?

No one has, except for her.

I have no idea what she got up to after graduation to

warrant her being here. She was insistent on leaving Jepsen for New York City and never wanted to move back. But after that, I don't really know. I have Instagram but I check it maybe once or twice a year. And to be honest, she probably wouldn't follow me, even if a lot of our graduating class did.

But now she's here. So obviously she knows something about the liquor business. Marketing, maybe? But why would she do that in Jepsen when she was living in New York?

"Let's get to the specifics," John David says, sitting down, his posture ramrod straight. "We'd like you both to work on developing moonshine cocktails that can be canned and sold in stores. We're losing our market share and canned cocktails are an area we aren't in at the moment. They need to be approachable enough for people who don't know that moonshine doesn't make you blind if it's made properly, but interesting enough to attract people who are into the brand already."

"So average people and booze snobs?" I ask.

John David's eye twitches. "Craft liquor enthusiasts."

"Same deal." I take one end of the rope toy my dog Murphy offers to me and hang on while he yanks it. Big Bubba's getting up in age, so he's already done with Murphy's young dog nonsense. "So, we just make up some cocktails and can it?"

"It needs to be more intentional than that." John David pulls his tablet out of his bag. "Market research on flavors, testing, serving an uncanned version at the bar, events, regional competitions to get opinions. Even more formal testing. Things like that."

Have I done any of this stuff before? Outside of a

marketing class I half paid attention to in my two years of college, nope. Will that stop me from trying to one-up Rose? Nope. If anything, it'll make me fight even harder to win.

"And you'll have to do the social media stuff," Dad adds. "Instagram and the TikTok stuff. Track the process, go to a few distillery events, things like that."

Another thing I don't know how to do, but could figure out. Dad and JD aren't exactly internet savvy enough to call me on it — they just know whether something makes money or not.

"So how many drinks will we need to make?" Rose asks, pulling out a notebook from her bag. I rarely take notes, but I know Dad is probably pleased that she's writing this down.

"We'd like to release the most popular drinks from the bar — the moonshine margarita and moonshine sweet tea lemonade," John David says. I know both drinks like the back of my hand. "But we'd also like two more to round it out."

Rose makes a few notes, her handwriting tidy and feminine. "So is one of us the lead on this, or...?"

"What do you mean by that?" I ask.

"I mean will one of us get the credit for it? Will one of us lead and the other executes?" she asks, her pen in the air.

"Or will one of us be the winner, you mean," I fill in for her. By the twitch of her mouth, I know I've hit the target.

"We weren't thinking of it in those terms," John David says, his eyes flicking between us. He's not the best at sussing out emotions, so I doubt he'll pick up on anything.

"Or do you want a competition?" Dad asks. Dad, on the other hand, is a heat-seeking missile for any weaknesses or vulnerabilities, and he catches on fast. "Because if you want a competition, I can sweeten the deal."

"In what way?" I ask.

Dad sits back, crossing his arms over his chest and assessing us. It's the same pose he got into when he was deciding my (many) punishments as a kid. I half-expect him to tell me I'm grounded.

"For one drink, I want you both to work together — fifty-fifty. And the drink has to pass our standards," Dad says. "And no passing it off as a joint project if only one of you came up with the entire concept."

Both Rose and I snort. The likeliness of us doing that is about zero.

"As for the other drink, both of you will present a few ideas to some potential buyers, some regulars at the bar, people like that. Then lastly, to us. The one that gets the best response is the one we'll take to market."

"Are you sure this is a good idea?" John David asks, frowning. "We just need this done, no extra BS."

"I think this is the way." Dad looks between the two of us again, slowly nodding like his own idea is finally hitting him. "What's wrong with a little competition to get the best out of someone? And why not sweeten the deal with a five grand bonus to whoever wins?"

Five grand? That could go a long way. On what? I don't know. But from the gleam in Rose's eye, I just know I want it more than she does.

John David's eyebrows shoot up, and he and Dad exchange a look.

"You're sure? Five grand?" John David finally asks.

"I'm sure."

John David eyes me, then Dad, an inscrutable look on his face.

"Fine." John David shrugs. "Two drink ideas at the end of the day. One joint. One individual. One winner."

"And a tight deadline — we want the final idea done in three months," Dad adds. "So no dicking around."

"No dicking around," Rose echoes, scribbling something in her notebook. I nearly make a smart ass remark about her needing to write that down to remember, but I hold myself back.

"I'll email both of you with a few details you'll have to keep in mind — ABVs, raw materials costs, things like that," John David says, picking up his phone. "You'll need to consider everything. And there's a lot to consider."

My stomach twists in knots, but there's a flutter of excitement too. I can see how this can boost the business — every party I've been to in the past few months has had canned cocktails, and people ask for them at the bar too.

This could really change things for me, if Rose doesn't get in the way.

At least I'll only have to see her at work and not—

"Oh and Wes, Rose is taking the spare room on your side of the duplex," Dad adds, as if this isn't a huge deal.

"What the fuck?" I blurt. "Since when?"

"Since her place fell through and you two are coworkers anyway." The way JD says it tells me it's a done deal. Without even asking me.

"You can't tell me someone's moving into *my* house," I point out. "What if I had someone lined up?"

I don't — my last roommate moved out to live with his girlfriend two weeks ago and it's not like the real estate market for regular people is big in Jepsen. The only other properties are bourgie cabins up higher in the mountains. Only wealthy people or professors at Crescent Hill, the prestigious private university about forty minutes away, live in those.

And I need a roommate to pay for my part of the mortgage. Waylon, who's a thousand times more responsible than me, convinced me to go in on a down payment with the inheritance we got when our great-grandfather passed away a few years back. It's cheap as hell with a roommate, but a little pricey without one.

"I know you don't," JD says, matter of fact. And I can't exactly pull someone out of my ass who can move in.

I look at Rose, who is just as thrilled about this as I am. Living with a woman would be weird enough, but living with Rose? She's probably going to smother me in my sleep. And I'm going to have to ignore how hot she is while fighting the urge to put a spider in her bed or something.

"You sure you want to?" I ask her. "I have the dog and I have a cat."

"I like animals." She lifts a shoulder.

"The cat's an asshole." He's cute and cuddly just often enough to remind me that he isn't a being sent from hell to annoy the shit out of me.

"But Murphy's a good dog. She needs a room, and you need a roommate. You'll be working together so you can carpool," John David says. Then, he turns to Rose and adds, "And since we're short staffed at the bar, would you be open to tending bar a few nights a week?"

"Sure," Rose says readily.

Fucking hell. I'm not too worried about myself at work —

again, I'm sure I can be an adult in front of customers. But working *and* living with Rose? I don't know how that's going to go. We had a minute long conversation and she looked like she wanted to lunge across the table and strangle me.

We'll see how long she lasts. Both of us are stubborn, but I can probably hang on longer than her.

John David and Rose talk more about the project and I half-heartedly listen, trying to remember what state I left my place in. I'm not nearly as tidy as Waylon, but I'm not a total mess. Well, mostly. Usually the women I bring home go straight up to my bedroom rather than lingering.

Eventually their chatter wraps up, and Dad and John David start to leave. We walk outside together, the dogs behind us.

"Can you excuse us for a second, Rose?" John David says, putting his hand on my arm.

He pulls me around the other side of the building, and the dogs trail behind us. I steel myself for whatever he's going to jump up my ass about. He should have been a fucking teacher with the way he loves to lecture.

"You're serious about this, right?" he asks, crossing his arms over his chest.

"No, I'm just going to dick around and tank the company that pays my family's bills." I run a hand through my hair and look past him.

He sighs, shaking his head. "Wes."

"Yes, I'm serious. Really fucking serious." My words are going in one ear and out the other. I can see it in his eyes. "You can really trust me."

"You've had a whole lot of ideas." He reaches down and looks inside of one of Bubba's ears, then the other. "And none of them have come to fruition. You're excited about an idea, then it loses its sparkle and you abandon it."

I hate that he's right. I'm not saying I'm as responsible as JD or Waylon, or even Ash, but I'm much better than I used to be. Most of my teenage years were spent getting into trouble, barely getting out of it, and giving Mom gray hairs that she dutifully covers the moment her roots start to show.

Then, shit hit the fan when I was in a sophomore in college at University of Tennessee. It's still a drunken haze, but I managed to break a whole window with my ass while streaking and rightfully ended up in a holding cell. As a broke college student, I couldn't bail myself out. Calling my parents or my Nana or JD would have been a recipe for a lecture. Waylon was just as broke as I was.

So that left Ash — he was already doing his thing down in Miami and had the cash to bail me out. But instead, he said, "No, you dumb fuck. Stay there and actually learn something for once. You can't be this stupid forever," before hanging up on me.

Ash is an asshole most of the time, but he saved me in the long run. I actually tried to turn it around — being more responsible, dropping out of college to get a job because I was just messing around anyway — and I think I've changed.

Getting anyone besides Waylon to believe it feels almost impossible at this point. I *need* this to work. To have concrete evidence that I'm not a fuckup. Turns out, fairly consistent decent behavior for a few years after a lifetime of being a little shit doesn't magically change people's minds.

But telling JD this would be like opening a vein, and he has the emotional range of a bottle of lotion.

"It'll be different this time," is all I say. "Rose and I have been competing since were babies and I can't turn down a fight against her. She'll push me to do better."

JD looks at me for a few more moments. "If you pull this off, I'll promote you to manager."

"Seriously?" I blurt.

"Yes." He checks his watch. "The drink has to do well. *Your* drink. And I don't want to see any of that bullshit rivalry get in the way. Understood?"

JD's eyes narrow and he doesn't speak. All four of us brothers look alike, with the same very dark brown eyes, so looking at him is almost like looking at myself a few years in the future. I doubt I'll have the frown lines, though.

"I promise, you'll just get a product that'll sell. Can I go now? I'm guessing Rose needs a ride to see her new place."

"Yeah." He nods, as if to dismiss me.

Fucking asshole. This situation's going to test my patience, but it's worth it if I can get a little more respect.

CHAPTER THREE

ROSE

Wes comes from around the corner, annoyance written all over his face. It's not aimed at me, though. I get the usual Wes half-smirk when he looks up.

The years have been way too nice to someone who was already good-looking to start. His smirk is even more maddening with the nearly perfect dusting of stubble along his jaw.

"I guess we're roomies now," he says, spinning his keys on his finger. "Come on, let's go."

He opens the back seat for Murphy, who leaps inside. I haul myself up into his SUV and buckle in, then text my dad that I got the room. He tells me that he'll drop off my stuff at Wes's so I don't have to go back and forth.

"Alright," he says, turning the car on. It rumbles to life and he pulls out. "You hungry? Because I'm stopping to get some food."

"Sure, I can eat." I check my phone. Today feels like it's

been going on forever, so the idea of eating and passing out for a nap sounds perfect.

But now I have all of these ideas swirling in my head, so I doubt I'll be able to nap. Five thousand dollars would go a *long* way for me. I could easily use that, plus my regular pay to move anywhere I wanted, assuming I budget things correctly over the next few months and find a roommate in my new city.

There's a *lot* to do, though. Market research, planning, checking prices of ingredients, thinking of flavor profiles. It's way more than just throwing together some drinks, so we need to plan. And planning with Wes could get messy.

"We should talk about how we're going to tackle this," I say.

"Right now?" he asks, pulling his sunglasses from the holder above the rearview mirror. "We just left the meeting."

"When else are we going to talk about it?" I ask. I jump when something damp brushes my arm, but it's just Murphy's nose as he rests his blocky head on the console between us.

"Tomorrow?"

"We need to *start* tomorrow. We have so much to do."

"You need a lot of runway to get ahead of me, then?" he asks, the corner of his mouth quirking up.

I close my eyes and take a slow breath. "I'm trying to get this done well. We can cooperate at least a little. We don't need to make it a dick measuring contest at every turn."

The words slip out before I can pull them back. Of course, he grins.

"A dick measuring contest?" He laughs. "You mean —"

"*I would totally win a* dick *measuring contest,*" I say,

imitating his voice and rolling my eyes. "There, I said it for you."

"You're the one who said it." He glances over me as we glide to a stop at a sign, that infuriating grin on his face. "Good to know where your head is at."

My face burns. I'm off my game and I need to stop digging my own grave. "Where are we getting food?"

"Jay's BBQ," he says, turning left. "That cool?"

"Sure." Jay's is my favorite. One thing my ex and I had in common was our love of food (and hatred of cooking at home), so we tried plenty of restaurants. None of them hit quite as good as Jay's.

We pull up to Jay's, which looks the exact same as it did when I was here last — a small building that you'd probably drive past if you weren't paying attention, with a little slanted roof and picnic tables scattered on the opposite side of the drive through. The smell of smoked barbecue cuts through the closed windows and Murphy stands, letting out quiet *boofs*. A drop of drool falls from his mouth and onto the console.

"Relax, Murph," Wes says as he pulls into the parking lot. "Be good."

He pulls into the drive thru and rolls down the window. Murphy squeezes his face between the headrest and the window, but Wes nudges him back.

"Hey, Wes," the cute blonde girl at the window says, leaning forward. "What's up?"

"Hey." There's a smile in Wes's voice — the smile that had every girl in our grade swooning without even trying. It has the same effect on this woman. "Not much. What specials do you have today?"

"We have ribs," she says. "I can hook you up with a full rack for the price of a half rack."

"You don't have to do all that for me." Wes rests an arm on the edge of the window, leaning toward her a bit.

"You're one of my favorite customers." The girl's cheeks flush and I nearly roll my eyes before remembering that I've been this girl before. Completely starry-eyed at a smooth smile with my logical side closed for business. "I can throw in two family sized sides too."

"That sounds perfect. Thanks. What about you, Rose?" He glances at me, and the girl finally realizes I'm there. She sizes me up like I'm her competition, which is the last thing I am.

I order the pulled chicken platter, then Wes and I settle on the sides we want to share. He adds a bone for Murphy to the order, then pays for both of us. When the girl brings our food, she lets her fingers linger on Wes's.

"I'll see you around at the Copper Moon?" the girl asks, naked hope in her voice.

"Yeah, for sure," he says. "See you around."

Wes pulls the bone from the bag and gives it to Murphy, who snatches it from him and settles into the back seat to gnaw on it. He hands me the rest of food and we drive off.

"Do you always get free sides and discount ribs?" I ask, putting the food bags between my feet. I'm not sure why I asked. It doesn't seem like he was intentionally flirting with her — it just happened.

"When certain people are working, yeah." He shrugs. Must be a regular occurrence, as I suspected. "It's not like I'm intentionally flirting with them. Why?"

"Nothing."

He studies me briefly, a dimple appearing in his cheek. But he doesn't say anything else. We pull off the main road, toward the edge of town.

Since we're going away from town, I expect the drive to his house to be long. But before I know it, we're pulling down a long driveway.

The home sits in a clearing and looks like a large cabin, maybe an old lodge if I had to guess. The front has two entrances, one for Waylon and one for Wes. It's much nicer than I anticipated, cozy and warm-looking.

Wes leads me inside. Inside is...hard to describe. It's definitely a man space — the decor is lacking, but the wood beams across the ceiling and the huge floor to ceiling windows showing off the equally large fenced-in backyard do a lot to make it feel inviting. There's a lot of neatly stacked clutter around, like stacks of books and bins. Several cat trees dot the massive living room space, and a chunky orange cat is perched on a tall one next to the back window.

The kitchen is open to the right of the entrance, and Wes plucks the bag of food from my hand. For whatever reason, he puts it in a cabinet.

"C'mon, your room is upstairs," he says after kicking off his shoes.

I kick off my shoes too and follow him upstairs. He points out the bathroom, which has a nice tub/shower combo, and his room, which has the same man-space energy as the rest of the house. The chair in the corner has clothes stacked up on it, and his bed is unmade, his green blanket rumpled at the base of the bed. Several reusable water bottles dot the other surfaces, along with a few graphic novels and things I can't identify.

"This is your room," he says, going to the room directly next to it.

It's the mirror image of his room but smaller, with a full-sized bed pushed against the wall, a dresser, and a chair in the corner. The view out the window is lovely, overlooking the backyard. It's much, much nicer than I expected. Tension rolls out of my shoulders as we head back down to the kitchen.

"So, some ground rules," he says, pulling the bag of food out from the cabinet. "First, these walls are thin as fuck. If you invite a dude over, just text me so I don't have to hear all of that."

"That's the first rule?" I ask, raising an eyebrow. "Not like, when I should pay rent? Or how we trade off on chores?"

I'm not telling him that my love life is dead and six feet under, mostly decomposed.

"I was just thinking about it." He pulls out the containers. There's a stool next to the big island and I sit down. "I guess for rent...same as what my old roommate paid — $600 at the beginning of the month. And as for dishes...I don't know. I just kind of do them whenever, so you can do them whenever too."

I roll my eyes and slide over my container of pulled chicken. "So what are the actual rules, then?"

"Besides a heads up before you bring company home — "

"If I do."

"If you do." He opens his container of ribs, then reaches over to grab a knife from a block on the counter. "Then I guess they're just things to know and not rules. I'm not a morning person at all, so keep it down before noon. And the animals. The cat's named Dennis and the dog is Murphy. They share three brain cells between the two of them and I never know which one of them has them at any given time."

I hold in a snort. There's clear affection in his tone despite the warning. "Okay."

"No, I'm dead serious." He points behind me, where Dennis is walking into the kitchen, tail in the air. "Just yesterday, Dennis got his head stuck in a plastic cup and nearly destroyed half the kitchen trying to get it off. Murphy almost ate a whole raw potato until I pried it out of his mouth. They're perfect, but they're not doing calculus in their spare time."

Murphy's tail thumps against the floor, like he's proud of himself, and Wes laughs.

"So basically, if you have food you need to leave out for more than a second, put it in the cabinet or shit'll go sideways," he adds.

Dennis purrs loudly like a little angel, butting his head against the base of my stool and sniffing my feet before moving on to Wes.

"Okay, I won't leave food out on the counter." I take a bite out of the pulled chicken and barely manage to keep myself from moaning. I'm so damn hungry and the food is unreal. "What else should I know?"

"If you hear what sounds like a woman screaming, just ignore it."

I stare at him for a few moments as he looks at his phone. "You can't just say that and not add context. Do you have bodies in the basement?"

"No. It's Waylon's dog, Duke." He slides the phone across to me and taps play on a video.

The video is of a fluffy dog laying in the yard in a light dusting of snow, with Waylon standing on the porch. Waylon asks Duke to come inside, but Duke barks back. And the more he asks, the more the Duke barks and howls back, to the point where it sounds like Duke is a woman screaming.

"Oh my god," I say, covering my mouth with my hand. "That's horrifying but kind of hilarious."

"Yeah. Scared the shit out of us when he adopted him." Wes takes his phone back. "He doesn't do it often but I figured I'd warn you."

"Good, because otherwise I'd think you had a murder den in the basement."

"What about you?" he asks, cutting in between two ribs. "You have any weird shit going on that I need to know about? Sleepwalking? Snack stealing? General chaos?"

"No, I'm a decent roommate." I'd lived with Erik for so long and he was so anal about certain things that I picked up the habits too. "I won't be too much trouble at home."

"At home?" He leans forward, propping himself up on his hands. It does nice things to his shoulders, but again, the quirk of his mouth reminds me of who I'm dealing with. "Do I need to remind you that we'll be working together? And given how much time you think we'll need to spend on all this, you have plenty of opportunities to be trouble?"

The way he says it plucks at a nerve I didn't even know was exposed.

"If we're able to schedule out the time that we'll work on things and when I'll be able to train at the bar, then we can minimize the time we spend together," I say, my tone more defensive than I intend for it to be.

"Woah, take a breath," he says. I actually do it instead of getting more riled up. "You wouldn't be as fun if we weren't at least a *little* different."

I can list off a lot of less-than-stellar things about Wes, but his sincerity isn't one of them. I trust him in a weird way — he doesn't take anything seriously, but he's not a true bullshitter.

"Whatever." I pull out my phone. "Can we at least set a time that we're going to start working? I need training for the bar and we need to plan for creating the drink."

He takes his time eating a rib, sucking sauce off his thumb in a way that shouldn't be even remotely erotic. But it is, somehow. He has nice hands, big and well-kept without looking like he's never done a day of manual work in his life.

"Fine. Let's aim for noon so we'll have time before the 4PM shift," he says.

"Let's do earlier so we can actually start working on the drink."

He sighs. "I'm not going to convince you otherwise, am I? Even though I just said I'm not a morning person."

"Nope." I gently nudge Dennis away from me with my foot since he looks like he's about to leap into my lap. Or more accurately, onto the counter in front of me. He's a round little cat, but he could make the jump. "And ten isn't even early."

"Fine. Ten." He sighs.

We go over a few more things while we eat, settling on what we need to plan tomorrow and how much training I'll get. We both finish our food and head upstairs. Once I'm in my room, I sigh and start to poke around a bit, making room for my stuff for when my dad drops it off. The closet has some winter gear, not that it ever gets super cold here, but there's more than enough room for my stuff.

I hear Wes in his room, puttering around. The walls really *are* thin. Why was he wondering about me bringing him guys when even back in high school he had a rotation of girls?

My face catches on fire just thinking about the stuff I might accidentally overhear. Where am I supposed to go if he has a girl over? Downstairs? What if they're super loud?

I flop backward onto the bed and run my hand over my face. I don't want to think about Wes fucking anyone, but the thoughts cut through anyway. I cross my legs to dull the ache that appears. I don't want anything to do with romance, but getting pounded into oblivion by a stranger would take the edge off my need.

Except this is Jepsen, and unless I find a tourist who wouldn't mind bringing me back to his hotel or Airbnb, I'll probably know the person or that person would be related to someone I know. The anonymity of New York City had me jaded, but it was perfect for an anonymous hookup.

I pull back the covers and slide under them. Even though I'm exhausted, I can't seem to settle in and shut my brain down. I try to take some deep breaths to steady myself, but that doesn't help either. Eventually I hear Wes head downstairs, then his voice outside.

I roll out of bed and peer outside. Murphy is playing with Duke, and Wes is standing next to a man who looks almost identical from above. Waylon. They're fraternal twins, but they look so similar that no one could deny they're brothers — they have the same dark eyes and dark hair, plus the height.

My phone buzzes on the bed and I sigh in relief – it's my best friend, Jo. She's the one person from the city who I'm still in touch with, the one person who's been a ride or die since we were roomies in college. If she and her boyfriend didn't already live in a tiny studio apartment, I would have stayed on her couch for a while.

"Hey," I say with a sigh.

"Hello, hello," she says. I squeeze my eyes shut so I don't burst into tears at her familiar accent. It's somewhere between British and American, leaning a little more British from her childhood going between London and New York City. "You got in so late last night. Are you settled?"

"God. I don't even know." I give her the full run-down of everything that's happened, from the raccoon situation to working with Wes to being his roommate.

"Shit, Rosie." She blows out a breath. "That sounds hellish. But at least you have the job and a ride, right?"

"I guess." She was always the one to look on the bright side, which I desperately need all the time. "I can't believe it has to be Wes Stryker, though. He drives me crazy in every fucking way. I can just feel the rivalry coming up again."

"Then maybe he'll be a good motivation to get it done and do a good job. Do better than him. That'll be a good boost, won't it?" Jo asks.

I mull over her words until they sink in. She's right. Winning against Wes is like a drug to me. But with everything that went down with Erik, do I even have what it takes to do that? I thought everything I'd built with Erik would help me get in the door somewhere else.

I was wrong. I could be wrong about this.

"But what if I lose?"

"Rosie." She sighs in a way that would seem pitying if I didn't know her. I can see her greenish-brown eyes softening even though she's thousands of miles away. "The Rosie I knew would be like fuck yeah, I can kick this man's ass."

I close my eyes again. I *was* that Rose at some point. I could kick anyone's ass if I put my mind to it, at least until I met Erik. Now I have nothing and I'm back home, living and working with a man who drives me crazy. I don't even know if this plan will work. What if I launch this product with Wes and it doesn't do well? Then where will I go? What if no one cares and the experience doesn't help me get a job in drink development somewhere else?

I don't want to think about it, but the thoughts keep creeping in.

"Well, I'll try to find that version of Rose somewhere," I say. I hear the sliding door downstairs shut and the dog bound up the stairs. "I've gotta go. But talk soon?"

"Talk soon. Love you."

"Love you too."

I hang up and let the phone fall on the mattress next to me. I can't fail at this. As tired as I am, I can't let Wes win.

CHAPTER FOUR

ROSE

Unsurprisingly, I toss and turn for hours that night before I finally pass out. But still, I wake up at eight-thirty like someone's poked me with a cattle prod even though the house is dead silent.

I watch a few YouTube videos, the volume turned low, instead of scrolling through social media. It's too much of an emotional minefield. My Instagram account is still up, though I purged all of the cringey flexing about the show. I only kept the few recipes I made completely on my own, plus pictures of me and Jo still up.

My relationship with Erik had been on the rocks for a long, long time — even if I was in denial — and all of my feelings for him are dead. Especially after what he did. But seeing him or what he took from me is just like stabbing a wound over and over again.

I eventually drag myself out of bed, go to shower and get ready, filling one side of Wes's sink with all of my skincare, hair stuff and makeup. He has his toothbrush, toothpaste, and deodorant out. That's it. Not that I'm surprised. He looks effortlessly good, and is literally not putting in that effort.

By the time I'm dressed, I expect him to be waiting for the bathroom. But nope, he's still faceplanted in bed. Murphy is resting his head on his butt, also asleep.

"Hey," I say softly. He doesn't stir. "Wes. *Wes.*"

"What?" he mumbles, his voice deep and rough from sleep.

"It's nine forty-five?" I say, unable to keep the question out of my voice. "We said we'd be at the bar at ten to start since we have so much to do?"

"Fuck," he grunts, lifting his head and pressing the heels of his hands to his eyes. "Are you serious right now?"

"Dead serious. It's either now, or we drag this out." I put my hands on my hips, waiting.

"Fuck," he groans again.

Murphy stands, stretching and yawning before hopping off the bed to greet me, tail wagging. At least someone is happy to see me. Wes stays face down in his pillow for another few beats before he rolls over onto his back and *oh*. He's pitching a very substantial tent in the sheets.

I turn to leave, my whole body heating. I'm not a virgin, of course, but I haven't seen a lot of dicks in my life. Even through a sheet, his looks way bigger than any of the ones I've ever seen.

Ignore, ignore, ignore. Surely the universe wouldn't be that rude to attach a nice dick to a guy who's already hot.

I putter around in my room, putting my braids up in two space buns just to kill time. Eventually, Wes knocks on my door. His dark curls are still wet and he looks tired.

"C'mon," he grunts.

He's almost hilariously crabby and sleepy-looking, yawning wide as we drive toward town. I let him crank up the music to stay awake, even though he chooses the most annoying station with a thousand commercials.

Rather than turning toward the bar, we turn in the opposite direction and park in front of a bakery that didn't used to be here.

"Coffee?" he asks as he slides out of the car.

"Please." I don't trust the ancient coffee machine in the corner of his kitchen, which looks like it would spit out tar instead of coffee. I need to grab a spare French press from my parents' house so I don't have to suffer through that kind of thing. I don't do well without decent coffee.

The coffee shop is surprisingly nice inside. Not too twee, but cute and whimsical, with light blue walls and vintage details. My surprise shifts into a jolt of dread when I recognize the guy behind the counter, Ted. We were friends back in high school — not best friends or anything, but close enough to where we kept up with each other on Instagram.

So, he knows everything. My heart rate picks up, and my face heats even though he hasn't even spotted me yet. The embarrassment of having flexed so hard about the show on Instagram, only to be right back in the place where I grew up is more intense than I could have imagined.

He looks at Wes first, nodding in greeting, before his eyes slide to me and widen.

"Rose?" he asks. "Holy shit."

"Hey." I wave, then let my hands drop before tucking them into my front jeans pockets.

"What are you even doing here?" He comes from around

the counter and pulls me into a hug. He smells like sugar. "I don't even think I've seen you come around during the holidays."

"Yeah, my family usually came to see me or I went to Nashville with them to see family." I tuck my hands into my back pockets, then hold the strap of my bag. "I'm just...well, I moved back. Temporarily."

"Damn, I can't believe it." He rests his hands on his hips, still smiling. Despite his clear pleasure at me being here, my face is still warm with embarrassment. "I never thought you would. I'd heard a few rumors that people saw you but I wasn't sure how true they were.

"I never thought I would either." A few people come in behind us, so Ted gets behind the counter again. Thank god. Hopefully he won't want to talk more and ask the questions I'd rather not answer.

"What can I get you?" Ted asks.

We each order large coffees, Wes's black and mine with oat milk, and breakfast biscuits. Ted and the other person behind the counter, who thankfully I don't recognize, start making our food. The other person working there must be new because Ted walks him through making it.

"Will I see you around?" Ted asks me as he hands over our coffee and the bag of breakfast sandwiches. "We should catch up some time. It looked like you had a lot of cool stuff going on and I'd love to hear about it."

"Um..." I glance at Wes, then at Ted, who looks so hopeful that I get another pang of guilt in my chest. "I'll be around. And yeah, we should."

"Cool." Ted smiles. "See you."

We wave goodbye and thankfully get into the car. Wes

takes a long swig of his coffee and sighs before we even start the car. I do the same, even though caffeine is going to make my jitters worse. Why am I freaking out, though? Ted has always been nice. All I have to do is tell him that the show didn't work.

But the shame and embarrassment of losing out on this opportunity have me in a chokehold.

"I forgot you and Ted ran in the same circles back in high school," Wes says, starting the car.

"Yeah, we did." I cup my coffee, looking out the window.

I can feel his eyes on me. "So what happened?"

"What do you mean?" I frown. "Nothing did."

He drums his fingers on his knee. "He was happy to see you, but you looked like you wanted to throw up. Not a normal reaction."

I sip my coffee, trying to hide my scowl. People always thought that Wes was just a fun, not-so-bright party boy back in high school, but I knew the truth – he's much smarter and way more perceptive than people give him credit for. I just wish he would aim all that perception at someone besides me.

"I was just surprised," I say instead. "And did you tell everyone that I was back in town? He said he'd heard rumors about me being here but I haven't even been out that much."

"No." He pauses, guzzling down even more coffee like it's iced instead of hot. "Well, I told Waylon. And obviously John David and my dad know. People might have seen you. So word travels."

"Way too fast." I nibble on the edge of my cup's lid, a nervous habit.

"I'm guessing you don't get that in New York," he says,

his tone light. Usually when people bring up New York to me there's a bit of ire in there.

"Nope. I can go a full day interacting with people without really saying much back there." I rest my elbow on the door jamb. "No one knows my business. It's great."

He huffs a laugh. "I bet people know more about your business than you think. And either way, isn't it nice knowing that people know you?"

My right eyebrow creeps up. "Not really. I'm not like you."

"What?" That wide grin of his lights up the whole car. "Dashing? Handsome? Charming?"

I roll my eyes. "Popular. And also, one of the youngest sons of one of the most prominent families in town."

And so ridiculously privileged and blind to it. I hope he's gotten some perspective in the years since high school but I'm not holding my breath.

He pulls into the lot of the bar — we're the only ones here. "Fair point. But also, not really. Yeah, people know all your shit, but people *know you*. And that's kind of good, isn't it? There's a lot of gossip but there can be just as many people who care about you enough to see if you're okay."

I blink, not moving to unbuckle my seatbelt. "That's a very optimistic way of putting things."

"I know." He shrugs and opens the door. "Sometimes optimism isn't all that bad."

I hold my tongue because I could bring down the vibe in an instant. But then again, I don't think much could bring Wes down.

We go inside the bar, which looks just the same as it did

the other day — rustic and approachable. He leads me to the back, where there's a tiny office.

"Hold on," he says with a sigh, flicking on the light. The space is already small, which is only amplified by the big desk in the middle of the room and a small love seat on one side. I sit down at the desk, but Wes stretches out on the love seat. He's so tall that his legs extend past the arm, and when he puts a hand behind his neck, his t-shirt exposes the tiniest sliver of stomach skin.

I open my laptop and pull out my notebook too, where I went a little bit crazy with the post-its and color-coding. John David sent over some background information on suppliers and costs that we'd have to keep in mind, so I did some planning and took notes last night.

"Here's what I planned last night," I say, pulling up my document.

Wes shoots me a side-eyed glance. "So you had me wake up early when you've done most of the work already?"

"I did most of the *planning*. And I need you to weigh in on it too because I really doubt you'll just go along with whatever I say. I'd rather lay it all out now so we don't end up wasting time bickering later."

"Whatever." He leans back, grabbing a stress ball that's sitting on a shelf. "What's the plan?"

"JD sent the information on ABV, packaging costs, things like that, which you'll have to read in your own time. But as for the planning, I think we should start with brainstorming based on the parameters JD sent, then start testing ideas with people," I say. "That lines up with Stryker Day at the distillery, the Jepsen Festival, and the industry convention in

Nashville. Then we'll refine it, let JD taste, and refine more. Then present it all to your dad."

The convention in Nashville is also hosting a cocktail competition, which caught my eye. I used to do them a lot — you create a cocktail based on a prompt, like a theme and a type of alcohol, then make it as you present to judges. But then, Erik got more into them. I didn't want to compete against him, so he took them and ran.

I nearly signed up last night, but my anxiety stopped me. Do I really need another path to failure right now? I don't. But still, I don't want to write it off yet.

"Yeah, John David's going to have a lot to say, so add time in for that." He puts down one fidget toy and picks up another.

"Okay, then." I scan the calendar and try to fit in extra time in spots. "Fixed it. I think. Do you really think that John David will have that many objections?"

"No, but he has a vacation home in my fucking business, so he'll have something to say." Wes says this casually, but his expression isn't as open and warm as it usually is. "You put the social media stuff in there?"

"Yes. We can just do it as we go and schedule posts. I know how to do all that," I say. "No other objections?"

"Not right now." He spins the fidget toy for a second before tossing it aside. "This is boring. Let's start your training."

"You don't want to start working?" I ask. "Or reviewing all the info JD sent?"

"Not particularly. Antsy." He stands up and stretches, revealing even more skin between where his t-shirt has ridden up and the waistband of his jeans. He has a tattoo of something I can't quite identify on his left side. "And relax, we'll start tomorrow. Full force. We can think of ideas while we handle the boring pre-shift stuff."

He starts leaving, so I guess I have to follow him. I close my laptop with a huff and trail behind. As we go, we pass by a collage of photos beneath a banner that reads "Wall of Shame".

"Oh, by the way, these are the people who are banned from the bar," he says. He gestures to the left side. "These are tourists – you probably don't have to worry about them. But the people on the right are locals."

I scan the right side. A lot of the faces are familiar. People I went to high school with, people I've seen around town.

"Wait, is that Catherine?" I ask, pointing to a picture of the petite brunette. It's one of the few photos that isn't a hazy, drunken photo taken outside. It looks like she's in a park, with someone cropped out next to her. "Didn't she and Waylon date in high school?"

"Yeah, and after. She can get fucked," Wes says with an alarming amount of venom.

"She knitted hats for newborn babies and was salutatorian?" I say, a question in my tone.

"She's also a cheating piece of garbage." He nods his head for us to leave and I follow him. "She doesn't dare to come back here anymore, but she has in the past."

"Oh." I blink. That's the last thing I would have imagined happening. We weren't friends back in high school, but she was the ultimate Nice Girl of our grade. I never thought she'd have the balls to cheat on a guy as nice as Waylon. Now I kind of hate her too.

"Okay," he says, stepping behind the bar. "I'm guessing you know the basics of how to run a bar, right?"

"Yep. I just need to know what to do and when, and where to find everything," I say, scanning the bar. Whoever did the closing shift last night did a good job — everything looks clean and set up for today.

Wes runs me through the boring stuff first — the POS system, their inventory, where cleaning supplies are, things like that — at lightning speed. Luckily, it's not so complicated that I can't keep up.

"And now, the part that's actually fun," he says, pulling out several glasses. "Our signature drinks."

I pick up the menus tucked between the napkin holder and a card holder. One side has food — there's a kitchen next door that handles that — and the other has drinks with names that are thankfully not annoyingly kitschy.

The menu is designed well, without too much BS on it, and the descriptions are fairly straightforward. Moonshine margarita. Moonshine Arnold Palmer. Things I could figure out on my own.

"It doesn't look too complicated," I say, putting the menu back. "I'm sure I can figure it out if I taste it."

"You think so?" He starts pulling out more ingredients, including Stryker moonshine and Big Bubba Bourbon. "Doesn't mean you can't pretend to listen to me, then, since you've figured it all out."

I cross my arms over my chest and lean my hip against the bar. "I didn't say I had it all figured out. I just said that I probably won't be too surprised by what you have to show me. It's not like the cocktails I made in New York."

"Which were...?"

"Custom ones. Bespoke ingredients, things like that." Our 'regular' drinks were pretty complicated. "I can handle whatever we make here."

Wes's eyebrow goes up, one corner of his mouth quirking up. It doesn't have his usual humor.

"So you're that good, then?" he says, grabbing the neck of the moonshine bottle. "Make a moonshine margarita the way we'd make it."

He hands me the bottle of moonshine and steps back, his eyes lingering on me in a challenge. I don't know what it is about that look that's like gasoline on a fire, but I take the bottle from him and pour myself a teeny shot.

I don't love drinking cocktails just to get drunk — I like them to taste good and be the kind of drink you savor. The whole reason I got into bartending was because of an experience I had on my twenty-second birthday (my twenty-first went about as well as you'd expect).

Jo took me to this hole in the wall cocktail bar and the owner started making us these crazy cocktails on the fly, telling us stories about how much the neighborhood had changed over the decades. We sipped the drinks for hours, never getting more than a solid buzz, having a good conversation. But that was more than enough, and I wanted to keep doing it.

Plus, bartending worked with my schedule and the owner needed a new bartender anyway. Then everything fell into place. Or out of place, depending on how I look at it. If I hadn't been bartending at that particular bar, I wouldn't have met Erik. And if I hadn't met Erik, I wouldn't be back here.

The moonshine isn't nearly as harsh as I expected, which changes how much I'll add to balance it out. I've made so many margaritas that I could do it passed out asleep, so it doesn't take long for me to put one together. I slide it toward him and watch as he takes a sip. He swallows, frowns, then takes another sip.

"Doesn't taste bad," he says, putting it down. "But you're missing the balance of it. It doesn't fit the people who come in here."

He grabs the same ingredients that I did, but also pulls out a different simple syrup. The way he moves behind the bar, like he's entirely in control and can bend flavors at his will, would be attractive if he wasn't using it to prove a point against me. The way his arms look when he shakes the drink adds insult to injury.

"Rule one of The Copper Moon — think about who you're actually serving drinks to." He pushes the glass to me. "Jepsen isn't New York City. Taste this."

I take a sip of the drink as he's made it. It's sweeter, for sure, but not saccharine or cloying. It's like he's taken the balance of everything and pushed it slightly in a different direction without throwing everything off. That kind of skill is subtle but something that comes from a lot of practice and knowledge.

I'm a little impressed. A little tiny bit. But mostly embarrassed. I should have known that. My face burns because he's right. It's something so obvious that I didn't even think about it. It's such a small thing, but that's all it takes for my confidence to be shaken these days. It's like every single mistake is amplified now, with Erik's voice taking up permanent residence in my head.

"And rule two is that everyone, even the most experienced bartenders and the people who were regulars before they started working here, get the full tutorial of every single drink." He pulls out even more bottles.

"So why'd you have me make one?" *Asshole.*

This time the quirk of his mouth has that impish quality to it. "Just because."

I bite back a *fuck you*. He's still my boss and my roommate, so even though we tend to work each other up, I now have reasons to stay on his good side. I hate that once again, someone has the ability to turn my life one way or another if I do the wrong thing. I need to get that five grand bonus and get the fuck out of Jepsen.

He walks me through all of their specialty drinks on the menu, having me taste each one. They're pretty good in a very straightforward way. Something for people to just throw back without thinking too much about it.

"Wait, what about this one?" I ask, pointing to the last item on the menu. "What's the *just trust me?*"

"Only I can make that," he says, tidying up our workspace.

"Why?"

"Because. It's a secret." He grins at me. "And no, no one else knows what it is."

"I'll just watch you make it once," I say.

"That's the thing — it's never the same thing twice. But there's a secret sauce in it that I include every time." He grabs some spray and covers the bar in front of us before wiping it down.

"Oh, so you just make a drink on the fly?" I scoff. "I can do that too."

He keeps rubbing down the counter for a few moments longer and harder than necessary. "Still, it's my thing."

"That's what I'm saying. I can make it my thing too." Okay, I'm poking at him at this point, but I rarely find anything that gets under his skin.

"Rose." He looks at me with a sigh. "Come on."

"Fine, whatever." I'm totally going to do it if someone asks me, though.

"Let's get back to it. Let me show you a few other drinks." He grabs a few bottles and starts showing me how they make moonshine Arnold Palmers.

Everything else about working the bar is more or less like the other bars where I've worked. Not long before the shift, Jasper, who I remember from high school, and a girl who I recognize but can't place come in. Jasper's hand is around the girl's waist.

Jasper's eyebrow shoots up in confusion when he sees me, but the girl smiles.

"Hey, you guys remember Rose from high school, right?" Wes says. "Rose, you remember Jasper and Sabrina? They're the other bartenders."

"Oh, hey," I say. Memories of Sabrina click into place. She's lost the baby face I remember, though she's still super cute.

Jasper nods a hello and Sabrina waves, her smile shy. When did they start dating? I thought Sabrina was Jasper's best friend's little sister? I'll find out soon enough.

"We handled most of the pre-shift prep," Wes says to them. "Besides some of the garnish prep."

"Okay, cool. We'll finish that up," Sabrina says. "Looking forward to working with you, Rose."

They disappear into the back, Jasper's hand tucked into her back pocket.

"So, any more questions?" Wes asks.

"How are the tips?" I ask, trying to sound nonchalant. The bars where I worked had wealthy customers. Some were assholes and stiffed me no matter how nice I was, but some of them left hefty tips that really saved my ass financially. I need all the money I can get.

"Depends." He assesses me in a way that makes me warm in ways it shouldn't, his gaze meandering up and down my body. "I think you could clean up."

I raise an eyebrow, suppressing a smirk. "Are you suggesting that I could get a lot of tips because you think I'm attractive?"

I expect him to shoot back a barb of some kind, but instead, his cheeks color. "Jesus, Rose. I have eyes, but does me thinking you're hot mean anything to you?"

It *does* mean something to me, as much as I don't want it to. My relationship with Erik had disintegrated to the point where we hadn't touched in weeks. And then he had to throw out every insult about my appearance as he could when we were in that final, blow out fight. I know it's because he didn't have a leg to stand on otherwise, but it still hurt.

So a guy as hot as Wes, even if he works my last nerve, thinking I'm attractive? Not just attractive — hot? It feels good. It feels more than good.

But it's Wes. How do I make his words not feel that way?

He probably tells a lot of women that. I don't remember ever seeing him without a date or a girl hanging off his arm in high school. He's the type of guy who thinks a lot of women are hot.

The tingly feeling across my skin fades, to my relief.

"Whatever." I dig through my bag, trying to think of a way to kill whatever energy has come over us. "I bet I could get more tips than you in a single night."

"Oh, you do?" A grin spreads over his face, his energy brightening. "You don't know what you just agreed to."

"I think I do." I try not to smile as wide as I want to. He doesn't deserve the satisfaction. He just deserves to lose. "What does the winner get? Besides the satisfaction and the money?"

He studies me for a few seconds. "What's a chore you hate? Don't lie."

"I hate doing dishes," I say.

"Then if I win, you have to do all the dishes for a month." His smile widens, confidence practically oozing out of his pores. I can't wait to crush his spirit.

"*When* I win, you have to get up before me and make coffee every day. Real coffee in my French press," I say. "Emphasis on before me, so no sleeping in."

His eyes narrow for a second before his smile returns. "I'm in."

CHAPTER FIVE

WES

When I lived with my old roommate, we kept things chill. We'd been roommates back in my two years at the University of Tennessee, so we'd seen each other in various states of fucked-upness — wasted, sick, exhausted, post-awkward hookup, all of it. Walking in on him in the bathroom when I was barely awake enough to process being alive wasn't a huge deal.

But Rose isn't anywhere close to my old roommate, so when I stagger out of my bedroom in my sweats and open the bathroom door, I'm slapped in the face with the vision of Rose in a tiny towel. I don't think my brain has fully registered that I'm awake, but my dick is already clocked in and very aware of Rose.

She's so small — how is the towel even smaller, riding up her thick thighs? The tops of her breasts are showing, her cleavage framed by her braids. Whatever she's rubbing on her skin makes it look shimmery and touchable.

What would it be like to grip her hips or ass or thighs, my

fingers sinking into her softness? Softness is my weakness, and she looks soft everywhere. And she's so petite that we could do a lot of fun positions and—

Then the lights finally turn on in my brain and I register that I'm staring.

"What the fuck, Wes?" Rose says, slamming the door in my face. "Did you pick the lock?"

"What?" I run both hands over my face, my stubble rough against my hands. "What the fuck, Rose? Why would I do that? The lock is just broken and I'm half awake from my nap. Sorry. You've been here less than twenty-four hours and I'm not used to having a roommate."

"Thanks for the heads up on that." She huffs. "I'll be out in a few minutes."

I lean against the wall across the hallway, hoping she doesn't come out before I get my dick under control. Dennis hacking up a hairball on the rug at the end of the hall distracts me long enough. By the time I've cleaned it up, she comes out in leggings and a t-shirt, a cloud of sweet-smelling scent in her wake.

Her eyes scan me from top to bottom, like everything I'm wearing and being is inconveniencing her. "It's all yours."

I push off the wall and step into the bathroom. The left side of the sink, which she's taken over, is covered in all kinds of lotions and face cream shit I don't understand. Whatever it is, it makes her smell good, like vanilla with a little something else. I take a few deep breaths through my nose. Not sniffing—just breathing very deeply.

I get dressed in my work clothes—jeans and a plaid shirt, sleeves rolled up for maximum effect. I have exactly one hair product, which I work through my curls to make them fall the way I want. Easy. I've never had trouble getting women's attention or adoration, and tonight isn't going to be any different.

"You good to go?" I call through Rose's door.

"Just a second," she calls back.

She opens the door moments later and my heart genuinely skips.

She's not wearing a ton of makeup, but her red lipstick is more than enough. Something about the color makes me want to taste her lips.

But her makeup isn't the end of it. Her braids are up in a bun that shows off the smooth softness of her neck. She's wearing a black tank top that shows a decent amount of cleavage, with a flannel shirt that looks a whole lot like mine over it. It's tied at her waist, where the waistband of her jean shorts sits. The shorts aren't much longer. It's hot outside and our bartenders wear shorts a lot since the bar gets toasty, especially at this time of year, but their thighs don't look as good as hers do.

She's going to clean up on fucking tips. Damn it.

"Ugh, we're twinning," she says, wrinkling her nose and apparently not noticing my gawking. "Hold on."

She shuts the door again, leaving me standing there dumbfounded. When she emerges again, she's wearing a plain green button-down in place of the flannel.

"Let's go." She nods toward the door.

I put Murphy into his crate, gesturing for her to go ahead of me to the car. Do I let her go ahead of me because I'm polite?

Maybe a little, because Nana would threaten to kick my ass if I wasn't vaguely gentlemanly. But it's also so I can get a good look at her ass in those shorts. It's the kind of ass I could stare at for way too long, lush and heart-shaped, so I peel my eyes away.

We climb into my SUV and I pull toward town, turning on some music. It's stuffy in the truck — or maybe I can just smell her light, sweet perfume more than I want to — so I roll down the window.

Neither of us says anything for a while. Every time I look to the right, I catch a glimpse of her thighs.

"A little unfair, don't you think?" I ask. "Using your feminine assets to defeat me instead of your natural charm?"

"Says Mr. Forearms." She curls one leg up under herself. "I know what you're up to with those sleeves. Rolled up sleeves are the peacock plumage of human men."

I can't help but grin. "You know that men know about that shit by now?"

"Of course. Men are extremely obvious in a lot of ways." She says it as if it's fact. She's so sure of herself and always has been, like she knows exactly what she's doing and why. I suppress a smile.

We arrive at the bar and I pull around to the back. Jasper and Sabrina should be the only ones here since they're wrapping up the day shift. But no, John David's fucking truck is back here too.

"Shit," I mumble under my breath.

"What is it?" Rose asks.

"John David's here for some reason." I pull in next to Jasper and throw the car into park.

John David is a living wet blanket. Hopefully he isn't staying or maybe he's just picking something up. He only shows on busy nights at the peak of tourist season when we need help, and even then, he hasn't done that recently.

We head into the bar, and I can practically *feel* JD's energy sucking the life out of the room. It's quiet besides the sound of Sabrina and Jasper restocking items and prepping the garnishes, their voices low. The bar feels naked without the bustle of music and people. John David is at a high-top table with his laptop, frowning at the screen.

"What are you doing here?" I ask him, not even bothering with hello. "You don't come to this shift anymore."

He looks up at me, the frown still on his face, then looks to Rose. "I'm here to supervise the shift."

"That's my job when you're not here," I say.

"And my job is making sure you do your job." He shuts his laptop and glances at Rose again, like he's trying to gauge her reactions. "I want to make sure that Rose is acclimating well and that she was trained to handle the bare minimum."

"Wes trained me," she says. "I feel very prepared."

John David slowly nods, his eyes narrowing. "Fine. I'll just observe, then."

"The entire shift?" I ask.

"If it warrants it, yeah." He tucks his laptop into the bag. "I'll help with preparing."

I sigh, digging a hand through my hair. Rose looks at me expectantly, her arms crossed.

"Just shadow me," I say, heading to the back.

She helps me with every task I do, staying quiet. I feel JD's eyes on us the whole time, even as he cleans up and preps for the shift. When I first started at the bar when I turned 21, he was here every single shift. How did I survive?

He didn't used to be such a dickhead, but I don't know when he changed.

At least I'm distracted when the bar finally opens. Most people who come in during the late afternoon are tourists looking for something to do at an odd hour before dinner, but a few of them sit at the bar.

"You're good to start on your own?" I ask Rose.

"Yep. Pretty straightforward, but Sabrina offered to help me out too." She rests her hands on her hips. "Does our bet start now?"

I glance over at John David, who's busy talking to Jasper and not paying attention to me. I don't have to try *that* hard to get great tips, especially since I make good drinks. But JD will be breathing down my fucking neck. Rose's eyes have that gleam to them that wipes away any sense I have.

"Yep." I smile. "Good luck."

"You'll need it more." She shoots me a smirk over her shoulder and goes down to a middle-aged couple that recently came in.

I attend to another group that came in toward the front.

For a while, things are pretty chill. I do a few things behind the scenes to make sure everything's organized, especially before JD gets to them. I serve a few people, but they're mostly concerned with hanging out with each other. Usually the tips can get big when there's time to chit chat at the bar.

I keep track of Rose as I work since I can make all of our most popular drinks in my sleep. She's already doing well and asks Sabrina a few questions from time to time.

Things start to pick up around seven, with people trickling in and settling at the bar. I turn up the music just loud enough to fill the space without people needing to shout. I actually like this part of the evening — talking to people, doing a lot of different things, making good drinks. I never have the chance to get bored.

"Hello, ladies," I say with a smile as a group of four women a bit younger than my mom come in. I don't recognize them, so they must be in from out of town. "What can I get for you?"

"Give me the strongest shit you've got," one of them, with a short blonde bob, says. She's wearing a crown and a sash.

I rest both hands on the bar, leaning forward. "That'll be our specialty drink. What flavors do you like? Fruity? Sweet? Something a little weird?"

"Ooo..." The blonde with the bob looks between her friends. "Why not something a little weird? For all three of us?"

"Weird it is, then." I grin, winking at her. "Don't say I didn't warn you."

"I don't think you could weird us out, hun." The brunette friend leans forward, practically thrusting her cleavage at me.

"What are you guys celebrating tonight? Bachelorette party?" I ask, nodding toward the blonde's crown.

"Divorce party!" Her friend, who has short dark hair, raises her hand in a high-five. "Because fuck her ex."

"Fuck my ex!" The blonde with the bob says with a grin, high-fiving her friend. "I can't bitch about men to a man, can I?"

"Bitch away. That's what I'm here for." I keep mixing their drinks and the woman takes me up on my offer.

That's the thing about being a good bartender — sometimes it's just about sitting there and listening to people get things off their chest. And this woman obviously had a lot to say. She talks at me while I make the drinks, and suddenly I know way too much about her husband's gambling addiction and inability to put the toilet seat down.

"Here are y'all's drinks," I say, sliding one of each of the drinks I'd mixed up. It's a little sweet with a hit of spice. "Let me know what you think."

"Thanks, hun," she says, raising her glass. "Want to drink with us?"

I usually don't unless it's a super slow night and the person's a regular, and even then I just drink a cider or something else that isn't boozy. I *definitely* won't do that with JD here. But the woman is looking at me expectantly, so I pour myself a little shot of soda.

"I'm on the clock, so I'll have to do soda." I raise my glass too.

"To new beginnings!" the blonde says. "With better dick!"

"And fuck all men except for..." the brunette looks at me.

"Wes."

"Fuck all men except for Wes."

I laugh. "I'll drink to that."

I throw back the soda and the women love the drink. They start talking at me again and I listen in until I absolutely have to move on to another group of people. But the job is done — they adore me, and as long as I keep giving them drinks (within reason) and playfully flirting, I could get a huge tip.

"Could you lay it on any thicker?" she asks as she comes

up behind me to pour a beer from the tap. "Those ladies all want to bang you."

"I'm here to win, not to be subtle." I start pouring a glass of frozen rosé. "Where are you with tips?"

"None of your business." She bumps me with her hip so she can get by. "We'll tally at the end."

I can sense JD before I see him. He lurks at the bar for a moment before I finally acknowledge him.

"What?" I ask, grabbing some glasses.

"Try not to spend too much time with one group," he says. "Everyone needs attention."

I resist the urge to roll my eyes. He has to find *something* to nitpick. "I know how to work this bar. I've been doing it for years without complaints. And believe it or not, people like it when you're personable."

His nostrils flare and his jaw tightens. It's a completely accurate dig so I'm not taking it back. "A group is coming in. Get to it."

I give him a smartass salute before I attend to the people who just walked in.

The group is made up of three youngish guys who immediately put me on high alert. They look like they're looking to pick up women — which I only know because I've been these guys before. Rose is pretty much their only target at the moment. Jasper will ward off anyone even looking at Sabrina in a weird way. Of course, they sit right in front of her at the bar before I can make it over.

"Welcome in," she says, her voice a warm purr that she's never aimed at me. But if she did, I'd be putty in her hands right away. If I didn't know her, of course. "What can I get you guys? Here's a menu."

I putter around a little, keeping one eye on them. Rose walks them through our bestselling drinks, pointing an elegant finger along the menu. The men look at her like she's giving the most compelling lecture they've ever attended. At least they're mostly looking at her face and not her tits.

"What's this drink *Just Trust Me*?" one man asks.

Rose turns the menu around. "I'll just make you something on the fly."

"It's my signature drink," I cut in.

All of them look at me, and for a brief moment, Rose looks like she wants to break a glass and cut me. This shit again. I don't know why I'm so defensive about the damn drink but it's *mine*.

"Is it?" Rose asks, putting one hand on her hip. "Because it just says to ask you about it, not that you're the only one who can make it. And it's literally just a drink on the fly."

"Let her make us a drink," one guy says, not taking his eyes off of her.

"We'll each make a sample of one," I say. "And you can decide which one's best."

"Deal." She smiles, then turns back to the guys. "Tell me what you like."

"Hm..." The one in the backward hat leans forward on the bar. He looks her up and down in a way that makes me grip the bar to stop myself from doing something stupid. "Why don't you do whatever you feel is best? I'm sure it'll be good."

"Okay. We can do that." Rose nudges me with her elbow. "Let's hop to it. Over here so they can't see."

We head over to the other side of the bar, our backs to them. I turn and assess the guys again, trying to ignore my annoyance so I can pick up what they might like. I grab some of our bourbon and a few other special ingredients I keep around. Rose's hand brushes against mine when we both go for the cherry liqueur, and her eyes narrow.

I let her have it first, and soon we're both done with our drink. Hers has 2 layers, one red and one deep brown, while mine doesn't look any different than a regular whisky shot. It's simple and masculine, which seems like their vibe.

"Want to drink with us?" one of the guys asks Rose as if I'm not standing here.

"Can't, sorry." She pushes the drinks toward them and smiles. "But I can watch you enjoy them."

One guy starts to say something but the glare I cut his way stops him. They each taste our drinks, one by one.

"This one. The flavors feel fancier. Like more stuff's going on without it being weird," one guy says, lifting the glass that had Rose's drink in it. The others do the same.

Rose gives me a smug smile. "I guess I win, then."

"I knew it was yours," one guy says. "It tasted pretty."

It tasted pretty? What the fuck? Did this guy get his pickup lines from a TikTok? I've never wanted to kick a stranger's ass for so little, so fast.

"Thanks." Rose smiles. "Just holler if you need me, okay?"

Rose shoots me a smirk as she passes behind me to check on another group. As she goes and after I'm a little bit away, the guys obviously stare at her and start talking about what just happened.

Something ugly surges up in me. Who the fuck do these guys think they are? Of course, there'll be hot women out there who you want to look at. But you don't fucking ogle them like they're meat. Especially Rose.

"I'm taking over that tab," I say, catching her by the sleeve.

"Who?" She glances past my shoulder. "Them? I have them handled."

I look back at them too. They're obviously still talking about her, their eyes flicking to her every once in a while.

"They're creeps." In the big scheme of creepdom, they're not bad but that's still too much. It isn't even about the competition at this point. I just don't like dudes staring at her like that.

"Maybe you shouldn't have accepted my bet if you can't handle men ogling me. I'm a big girl and I can handle myself. We're in fucking Jepsen, not Manhattan." She rolls her eyes. "Don't be butthurt that they liked my drink more. And don't steal my tips."

She glides past me, smiling at one of our regulars, Dan. I grind my teeth and start making a moonshine margarita for another customer.

I taste the cocktail with a little straw even though I know it's good, my chest tightening. It's fucking dumb, but this is my place — the thing I'm good at. And the fact that she can just swoop in and do so well pisses me off more than it should.

But showing that I'm pissed would only satisfy her more, so I head back down to the women having the divorce party to check on them. I'm all smiles and they're thrilled to see me.

Refilling their drinks and listening to them roast men are a good distraction, especially when I feel John David's eyes on me. He's been at the end of the bar with a glass of water, watching everything going on. He doesn't even have his phone out.

After a while JD summons me over.

"You weren't going to sleep with any of those women, were you?" John David asks, one eyebrow going up.

I hate how he can just arch his eyebrow and make me feel like a toddler who just got caught eating Play-Doh like it's a block of cheese.

"You really think I would?" I try to brush off his words with a scoff. "Jesus, JD. Why are you so concerned?"

I nearly make a jab at his complete lack of a dating life, but I hold back. I don't know — and don't want to know — if he's casually hooking up with someone on the side. Maybe he is.

"I need to stay on top of you," he says. "You know how much our company's reputation matters."

I slam the top of the cocktail shaker down harder than I have to. "Thanks, JD. I had no idea that the reputation of the company that keeps our family afloat mattered."

"Don't be a smartass." He crosses his arm over his chest. "There's a lot at stake here with what you and Rose are doing and with the bar. The income here is important and if it gets a sleazy reputation..."

He trails off and lets me fill in the worst-case scenario. The entire business tanking would mean my entire family getting fucked over. Yeah, we're several steps removed from that but it's not like the business is a permanent thing. That's the entire reason my grandfather passed the business to my dad, and why my dad is trying to get John David to take over after him – longevity.

"Yeah, yeah," is all I say.

I throw myself back into the shift, toeing the line between serving people well and making sure JD stays off my ass. Eventually two AM comes around and the customers clear out, leaving us to close. JD hops up without saying a word, helping us wrap up.

"So, how do you think the shift went? Aside from me treating a party that left me a forty percent tip extremely well?" I ask as I clean a glass.

JD pauses. "Fine enough, but could be better."

I put the glass down so I don't crush it. *Maybe* I could have been faster with everything, but for fuck's sake, I know that everyone was taken care of.

"What more could you possibly want? Within reason?" I ask, forcing my voice to stay low so he doesn't accuse me of freaking out. Even though my blood is simmering.

"You just seemed preoccupied with those women. With socializing with the customers. No one was left without service this time, but that's just this time," JD says. "Stay focused."

I inhale through my nose slowly, then let it out just as slowly. JD's a grumpy asshole, but he's just efficient and polite enough to be a good bartender — it's not like he doesn't know what he's doing.

I *know* I did well enough. That one group didn't make or break the whole night for anyone.

I head to the end of the bar to cool down, and as I do, the insecurities set in. Maybe he has a point. Flirting is fun and all, but is it going to make me seem like the kind of person who can take a bigger role in the company? Probably not. I just don't know how the fuck I can ever impress him.

"Let's calculate tips," Rose says, snapping me out of it.

"Fine." I go to the register, pulling out the cash tips we received and our receipts.

I count the cash in front of her, then add up all the tips from the receipts. Fuck. She kicked my ass on her first fucking day. By a good margin.

"I win!" Rose says with a satisfied grin. A dimple I find both cute and irritating pops up in her cheek. "I'm so excited for my morning coffee."

I heave a sigh. I get roasted for trying to get more tips and lose anyway? Just the right ending for the night.

"Fine, you win," I say. "Just don't complain if it tastes like ass."

CHAPTER SIX

ROSE

Depositing all those tips is going to feel really damn good. If I keep having nights like those and I get the bonus, moving will be easy.

I get dressed the next morning without Wes barging in on me mostly naked. I find him downstairs, watching a YouTube video on making a French press coffee. My heart skips a few beats when I take him in. He's not wearing a shirt, his sweats slung dangerously low on his hips.

He must be making good use of those weights I saw in the garage. His shoulders are broad and muscular, his shape well-honed body of a fighter. His back...just...his back. The muscle underneath his skin, the tattoo, which I now see is of a forest.

The man is perfect. Physically. And I need to stop lusting after him somehow.

Murphy trots up to me, tail wagging, and backs into me so I can give him a few butt scratches. I bend over and oblige him, scratching the spot that makes him lean into my touch.

"Morning," I say, forcing cheer into my tone even though I'm pretty much dead before my first cup. "Is my coffee ready?"

He shoots me a glare over his shoulders that quickly turns into a heated one, aimed right at my tits. Which are pretty much falling out of my tank top.

I stand up, yanking my tank top into place. But it's too thin to hide the fact that my nipples are hard.

Good lord. A single look from Wes is like a kiss on that sweet spot on my neck from anyone else. I'm putty without him putting a hand on me. Will being around him often kill the lust I have for him? And how can I speed that process up?

"It's gonna taste like shit, sorry," he finally says, clearing his throat and looking back at the counter. "I'm following a fucking YouTube tutorial when I'm half awake."

"It's just the concept of you making my coffee because you lost that'll make it delicious." I pull out my creamer and put it on the counter next to him. "By the way, I like a lot of this oat milk creamer."

"Noted." He pours the rest of it into a mug for himself.

After we slam our coffee and Wes gets dressed, we head into town.

We park at the bar, then walk over a few blocks to a new breakfast and lunch spot. It's another cute cafe, but with more table service. Still, people are sitting with laptops or books. Is it better that he took me here rather than the other cafe where I was recognized? I'm not sure why being here is worse than working the bar, but it is — maybe because I don't have an escape route or an excuse to dip out of a conversation.

"What's up, man?" the guy behind the counter says to Wes, shaking his hand. "What're you doing here?"

Does Wes know everyone here? The town's not that big, but god. Something tugs in my chest. Envy? But half the reason why I wanted to move to New York was the anonymity of it. But then again, if I were as likeable as people think Wes is, I wouldn't mind people knowing me either.

We order banana nut pancakes, and the guy behind the counter gives us a number to put on our table. Wes guides us to a table that's more or less in the middle of everything and settles down. He sighs heavily.

"What? We haven't even started," I say.

"I'm not really looking forward to the dull parts." He pulls his laptop out too. "I just like making the drinks."

"The competition is about all of it." I pull out my laptop too.

"No shit. Just because I'm not looking forward to it doesn't mean that I won't leave you in the dust." The corner of his mouth lifts.

I roll my eyes. Before I can say something back, someone catches my eye.

"Rose? Is that you?" one of my mom's friends, Anne, says with a smile.

"Hi." Shit. How quickly can I crawl under this table? "How are you?"

"I'm good, I'm good." She squeezes my shoulder. "How long are you home? How's that TV show going? I saw that boyfriend of yours on a different show just the other day."

My stomach drops and my face gets hot. I guess my mom

hasn't been keeping everyone up to date on my failures. Wes's eyebrow quirks up in question.

"Oh, we broke up a few weeks back," I say, trying to ignore Wes's eyes on me. "And the show's not happening. At least for me."

"I'm sorry to hear that, honey." She sounds genuinely sorry for me, which makes it so much worse. "So, are you bartending down here, then?"

I can only nod.

"Good. You shouldn't let those skills go to waste. Especially if you were good enough to at least get a TV deal like that." She glances past me. "I'll see you around, hun. Need to grab this food and head out. It was nice seeing you."

"It was nice seeing you too," I say, forcing a smile.

Anne leaves us, and the silence over the table is deafening. Wes is looking at me like the questions are moments from bursting from his mouth.

"Go ahead and ask because I can tell you want to," I say, opening a browser, then my email.

"You had a boyfriend who's on TV or will be on TV?" Wes asks.

He's asking about Erik first instead of the TV show that never was? That's a first, not that I've talked about this much at all. And somehow, it's worse.

"Yes. He's had a mixology site for a long time and now he's branching into TV appearances. And a show," I say. *Because of me.* Nearly all the recipes for the past three years are ones I created. I fixed his SEO. I helped his following grow on social media by almost tenfold.

And none of it matters now. All those days spent discussing how I'd be a part of the show and how we'd both work together, were a waste. I was just a side character in the story of his life in general, not just on our almost-show. Not even — he wrote me out all together and hasn't looked back. Even with my presence online, people moved on from me like I never existed.

"But you were going to be on TV also?" Wes asks. He pauses when someone arrives with our pancakes and coffee. We make space. The carb coma I'm going to go into after eating these is going to be deep.

"Yes. He'll still have a show, but I won't be on it." I start digging through my email for the one John David sent with some basic information we needed as a jumping off point. "Can we get to work now?"

"What was the show?" he asks instead.

I type a little harder than necessary. "It was about bartending. Check that email John David sent for the info on marketing trends."

He finally does as I say, though I catch him looking at me from time to time. I wish I could see into his head. Is he impressed by the fact that I was almost on TV? Or is he caught up on my ex?

"Got it," he murmurs. "So the show fell apart because you broke up?"

I take a deep breath and let it out, trying to seem as laid back as possible about it. It's in the past. "Basically. Shit like that happens more than you think."

He can see right through me, though, and I hate it. At least he leaves the topic alone and we start working in silence.

My head is all over the place but eventually I focus on the problem at hand. Our budget isn't that big for all of this, so I don't have a ton of money to get some deeper research done. It's fine, mostly, but I don't want to just do *fine.*

I sit back and sigh, cutting into my pancakes.

"I wish we had a little more of a budget for this. Unless JD's cool with us spending a ton on some of these online tools, we might not get all the information we need," I say. "Or maybe we could get a little money for surveys?"

Wes sits back too and stretches. "Why don't we just ask people around here?"

"It's not a great —" I almost say sample size, but he's already looking around at the other people minding their business.

"Yo, Bud," Wes says to a guy behind him. He's wearing a camo hat and an orange t-shirt, which looks incongruous to the dainty teacup next to him.

The guy turns and smiles, giving Wes a fist bump. "What's up, man?"

"You want to answer some questions about cocktails?" Wes asks.

"Sure, I guess." He turns around fully. "What about them? Besides the fact that I like to drink them."

"We're trying to figure out what people might like." Wes glances up at the ceiling, like the answer's written there. "Actually, why not come down to the bar after this and try some stuff?"

"Uh, hold on," I say. "That's not in our plan."

"C'mon. It'll be helpful, probably." Wes drums his fingers on the table, scanning the room. "And we can do social media. We haven't really done a lot of that."

He has a point. But what is he going to do? Round up a

bunch of people in the diner and take them to a bar to taste drinks?

As it turns out, yes — he manages to gather four people: Bud, who we both went to high school with, Doris and Don, an older tourist couple, and Oz, a man a few years younger than us who has to be baked as a cake from the look in his eye.

After we finish eating, we all walk over, with Wes leading the way.

"Alright." Wes steps behind the bar and rests his hands on it. "You got your phone?"

"Yes. But we don't have a plan," I say, pulling out my phone. I splurged for one with an amazing camera last year when I was doing content for Erik's site, while Wes's is a few years old with a ridiculously cracked screen.

"A plan is boring," he says, in true Wes fashion. "Why not wing it?"

I glare at him and he gives me that irritating, handsome grin back. Trying to convince Wes to stick to a plan is like asking a feral cat to walk on a leash. And admittedly, sometimes his spontaneous ideas are better than my well-planned ones, not that I'd ever tell him that.

"Okay, winging it," Wes says, taking my silence as agreement. He runs a hand through his hair and looks at everyone. "How about all of you sit at the bar and we can take videos of tasting a few of our ideas for a canned moonshine cocktail?"

The small group murmurs in agreement and sits at the bar. I go down the bar so I can get everyone in a photo, snapping a few. Wes puts a bottle of Stryker Moonshine and Big Bubba Bourbon on the bar, posing them just as well as I would. He rests an elbow on the bar and smiles again, looking like he's made to be in front of the camera.

"Okay cool," Wes says, resting his hands on the bar. "So, what kind of moonshine cocktail would y'all like to drink on a summer afternoon? We're already doing the moonshine margarita and sweet tea lemonade."

"A beer," Oz says.

Wes and I exchange a look.

"We're thinking cocktails rather than beer," Wes says. "Like something you'd drink at the beach."

"I love the beach," Doris says with a sigh.

"What? You hate the beach, Doris. You complain the whole time. That's why we came to the mountains," Don says, crossing his arms over his chest. The movement strains his blue polo shirt, which coordinates with his wife's.

"Well, I like beach cocktails." Doris huffs. "Something fruity."

"We can run with fruity," I say. I take a step back and scan the ingredients we have. "Let's see a few options. Can you grab the fruit moonshine we have, Wes?"

I pull out all the fruity mixers we have, plus some coconut milk, and Wes grabs all the moonshine. We put it all in front of us.

"Let's see..." Wes starts sliding ingredients toward himself. "The beach...like a piña colada?"

"Pineapple's supposed to be good for a lot of things," Bud says with a goofy grin. Wes shoots one back to him and I roll my eyes.

"What's pineapple good for?" Doris asks with a smile.

"Uh..." Bud's cheeks flush. "Nothing."

"No, I want to know." Doris leans forward and looks to me. I'm sure as hell not telling her.

"Semen, Doris. Semen." Don sighs and rests his elbow on the bar. "Makes it taste better."

"Maybe you should have a little more pineapple, then." Doris glares at her husband.

Oh my *god*. I stomp on Wes's foot so he doesn't laugh, and he turns to let out the fakest cough I've ever heard. I did *not* need to know anything about their habits in the bedroom.

"Anyway!" I clasp my hands together. "Fruity flavors. Pineapple."

"Isn't pineapple a vegetable?" Oz asks. "Like how tomatoes are fruits?"

He can't be serious. But he is. I pull it together and say, "It's a fruit."

"No, I'm really sure it's a vegetable. It has the green part," he says with a breathtaking amount of confidence for someone who's so wrong.

"If the green bit was the only thing that made a vegetable, then strawberries would be vegetables," Bud thankfully points out. I don't think I could hold it together if I answered.

"I'm Googling this shit," Oz murmurs, pulling his phone from his pocket.

"Pineapple juice and what?" Wes asks, scanning the moonshine options. "Let's try a few flavors out."

Wes starts mixing pineapple juice with some other juices, plus moonshine, and I do the same. I split my drink into several small taster glasses, and Wes does too. We slide the samples to everyone. I study their faces as they take a sip.

Doris daintily tastes it and nods, and Don's face is inscrutable.

"Pineapples are fruit," Oz says with a sigh.

"Like we said." Bud takes my drink and throws it back. "Tastes good."

"What's good about it?" I ask, pulling out my notebook. I quickly scribble down the ingredients.

"Dunno. It's fruity. It's kinda sweet." Bud shrugs.

Not the most helpful, but it's something. I taste it again too. It's a bit too sweet, almost cloying, but you can't taste the alcohol.

Everyone else gives their comments, which again, are varying levels of helpful. I wish we'd been more methodical about it all, but of course, we had to wing it.

I push down my annoyance. At least we're working toward something, right? Wes keeps creating drinks, giving out samples and getting vague feedback. It helps. Sort of.

"Oh shit, we have some passionfruit juice," Wes says, pulling it out from deep in the fridge.

"Would that be expensive production-wise?" I ask.

"We can just try a little. No need to set it in stone." He tops off his drink with the juice. "Looks pretty too."

"Let me get a photo," I say.

I position the drink and snap a bunch of photos. Then I do the same with mine, and taste his.

"I think it could use a little bit of something." I scan the ingredients. "Here."

I tweak the drink with a few more ingredients before tasting it again. The flavor explodes over my tongue — it's perfect. Fruity, but not cloyingly sweet. Definitely beachy.

"I like this," I say to Wes.

"Yeah?" Wes brightens, taking the glass. "That's solid. Y'all want to taste this?"

We recreate the drink, adding in the ingredients we included to make one joint drink. I jot down the ingredients and the amounts, though they're not super exact.

"This is so good," Bud says. "Feels kinda fancy without being too much."

"This is heaven." Oz slams the rest of the drink. He looks pretty toasted.

Doris and Don agree that it's great too. We take a few photos of them enjoying the drink, plus the final product with a bit of garnish, just for fun.

"Whew, I'm tipsy." Doris rests her head on her husband's shoulder. "This is a lot of fun. We should go to the beach, Donny. I'm gonna get you some pineapple and we'll have a great time."

"Annnd that's all we need from all of you today," I say quickly, before Doris goes on. Don is getting a little handsy, despite his earlier annoyance with his wife.

"You can get a free meal on us at the tavern next door," Wes adds. "To soak up that alcohol."

A good call — we were a little bit sample happy. Everyone thanks us and files out. I blow out a breath and start to clean up.

"See, that was kind of productive," Wes says, wiping down the bar. "Even if we winged it. We got our joint drink down, and we didn't think that would work as well as it did."

"True." I take the glasses and start carrying them to the sink. "I think we could serve it at Stryker Day and get even more feedback. Maybe something more formal, if you want me to type up a survey."

"Yeah, sure." He dries his hand and offers it to me in a high five. "Nice teamwork."

I pause, then slap his hand. So apparently Wes and I can work together, at least a little. Maybe this won't be as bad as I thought it would be. For the first time since this started, I have some hope that we'll make it through without driving each other insane or competing on every little bit of this project.

"Nice teamwork, yeah," I say.

CHAPTER SEVEN

ROSE

John David Stryker Day — specifically, John David Stryker the first — is a bigger deal than I remember it being. Every year the distillery throws an event to celebrate the founder of Stryker Liquor's birthday, with drinks, music, and free food.

And this year, Wes and I need to play nice while we serve up the idea we put together at the impromptu focus group the other day and film stuff for social media. It's going to be a pain in the ass juggling both, but apparently they don't even have a full time social media person. It's just an intern who does kind of a half-assed job.

Wes sighs, looking at the crowd waiting to come through the double doors at the front of the distillery.

"Can't believe we still throw this bullshit event every year," Wes says, resting his forearms on the heavy wooden bar in front of us.

"You don't like it?" I ask. "It's kind of fun. An excuse to party."

"The event's not the problem. It's the reason behind it,"

he says. "My great-grandfather was a fucking nutcase who just happened to be good at business. Not the kind of person who we should be holding up as an example in any way, even if I owe my life to him."

I glance at the portraits lining the wall of the distillery, starting with an old photo of John David Stryker the first. He does look a bit rough around the edges, with a big bushy beard and patched-up outfit. Wes's grandfather looks a bit more dignified, wearing a suit, and his father looks just like he does now in a more casual dark blue button-down shirt. I'm guessing JD will fill up the last spot whenever their dad retires.

"I mean, he was making moonshine in his backyard during prohibition. It's not like he was the most law-abiding citizen," I point out.

"Yeah." Wes rakes his hands through his hair. "But it's not like my grandfather is any better. Did you know he faked his death when I was a kid? Just to see how my dad would do running the company?"

"*What?*" I gape at him, waiting for him to show me he was joking. He doesn't. "I'm guessing that fun fact isn't included in the tour."

Wes barks a laugh, like he wasn't expecting to. Then again, we don't really have normal conversations like this often — I'm surprised too.

"Yeah, definitely not. Fun core memory, right there. Thankfully Dad did a better job than he'd ever do so the old man retired. He was too chaotic to run it anyway and probably would have run it into the ground if he had enough time."

"Hello, hello!" Mrs. Stryker says before I can respond.

Everyone in town knows Mrs. Stryker — she's a former beauty queen, and still looks the part. Not a strand of her dark hair is out of place and her makeup is almost professionally perfect. Unlike me, Wes, and the others working at the distillery, who are in Stryker Liquors t-shirts, she's in a nice button-down shirt with the Stryker Liquor logo on one side tucked into nice slacks.

She's also known for having her hand in everyone's business in town, like the epicenter of gossip. My mom says if she wanted to, Mrs. Stryker could probably hold the whole town hostage with all the dirt she has on people.

She air-kisses me on the cheek, then does the same to Wes before checking her lipstick in the front camera of her phone.

"Are y'all excited?" she asks with a beautiful smile. "It's a nice turnout this year."

"Yeah, it looks like a crowd," I say. Even if she's not making any decisions about the drink, I still want her on my good side.

"Let me fix your hair, Wesley," Mrs. Stryker says with a tut, reaching for Wes's head.

"Ma, please," he says, stepping back. "It's fine."

"Well, you two are going to be in a lot of pictures and on social media, no?" She adjusts his loose curls anyway, and actually makes them look better. "We should kick that up a notch. I'm thinking of doing a photoshoot with Big Bubba and some of the other Bubbas."

"Other Bubbas?" I ask.

"Big Bubba is just the oldest male lab our family has at any given time," Wes says, pushing his hair back to how it was. "There's a whole family tree of them."

"And speak of the devil," Mrs. Stryker says, her face lighting up. She leans down and Big Bubba himself comes trotting up to her. "Hi, Bubba. Where's your pappy?"

Mr. Stryker doesn't seem like anyone's pappy, but he appears behind the dog, so I'm guessing she's referring to him. He claps Wes on the shoulder and nods hello to me before kissing his wife on the temple.

"I think I want y'all to do a demonstration," he says without preamble.

"For what?" Wes asks, petting Bubba's back hip.

"For what you've been working on," Mr. Stryker adds. "JD said that you had some kind of focus group the other day at the bar."

I exchange a glance with Wes, hoping my panic isn't written across my face the way it's making itself known in my chest. We have the drink, sort of, but a demo involves some prep, right? I'm not a spontaneous presentation kind of girl.

"We...haven't really prepared anything?" I say. "We have the drink, but we haven't coordinated on a demo yet."

Mr. Stryker levels us with a look. A challenge. My panic evolves to irritation. What is he getting out of this? Keeping us on our toes, but to what end? I can feel Wes's emotions mirroring my own without even looking at him.

"I'm sure y'all can put something together." Mr. Stryker tucks his hands into his pockets. "Might as well test your idea for a crowd."

"I can film it for social media too!" Mrs. Stryker adds, her eyes brightening. "I have a tripod somewhere."

"Sounds good." Mr. Stryker looks at his watch. "We're opening the doors in just a few minutes, so y'all should get to it. We'll get someone to cover the bar for the next half hour."

I give him a tight-lipped smile and look over to Wes. "Let's go figure something out, then."

Wes guides me back to the office without a word. Once we're inside, he flops into a seat and groans.

"Of course he'd do some shit like this," Wes says, running his hand through his hair. "He takes power trips like they're his daily vitamin."

"He's our boss, so we need to figure something out." I'm too worked up to sit, so I pace back and forth. "I wish he'd given us parameters or something."

"Have you ever done a demo before?" Wes asks. "For that TV show you were going to be a part of?"

"Not for that, but I've done competitions." I take a deep breath through my nose and try to calm down.

For competitions, I usually spend a ton of time preparing. Hell, I finally entered the competition at the convention in Nashville in a few weeks and that doesn't even feel like enough time to get ready.

"Oh, cool, so we can wing it." Wes puts his feet up.

"What? No," I say, my eyes widening. "How did you jump from me having done something kind of adjacent to us being ready to wing it?"

"Because you're with me." He grins. "I'm confident in front of a crowd. Just give me a little prompting and I'll sort it out."

I swear to god. This man is going to drive me to madness or make me end up in jail. I'd need a running start to jump up and strangle him because he's so tall, but I'm fast.

"More like you're cocky." I press the heels of my hands to

my forehead to ward off the headache that's coming. "Wes. We need to put together a plan. Quickly."

"What's better — a plan thrown together in the half hour we have, or accepting our fate and just rolling with it?" He steeples his fingers together, like he's about to give a Ted Talk on being a reckless dickhead.

"The first thing."

"Nah, the second thing."

"What was the point in asking if you were just going to shoot it down?" I look around for a pad of paper to take notes. "You know what? Never mind. I'll plan something, then you can go along with it."

"Fine with me."

Wes sits there, watching me scramble to think of how to present this drink. It's not that complicated and I don't need to know the history of the ingredients. Wes probably knows the history of the distillery to fill in some gaps. Do we even have all the ingredients that we need?

I usher Wes to follow me, so we can grab the ingredients and tools for the drink from the bar station where we were supposed to be serving it first. The event is already bustling, with people clustered around different stations they've set up in the big grassy area behind the distillery.

I'm already sweating my ass off and we haven't even started.

"Y'all ready?" Mr. Stryker asks, studying us.

"Yes." I try to smile even though I'm both furious and nauseous.

"We have a drink demonstration over here for anyone who's interested," Mr. Stryker calls over the crowd. "A new drink we have in development."

I hang onto hope that no one will be interested, but soon a small crowd gathers in front of us.

"Hey, I'm Wes Stryker, and this is Rose," Wes says before I can even open my mouth. "Are y'all ready to see one of our newest drinks?"

One woman lets out a *woo* but the crowd stays dead silent otherwise. Amazing start.

"We don't have a name for it yet, but this drink is perfect if you like tropical drinks," I say, grabbing a glass.

"We should call it the piña moonlada," Wes adds. He pushes the ingredients forward, turning the labels so they're visible.

"That's terrible," I blurt. My eyes flick to the phone on its tripod, avoiding Mrs. Stryker behind it. "And it's not really like a piña colada at all."

Wes's grin shows me he's joking around, which only makes me want to pinch him. "But it's memorable. And who doesn't like a piña colada?"

"True," I say, even though I hate them. "So —"

"We'll start with some pineapple juice," Wes says, grabbing the juice and the stainless steel shaker. "Just eyeball it."

He can eyeball it since he does this every day, but isn't the point of this to show what the drink we're going to can and sell will taste like? What happened to walking through the ingredients list before we jump right in?

"We recommend two ounces," I say, holding up a jigger with the 2 oz side up and tapping it.

"Or let loose a little." Wes caps the juice and puts it back. "We have fun when we let loose, don't we?"

I'm so taken aback at this blatant lie that I let out an incredulous laugh. "Do we?"

"Of course." He winks at me, one side of his mouth lifting higher than the other.

An alarming number of men have winked at me, and each one gave me the heebie jeebies. But with Wes? I swoon against my will.

"Sure," I choke out, trying not to mess with my braids or dry my sweaty hands on my jeans. *Pull it together.*

"Same deal with the orange juice — just add a little bit more OJ than pineapple juice." He grabs the orange juice next.

I try to lunge across the table to reach the rest of the ingredients, so I can take control of this again. But the table is too long and I end up missing it by a few inches.

"Want some help?" Wes asks, sliding the ingredients my way.

"Thanks." My face gets hot as I take the ingredients. "Next, we'll add 2 ounces of lime juice and one ounce of passionfruit juice. Lastly, 2 ounces of coconut moonshine."

I measure out each ingredient, dumping it into the shaker.

"Then you shake it," Wes adds, putting his hand out for the shaker.

"You think I can't shake this on my own?" I ask, trying to keep a smile in my voice.

"You can." He puts his hand up. "Just trying to be a gentleman."

"Oh? You?" I say before I can stop myself. Thankfully, the crowd actually laughs. "Fine, then, go for it."

He laughs too and takes the shaker, shaking it. A lot of eyes in the crowd go to Wes's arms. Glad it's not just me that's mesmerized by them.

"After you give it a shake, strain it into a glass." He puts it down in front of me, presumably to finish.

He rests his hand next to me and leans against it as I pour, partially boxing me in. Even though he's on my last nerve, his big form behind me instantly lights up a primal part of my brain that doesn't need to be activated right now. If he leans forward just a little bit, he'd be pressed against my back.

"Then, you just top it off with a bit of soda water." I crack open a can and top the drink. "We'll put a bit of pineapple for garnish today, but we're testing this drink out to see if people would like us to can it and sell it."

I put a small wedge of pineapple onto the edge of the drink and push it forward.

"So, any questions?" Wes asks, resting his hands on the table.

I didn't think of having questions as a part of it, but maybe we'll be able to salvage this. I didn't mean to rip into him, even if people wrote it off as a joke. Mr. Stryker is watching us, his arms crossed over his chest. Is that just his general demeanor, or is he annoyed at us?

"What if I don't like orange or lime?" a woman asks. "Can I replace it with something else?"

That's almost...the whole recipe... what is she expecting? I look to Wes to answer because I'm not sure if I can give her one.

"You can just add more pineapple juice," Wes says. "It'll be different than the drink we plan to sell will be, though."

"Oh, I don't like pineapple either." The woman's shoulders sag. "What about apple juice?"

"Probably not, but you can try it," Wes says.

The woman looks so confused. "Pineapple? Apple?"

Wes and I exchange another glance.

"They're two different fruits," I say, slowly and hopefully not letting my confusion into my voice.

"Oh. I've never had an apple," the woman says.

How is that possible? This woman has to be forty years old at a minimum. I can tell Wes is moments from bursting out laughing, so I step on his foot.

"So, that's everything," I say before the question session gets out of control. "We'll be serving these drinks for the next half-hour or so, if you'd like to give it a shot."

"Thanks, everyone," Wes says.

The crowd claps half-heartedly. I let out a breath, my shoulders sagging. Some people who work at the distillery swoop in to give us some more glasses, ice, and ingredients.

"That wasn't too bad, was it?" Wes says to me.

"It wasn't great. Your dad looks unimpressed," I say, glancing over to where Mr. Stryker is talking to JD.

"He never looks impressed, trust me." Wes snorts.

My irritation is stewing, escalating into true irritation. Maybe Wes hasn't done anything to impress his dad. But I could, and this little stunt is putting me steps back. He has no idea of how much extra shit I need to do to get ahead compared to him.

People start lining up to try the drink, so I can turn my attention off of him. We sling drinks, including to the woman who's never had an apple before. As the line trickles down, Mr. And Mrs. Stryker step up.

"Let's give this a try," Mrs. Stryker says. She slides my phone to me. "And here's your phone. We recorded the whole thing. I sent John David a copy as well."

"Thank you." I tuck my phone back into my pocket. They'll expect us to post something about this on social media. How am I supposed to edit down this video to make it look like Wes and I are getting along?

Wes mixes up two drinks for his parents and slides them across the table. Mrs. Stryker takes a dainty sip, then nods, and Mr. Stryker does the same without any reaction.

"Thank you. It's lovely," Mrs. Stryker says with a smile.

Mr. Stryker just nods. Someone catches their attention and they both drift off to another conversation. I relax for the first time this whole day, before I realize how much we fucked up.

"Did you have to do that?" I ask him.

"Do what?" His brows furrow.

"*That*. The whole thing you just did, making us look like we're a complete hot mess," I hiss.

"Rose, we had like fifteen minutes to throw that together. We *were* a hot mess," he says. "And I think you did fine. I know I did."

"Wes. That was all over the place. It didn't look good." I grip the edge of the table and try to pull myself together, but I'm so over this shit. I'm over his cavalier attitude about all of this. This stuff matters to me. He can get a bunch of other chances, even if his father is a dickhead, but I only have one shot with this particular thing. But does he care?

Probably not.

I knew the other day was a fluke. Wes's flavor of chaos is just a pain in my ass.

"Y'know what? Never mind."

I brush past him to get some space. We've barely just begun and I'm so tired of his bullshit.

CHAPTER EIGHT

WES

Nana Brunch, as we started to call it, began a few years back when both Waylon and I had moved back to Jepsen. She's always wanted us to know how to cook just in case — or, as Nana said, "I'll be damned if I have some useless ass grandsons."

When she had a knee replacement a year or so ago, Waylon and I came over to cook for her and the tradition stuck to Sundays a few weekends a month.

We pull up to Nana's little house on the edge of town, a one-story ranch style house painted her favorite shade of yellow. Her garden is purposefully chaotic, overrun with flowering bushes and plants beneath the wraparound porch and hanging plants hanging from it.

She steps out onto the porch when she hears us coming, shading her eyes from the sun. She's in a hot pink mumu, her long white hair up in a bun on top of her head, and cat slippers. She changes her glasses a lot for someone with the worst prescription I've ever seen, and this time they're bright yellow cat-eyed ones that clash with her clothes.

Nana says she stopped giving a shit about what people thought of her decades before I was born. I can't imagine her ever caring about other people's opinions. She straddles the line between the hippie population and the extremely southern population of Jepsen, which means she's more than willing to tell you exactly what she thinks in a sweet southern accent, then give you a weird tea to cure your insomnia that you don't even have.

"Well if it isn't my grandsons, deciding to show their faces," Nana calls out as I hop out of the car. She still has a smoker's voice even though she quit before we were born.

"Hey, Nana," I reply with a grin.

"Y'all are late." She rests one hand on her hip. "I'm hungry as hell."

"Sorry. We had to go to the store and wrangle the dogs."

Waylon lets Duke and Murphy out of the backseat, and they go bounding up to Nana, tails wagging.

After cooing over the dogs, she pulls us each in for a big hug and a wet kiss on the cheek. She always smells like comfort and home. I spent a lot of days at her house when my parents got sick of my bullshit, so in some ways her little house is more home than my parents' sprawling mansion.

We head straight to her small kitchen, petting her ancient Maltese Coco and her cat Sugar on the way. There's barely enough space for all three of us, so we banish the dogs to the edge of the kitchen. It doesn't help that she has all kinds of knickknacks, pieces of art, and plants on every windowsill, making it feel cluttered. But it's cozy.

"What're you making us today?" Nana asks, easing into a chair in her breakfast nook.

"Biscuits and sausage gravy," I say, unpacking the groceries.

"Good, good," she says. "Make some coffee, would you, Waylon?"

"Wow, not me?" I arch an eyebrow and grin at her.

"Whatever you make can't be called coffee, sweetness." Nana laughs, scooping up Sugar. "I don't know how you survive."

The memory of seeing Rose's big, lush tits practically spilling out of her tank top when I made her coffee the other day come floating up against my will. If making coffee every morning came with that view, I'd do it with no complaints.

I focus on unpacking everything so things don't get awkward. Thankfully I took the edge off in the shower this morning so I have a little bit of control.

"Oh, I saw all that Stryker Day stuff on Instagram," Nana says, pulling her phone out of her bra. "Y'all did a nice demonstration."

"Since when are you on Instagram?" I ask, setting the sausage aside and going into the lower cabinets for the cast-iron skillet.

"Since your cousins talked me into it." Nana looks at the screen over her edge of her glasses. "I can see photos of all my grandbabies, those dogs that ride on skateboards, and Chris Hemsworth in one place."

"Jesus, Nana," Waylon says, opening Nana's stuffed pantry. "Chris Hemsworth?"

"I'm old, I'm not dead." Nana laughs, still tapping around. "Here you go — here's the post that's blowing up.

Everyone thinks you're very handsome and that you and Rose look cute together."

"We look *cute* together?" I ask. She extends her phone to me and I take a look.

The video is a clip of us doing the demo. I'm not sure what people are thinking, but all I see is us exchanging snippy comments and trying to smile around it all.

But I check the comments and Nana is right — there's a lot of thirsting for both of us, and people asking if we're dating. I kind of hate everyone being a creep to Rose.

"People are crazy," I say, handing Nana the phone again. "Nothing's going on besides the usual."

"Looked a little flirty to me too." Waylon grabs a bowl from a different cabinet, then flour from the pantry. "At least flirty in the way you two get."

"Flirty?" I scan Waylon to see if he's joking around but he looks like his regular self. "C'mon. I'm just trying to mess with her, not flirt with her."

I feel guilty about dicking around during the demo now since she was so pissed. I still think we did well — seriously, how well could we have done with next to no notice? — but I could have been more cooperative.

"Just calling it as I see it." Waylon shrugs and washes his hands.

"Well, you always had a little crush on her, didn't you?" Nana asks.

I'd practically lived with Nana back then since my dad and I were fighting all the damn time. As a wild ass teenager, having someone to rant to without judgment literally saved me. But unfortunately I told her pretty much everything, from bullshit from my dad to dating to school. And Rose was involved in that.

"I didn't have a crush on her in high school," I grumble, slicing open the package of sausage open with a little too much force. The dogs perk up, like I'm going to sling more across the room. "If anything, she was my nemesis back then."

"Nemesis?" Nana bursts out laughing, which sounds more like a wheeze than anything. "Who are you, a Bond villain? Get a grip."

I can't help but laugh too. "Fine, she was my rival. *Is* my rival since she's standing between me and finally moving up into the company beyond the bar."

It's been a while since I've spoken to Nana since we didn't come over last Sunday, so I explain what's going on with the drink – what Rose and I have to do, along with Dad's plan to pit us against each other. And of course, JD's offer to promote me to manager.

"That's so like your father," Nana says, hiking Coco up under her arm. "Pulling some nonsense like this to get y'all to be at each others' throats."

"I know." I stab at the sausage in the pan, breaking it up. "But maybe it'll help? I still can't please JD but I think I could if I make a killer drink if she's pushing me to do better."

"I remember that you always gave more of a shit in classes she was in," Nana says in a tone that makes me turn and look at her. She puts her hands up. "I'm just saying. The Insta comments might be right."

I can't believe Nana's calling it Insta, but I brush that off.

"Nana, that was high school," I say again. "And also,

even if I did have a thing for her, so what? She could barely tolerate me then and she barely can now."

"Yeah, high school," Waylon says, crumbling cold butter into the flour. "Who's to say you can't be friendly *and* still have the rivalry going? Since that seems like it'll be impossible to end if you're trying to win against her. She doesn't have to hate you."

I stop stabbing the sausage with the spoon. "Just...be friendly?"

Waylon raises an eyebrow at me. "Have you seriously not considered that?"

"Not really." I spot Murphy trying to crawl across the floor to get a bit of sausage that flew off the pan. "Get back, Murph."

He just lays down halfway to me, his legs splayed behind him.

"I think y'all could get along," Nana says. "You're grown now. No need to let old stuff from when you were little get in the way."

I scoop up some sausage and put it in a bowl. They're not *wrong*. And it's not like we have any serious beef from the past that I'm aware of. I just drove (okay, still drive) her nuts and we were always down each other's throats, trying to win.

"We'd probably be more productive if I tried to keep myself from driving her crazy," I admit.

"Exactly," Nana says. "Clear the air. Then make the best drink you can, win the competition, sell that shit, and get to where you want to be."

"Might as well give it a shot," I say. An apology shouldn't be hard at all.

As we finish cooking, the conversation shifts to Waylon,

who talks about what's going on at the vet clinic and the latest terrible date that Mom set him up on. Nana's exasperated with Mom, as always. I have no idea how Mom became the polar opposite of Nana, all prim southern belle, but she managed to. Once we eat breakfast, we linger for a few hours on the porch, watching the dogs play in the yard, before we head out.

Nana kisses Waylon on the cheek first, then pulls me into a fierce hug.

"Don't forget to bury the hatchet with Rose," Nana says, fixing my hair. "It'll make your life a lot easier."

"I won't forget."

Waylon and I climb into the car with the dogs and head back to our house. The drive isn't long, but I get enough time to think about how I could approach Rose about this. I'll start with the apology, but then what?

Since she doesn't have a car, she's at home where we left her. I find her on the couch, watching some reality TV show in her pajamas. She has a scarf over her braids, which are wound in a bun, and a star-shaped zit pad on her cheek. Dennis is curled up on the arm of the couch in a loaf shape, eyes squeezed shut.

"What's up?" I ask. "You want some leftovers from my grandma's?"

"Sure?" She raises a skeptical eyebrow at me, but the skepticism turns into a smile when Murphy trots toward her. He flops at her feet.

"They aren't poisoned." I snort. "It's biscuits and gravy. Still warm."

"Yeah, thanks, then." She stands up. Her t-shirt is so long that it looks like she's not wearing any pants. I pry my eyes away from her legs. Burying the hatchet doesn't involve gawking at her.

I hand her the food, then go to get her a fork. She looks up at me in surprise when I sit down between her and Dennis, handing her the fork.

"Thank you," she murmurs.

We sit in silence watching TV. It's a show where a bunch of men are competing to date one woman, who has to be the most boring woman in the world. She's like if skim milk were a person.

I watch Rose eat out of the corner of my eye. Well, "eat" — more like devour. I like cooking for people for the same reason I like bartending. It's an easy thing to do that makes people feel good.

"Sorry about the other day," I say, just to get it out. "At the demo. I shouldn't have dicked around."

Rose's eyes widen for a moment. I don't think she fully heard me until she says, "Thank you. That's really nice of you."

"Nice, or basic, trying-not-to-be-a-dick courtesy?"

She smiles. "It can be both."

We watch more of the show. How does she watch this for hours on end, and why am I getting a little invested in this shit?

"You remember why we started competing? Beyond the baby pageant situation?" I ask when a short, unskippable commercial comes on.

"Not really, why?" she asks, sucking a crumb off her thumb. My eyes linger on her mouth, trying to ignore the thoughts of how good it would feel for her to do that to me. This lust is clouding my thoughts.

"Dunno." I extend my hand to Dennis, who's gotten up from his spot and started to climb down, probably to step all over the biscuits. He lets me scoop him up and settle him on my lap.

"You sure you don't know, or are you just hiding something?" Her eyes slowly narrow. Even without makeup, her lashes are ridiculously long.

"Okay, fine," I say, resting my hands on Dennis's back. "I was just thinking we could just...make things less...bicker-y."

"Bicker-y?" Rose presses her lips together, like she's trying not to laugh.

"You know what I mean," I say with a sigh. "Just bickering less. So we can get this shit done. I mean, a lot of it's my fault, but...I don't know."

This shit sounded a lot better in my head.

Rose's eyes turn confused, then soften. "So...you're saying you don't want to drive me nuts anymore?"

"I don't *want* to, but I'm not perfect." I smile.

She bites her bottom lip for a moment.

"Okay," she says softly. "That sounds good."

"Good." I relax.

We'll just have to see how much patience we each have.

CHAPTER NINE

WES

"Fuck off," I grumble to Dennis, who's sitting on my chest. Despite my warning, he tries to put his grubby little paw into my mouth. "Dude."

Dennis meows, purring and walking all around and over my head. I try to bury my face back into the pillow, but then he walks on the *back* of my head.

"Fine, you little shit," I say, rolling over and scooping him up. He's purring his ass off, giving me a slow blink. "No remorse, huh? I guess I have to get up anyway."

My brain comes more and more online, and I shuffle downstairs to make Rose's coffee, Dennis in my arms. I wish I hadn't agreed to this being Rose's prize. I don't understand how she wakes up relatively early after we get home around three in the morning. Maybe because she has the coffee.

I've gotten the hang of the French press, even if the time it takes feels entirely too long for a drink you need first thing in the morning. As I wait, I play with Dennis, tossing his stuffed catnip banana for him to fetch and bring back to me. He's better at this than Murphy.

Eventually he flops to the ground, exposing his belly. I know better than to pet his belly directly, so I scoop him up again to pet him.

"You're a menace to society," I say in a dumb baby voice that I only whip out for animals. "You're a fluffy little asshole wrapped up in cuteness."

Dennis purrs, butting his head against my chin and chirping.

"A little asshole wrapped up in cuteness?" Rose says, Murphy behind her. Murphy's been sleeping in her room lately, the traitor.

I whip my head around and find Rose watching me, amusement brightening her eyes. My face gets hot despite myself.

"A *fluffy* little asshole wrapped up in cuteness," I say, gathering myself. I check the timer on my phone. "The coffee is almost ready."

"No, we're not skipping past the fluffy asshole stuff." She saunters into the kitchen. Thankfully she's wearing more clothes today — bike shorts that hit her mid-thigh and a loose tank top — but I still can't keep my eyes off of her.

"It's self-explanatory," I say, walking over to put Dennis down in front of the window. Hopefully the birds and squirrels will hold his attention. "He's fluffy and a little asshole."

"Still. That's cute."

My phone goes off and I pour us each a mug of coffee. I top hers off with her creamer, getting it to the exact shade she likes it.

"Here you go." I slide her mug to her.

I watch her intently as she picks up her mug and takes a sip.

"Mm, perfect," she says, closing her eyes and shaking her hips. "I've trained you well."

The low purr of her voice makes my cock ache. I'd gladly let her train me to do a lot of things.

Maybe making coffee for her every day won't be so bad if I get that kind of reaction.

We finish our coffee, sorting out what we'll be focusing on today — our individual drinks — and get dressed. After we drive to the bar and head inside, she puts down her bag and starts grabbing all the different flavors of moonshine that we have.

"Wow, jumping right into it?" I ask.

"I just had an idea and I want to make it before I forget." She bends over to grab a glass and a shaker, her shorts riding up her thighs.

"What's the idea?" I ask. I haven't had many ideas yet, but once I get around the ingredients, I'll think of something.

"I won't tell you until I'm done with it," she says, grabbing a bottle of moonshine and a shot glass.

She gets to work and I start to work too, grabbing a few random items. We have all the information on ingredient pricing so we know not to use a ton of expensive shit that'll cut in the margins.

Rose starts mixing drinks, shaking a cocktail shaker with one hand while scribbling down notes with another. I just start mixing some things together based on how I feel and what could possibly taste good. A lot of the customers I make drinks on the fly for like something a bit sweeter when it comes to mixing with moonshine. Lower quality moonshine can be like drinking straight up rubbing alcohol, but ours is much smoother.

I taste my drink. It's not quite right, and I'm not sure how to fix it. I switch up my moonshine, picking our cherry flavor, which has some moonshine-soaked maraschino cherries, and some coke. This hits right.

Meanwhile, Rose is cutting something up in a very elaborate way for some reason. Eventually she finishes and puts it on her glass.

"Taste this. The garnish is just for practice," she says, pushing the drink toward me and putting a tiny straw in it for me to taste. The garnish is an orange slice, cut into a rose. It looks pretty cool, to be honest.

"Practicing what? Cutting oranges into the shape of your namesake?

She tucks her braids behind her ear and doesn't meet my eye. "I'm going to be a part of the cocktail competition that the convention sponsor is holding when we're in Nashville. That garnish is part of my presentation."

"Cocktail competition?" I raise an eyebrow and lift the glass to my lips. I've never heard of those before. If I had, I would have entered.

"Yeah. I did them all the time in New York." She bites her bottom lip and looks at me, then the drink like she wants me to taste it.

I take a sip. It's good — really good — but there's a lot going on. One flavor hits me first and melts over my tongue, but then more complex, almost savory on the back end.

"What does it involve?" I ask. "Just making a drink recipe and having it judged?"

"Yes and no." She watches me take another small sip. We're not trying to get drunk here, so I take it slow. "There's usually some kind of rule — like you have to use the sponsor's liquor or some ingredient. Then you have to do a presentation while you describe what you're doing and why to some judges."

"Huh." It's not something I'd personally do — I'm good in front of a crowd, but the idea of a whole planned presentation doesn't sound fun.

"What?" She narrows her eyes. "The cut off date is closed for entering."

"Relax," I say with a smirk. "You thought I'd join just to compete with you even *more*? It's not my scene."

"You're a little chaotic, so maybe." She rests her hands on her hips and glances at the drink in my hand again. "Are you going to tell me what you think of the drink?"

"I like it," I say, because there's no point in lying. It's *really* fucking good, citrusy and a bit smoky from one of the peppers. "But it's kinda complicated."

"Complicated?" She frowns. "How so?"

"Complicated is the wrong word, I guess." I take another sip. "Sophisticated, I think."

She rests a hand on her hip. "Is it, though?"

"I'm telling you, yes. There's citrus as the main flavor but there's a lot more there." I ask, mulling it over. "Whatever — if it's not something simple like lemonade, it might not go over well with the people who like our drink. Or at least that's my gut feeling."

She takes the drink back from me and takes a sip from the opposite side of the glass, leaving a lipstick print on it.

"Fine, good point."

"Try this. Cherry coke." I push my drink toward her. "Easy, and the cherry moonshine is a favorite."

She takes a sip, her lips pressing where mine were. Slowly, she nods.

"It's nice," she says, pushing it back to me. "Straightforward."

"One of the few times you've said that as a compliment." I swirl the drink around.

"What is that supposed to mean?" she asks.

"We're like yin and yang." I gesture between the two of us. "You're extra — in a good way — and I'm chill. You make shit complicated — which isn't always a bad thing — I'm straightforward."

She mulls that over. To my surprise, she doesn't look annoyed at all.

"I guess so." She shrugs. "Back to the drawing board, I guess."

We go back to working on our own for a while. I'm pretty satisfied with the cherry coke moonshine, so I start dicking around with some other flavor combinations. Some taste terrible, like vanilla creme, but other ones have potential.

"Why wouldn't you want to compete?" she asks out of the blue, taking a step back and looking at the higher shelves where we keep the moonshine flavors people rarely order. "You like making drinks. You like competing. It's perfect."

"There aren't exactly a lot of competitions around here," I say, trying to see what she's looking at. We used to do a lot of seasonal flavors, which are up on that shelf collecting dust.

I've never liked any of them. "And it feels like it takes the spontaneity out of it. But hey, it sounds like your thing so that's cool. Bet you're good at it."

She looks back at me and blinks like she can't believe what I've said. I guess I did compliment her without a smartass comment following it. But I'm not going to bullshit her on it, especially since we've come to a truce or sorts. She's good at what she does. Maybe not as good as me, at least around here, but still amazing.

"Thank you," is all she says, her voice quiet. Then, she points up at the shelf. "Where's the ladder? I need to grab that gingerbread moonshine."

"No, you don't," I say.

She frowns. "Why?"

"Because gingerbread moonshine tastes like the Gingerbread Man's asscrack. There's no way you can make that taste good."

A wicked grin spreads across her face. "Wanna bet?"

"I can't even bet you on that because you'd be breaking some kind of natural law making that taste like anything but garbage."

"Fine." She marches past me and toward the back closet. I sigh when she returns with a short ladder. "I'll do it myself."

She opens the ladder and starts climbing up it. Her ass is right in my face, and I only have a thimble-full of self control to not look at her. I give up and check her out. Shit. I want to just *touch* her. I've never seen a more perfect ass on any woman before — the way it perfectly matches her thick thighs and the curve of her hips is art.

As she steps back with an armful of moonshine bottles,

she starts falling back. She lets out a squeak and I catch her, one hand on her ass and the other around her waist.

She freezes, and so do I. Even the tiniest shift could send all the glass bottles in her arms to the floor so I squeeze a bit tighter. By mistake. But it feels so good that my cock starts to harden. As if she isn't a slipped hand away from breaking her neck.

I lift her off the ladder and slowly start to move her. She starts to kick her legs, but I hold her tighter, my arm brushing the underside of her breasts.

"Wait, wait, hold on," I say, holding her closer. She's light, but she's holding an armful of glass. If she squirms more we'll have a lot to clean up. "Let me get you so you don't drop that."

I slowly bring her down and onto her feet. She doesn't quite meet my eye as she murmurs a thank you. I don't miss the waver in her voice or her hardened nipples through her shirt. My cock is being an asshole and won't calm down, so I turn to the bar and start wiping it down, even though it's still clean.

"Um, a better bet than that drink," she says, straightening her shorts. "The Jepsen Festival this weekend."

"What about it?" I ask. The Jepsen Festival is an annual event in town, and it's one of my favorites. It's all shitty fried food, goofy events, and rickety carnival rides.

"We're supposed to test our drinks on the public, right? We can do that with each of our drinks and hand out a survey," she says. "Whoever gets the better response gets a favor."

"Sure, works for me," I say. Thinking of competition is safer than thinking of her ass. "I'm in."

She pours herself a little bit of the gingerbread moonshine and tastes it. Her face goes through a full range of emotions, ending in disgust. I burst out laughing.

"Ugh." She wrinkles her nose and pushes the bottle of gingerbread moonshine away. "This really does taste like the Gingerbread Man's asscrack."

CHAPTER TEN

ROSE

It's ridiculously hot already, and that's even with the tent above us. I'm wearing a tank top and denim shorts, my braids up in a bun on top of my head. Sweat drips down my chest and between my breasts and I'm just standing here, watching Wes haul things out of the back of his car.

After he flipped me around the other day, picking me up like I hardly weighed a thing, I know he's more than capable of doing all the heavy lifting.

I know I wasn't imagining the hardness pressing through his jeans and against me. It was too big not to notice. Now I can't stop thinking about it no matter how hard I try. Between that and the time I walked in on him in bed, I completely understand the rumors about what he's packing. They're based on actual experience.

And now that he's actively trying to make an effort to drive me less nuts?

I don't know. But I assumed him toning it down would make me *less* confused, not more.

The simple mental switch from assuming the worst of him to assuming that he's just playing around has been way more powerful than I thought it would be.

"Yo, Rose, look alive," Wes says.

"What? Sorry." I go back to filling a few cups with ice before popping them back into the cooler.

We mixed up two big batches of the cocktails we wanted to test on people, so I'm pouring about fifteen each. That should be a small enough sample for us to get good feedback. Whoever gets a higher average on the score card we're giving out wins.

Wins what? Just the satisfaction, I think. Watch him pull something out of his ass as his prize.

Wes appears next to me and starts filling some of the cups. He's in shorts and a tank top with the sleeves ending at the shoulder, sunglasses on. He's less relaxed than usual, a frenetic tension in his movements.

"You good?" I ask.

"Yeah." He looks around. The festival started this morning, with rows and rows of booths on one side, an exhibition section with the 4H club presentation, baby pageant, dog pageant, and other events, and some rickety looking rides that are probably the same ones from when we were kids. "Should be a good turn out."

"Always is." The Jepsen Festival is admittedly one of my favorite events from my childhood — all of the greasy foods, the goofy games, the silly events. It's the perfect beginning to summer.

When I described the event and all of its traditions to Erik he brushed it off as something "quaint", like I grew up churning butter and doing math on an abacus. I never brought it up to him again.

"We good to go?" Wes asks, checking the time on his phone. They don't allow anyone to serve liquor until after twelve, though we're the primary ones serving it. The other booths from restaurants are serving beer and wine.

"We're good."

A slow trickle of people start to come into our area. I figured that since it's early, most people won't want to drink. But to my surprise, we get a few takers, who then fill out our survey.

"Hi, sweetness," a tall, older woman says as she saunters up a half hour later. She's wearing a violently purple mumu and matching cat-eye sunglasses. Her white hair is piled into a neat bun on top of her head, and based on the size of it, her hair is probably almost down to her waist. The combination of her outfit and her presence — she's tall and big-boned, not at all frail with age — is a lot all at once.

"Hey, Nana." Wes lights up and he goes out from behind the booth and gives her a hug.

"This must be Rose," she says, squeezing Wes's shoulder.

"Yeah, it is. Rose, this is my grandma," Wes says.

"You can call me Nana," she adds. "Everyone does."

"You know who I am?" I ask, drying my sweaty hands on my shorts before extending one.

"You a hugger?" she asks, going behind the booth. Before I can do more than nod, she wraps me in a hug, smushing me into her large bosom. She smells like fresh peaches. "And yes, I do. Wes told me *all* about you when he made me brunch the other week."

"Nana..." The tips of Wes's ears flush. "I mean, we work together and we live together, so —"

His grandma waves him off and gives me a conspiratorial look that makes me like her immediately. "You're giving him a run for his money, aren't you?"

"Yep." I grin. "Do you want to try the drinks we've been working on?"

"Of course."

We each pour our drink into taster glasses and slide them to her. She takes a sip of Wes's, nodding, then takes a sip of mine.

"They're both pretty damn good," she says, finishing each of them in a single gulp.

"There isn't one you like more than the other?" Wes asks.

"Why? Are y'all competing with this too?" Nana puts a hand on her generous hip.

"Maybe," Wes says slowly.

"You're a terrible liar." Nana laughs. "Just because you're as transparent as glass, I'm not going to tell you."

Wes groans. "Can you at least fill out a card about what you liked and what you didn't? It's anonymous."

"Fine, fine. Even though you know my handwriting, I'll let Rose handle it," she says. I hand her a card and a pen, and she starts filling it out. "When are you and Waylon coming to cook for me again?"

"Whenever you want," Wes says. "Maybe the Sunday after next? What do you want us to make?"

"The biscuits and gravy y'all made last time were good." She hands me the card.

"Wes cooked that?" I look between the two of them, tucking the card into the file folder I brought. "Wes, you said they were from your grandma's house."

"From her house — because I went there and cooked it." He gives me one of those cocky smiles of his, but there's a sense of real happiness behind it. "Are you surprised? Cooking and making cocktails are all about flavor and technique."

"True, I'm just..." Weirdly aroused because those were the best biscuits and sausage gravy I'd ever had? And because the image of him at the stove, cooking with skill, is crazy hot? "Yeah, I'm just surprised."

"You should come to my house the next time the twins cook for me," she says. "I taught them well."

"Yeah, I should."

"Good. Then I'll see you soon." Nana pulls Wes over and gives him a kiss on the cheek, then does the same to me as if we didn't just meet three minutes ago. "Gonna get some of those catfish nuggets before everyone else does."

She hurries off like the catfish nuggets are a rare jewel ready to be stolen.

"She's cool," I say once she's out of earshot.

"Yeah. She's the best." Wes smiles. "And based on what her card says, she liked my drink more."

"Hey! No looking at the cards early." I take the card from him and put it back into the folder. "We need to keep it a surprise."

"Fine." He turns on the charm as more people show up.

Two hours pass and we hand out samples and sell drinks as fast as we can. Eventually Jasper and Sabrina show up to take over for us.

"Don't forget to get the feedback cards when you give out samples," I say to Sabrina.

"Will do. You guys go have fun," she says. "Try those catfish nuggets."

"What's in these catfish nuggets? Drugs?" Wes asks, sliding on his sunglasses.

"Maybe we should try them." Just the thought of fried food makes me hungry.

We wander down the rows of booths together, eyeing all the food options. The line for catfish nuggets is at the far end, near where the exhibition section is, and it's long.

"Want those? Might as well see what the fuss is all about," he says.

"Sure. I love catfish anyway." We get in line. The sun is beating down on us hard and I shade my forehead with my hand. "I haven't had it since I left here, I don't think."

"You haven't had catfish in almost ten years?" His eyebrows shoot up. "Even though you love it?"

"The southern food in New York is mediocre at best, if I'm being real. Flavor-wise it's fine, but it's missing something I can't put a finger on." We take a step forward. "And so overcomplicated. Like I don't want chicken and waffles with a hot honey syrup and a bunch of extra BS. I want something made by a woman with old ass pans and fingers that don't even feel heat after decades of cooking."

"The legit shit."

"Yeah." I never realized how much I missed things like that until now — the intangible stuff about Jepsen that keeps popping up from time to time the longer I'm here. "I'm not the best cook."

"Admitting a weakness?" Wes tucks his hands into his pockets. "You're softening."

"I won't starve and that's all that matters." I take a second to study his biceps. He's ever so slightly sweaty and it makes his skin glisten in a way that makes him look even better.

"There's a huge rift between not starving and not hating what you eat." His sunglasses are dark enough to hide his eyes, but if I'm not imagining things, he looks genuinely concerned for a second. "Wait, how are you so into coffee while not knowing how to cook?"

"Food is annoying to prep. Coffee smells good and there's more of a science to it," I say. "And fewer dishes."

He just nods and we walk forward more. The line is moving fast, and within minutes we have catfish nuggets, hush puppies, and fries in little paper baskets, plus a fork. Everything is small enough to eat with our forks in one bite. They live up to the hype, being just as crispy and perfectly salty as I'd hoped. We end up wandering through the exhibition section as we inhale our food.

The 4H club kids show off their animals, and competitors show off their unusually large vegetables. A larger crowd is toward the end at the baby pageant. Parents and their babies are standing in a line, bouncing them and killing time before the first "event". There are two divisions — six months to a year, and one from a year to two years.

All of the babies are dressed up in one way or another, and it's absolutely adorable. I've always been on the fence about wanting kids, but seeing all these babies looking extra cute has me leaping toward the baby side of things.

"Oh, look. It's the first place where I beat you," he says with a playful smirk. He's already inhaled his food so he tosses the empty basket into the nearby trash can.

"God, will you ever let that go?" I let my head fall back and sigh.

"Nope." He grins. "Because it's funny as hell."

It *is* stupid but fine, it is a little funny. The baby pageant required zero skill. We barely had a grip on object permanence, much less the meaning of competition. Yet it was the beginning of whatever we have going on now. Or whatever we had, since he's actually making good on his promise to rile me up less.

But I'm trying too. I don't *have* to react to his nonsense. Or I can just take it as a joke instead of something else.

"Speaking of, how did you win while Waylon didn't place?" I ask. A dad lifts his baby up in the air, making her laugh.

"Because Waylon was too busy crying his eyes out. We were total opposites — I was the easy baby and he was always upset about something," he says. "Then it switched when we became toddlers and I made my mom's life a living hell."

There's a wistfulness in his tone that I don't miss. I don't know how Mrs. Stryker is as a mother, but maybe he's guilty for being difficult? I don't know, but I don't press him on it.

"Yo, Kenny," Wes calls out.

A man with Wes's same dark hair, but green eyes catches Wes's eye and nods. He and an Asian woman holding a baby next to him – his wife, I assume - come over. I recognize them both in that vague way I recognize a lot of people around here.

"Hey, what's up," Kenny says, clapping Wes on the shoulder before addressing me. "I know your face, but I don't remember your name, sorry."

"It's fine. I'm Rose. We probably went to high school together."

"Ah, right. Wes's rival," he says with a grin. I glance up at Wes, whose ears turn pink. How much has he talked about me in the past? I didn't think our rivalry was that huge of a deal. "I'm Kenny and this is my wife Bex and our baby Gabi."

"Oh, we had AP European History together," I say, my memories clicking into place. Bex was the cheer captain and Kenny was the captain of the football team - both were a year ahead of us. Cliché as hell, but hey, they're still together.

"Right, we did." Bex smiles. I remember her being nice.

Gabi, who's probably around eight months old if I had to guess, reaches toward Wes. Bex happily hands her off and Wes holds her like he holds babies all the time, bouncing her a little and smiling. I'm not sure why I'm so shocked — the Stryker family goes beyond his immediate family, and those parts of the family definitely have other kids. Is the fact that he's holding a very adorable baby getting me, or is it the fact that his bicep looks extra delicious flexed like that? Or both?

I need to get a grip. How long have I even been staring at his arms? They're chatting away about an upcoming family event and I've barely paid attention.

"We'll be starting the first round of the baby pageant in just a few minutes," a woman says into the mic.

"Good luck," Wes says, handing their baby back.

"Okay, good luck, babe," Kenny says, kissing his wife, then his daughter on the forehead.

"Say bye to daddy and Wes and Rose!" Bex holds up the baby's little fist and makes her wave before heading to where the other babies are getting lined up.

"Hey." Wes nudges me with his elbow. "Over-under on what baby'll win."

"What?"

Wes looks at me with mild exasperation. "The babies. Who are you betting on for the win?"

"First of all, I didn't realize this was the kind of thing you bet on. Second of all, you can't bet on *babies,*" I hiss.

"Why not?" Wes's grin spreads across his face. "What's the baby going to do? Lobby congress to stop baby pageant gambling? The parents probably won't complain either. It's all fun. Do you want to be boring, or do you want to win a little cash?"

I narrow my eyes at him. God, that smile of his. There's trouble written all over his face, but it's the kind of trouble you have to try just once. He still drives me crazy with nonsense like this, but he's undeniably gorgeous.

"Fine, I'm in." I scan the babies. "How are we supposed to judge? They're all cute."

"It's subjective. I'm betting on Gabi since she's a Stryker, so you have to choose another baby for the pageant part." Wes pulls out his wallet and checks how much cash he has before tucking it back into his pocket. "As for the race part, six-month-olds to a year old...hmm..."

"This is a total shot in the dark. You can't tell what babies will be fast just by looking at them," I say.

"Look at that kid.' He gestures toward a baby dressed as a dinosaur. "He's determined."

I take a closer look. The scrunch of the baby's face says it all. "That baby is one hundred percent pooping."

"He's lightening the load for better aerodynamics," Wes says with confidence. I hold back a snort. "I'm betting on him. Gabi and dino suit. Gabi for the overall win."

He looks at me expectantly and I press the heel of my

hand to my forehead. Why do I want to give into his nonsense? It *is* kind of fun, even if it's dumb....

"Fine, I'll go with cute little afro puffs baby girl for the pageant and race car driver for the race," I say. "Afro puffs for the overall win."

"How much?"

"Five dollars tops," I say. "I'm not losing more than that for this foolishness."

"Is this a betting pool?" a man asks from behind us. "I'd bet on my son any day."

"Hell yeah, why not?" Wes's grin widens.

Once that one man is in, a few of the other bystanders hop in too. Eventually the pool is up to a hundred bucks.

"Now this will be exciting," Wes says. I sigh and he gently bumps me with his shoulder. "I wouldn't stick around if Kenny and Bex's kid wasn't in this. I had to jazz it up a little bit. Loosen up."

When people tell me to 'loosen up', I usually throw up my defenses. I'm loose enough, thanks. But something about Wes's excitement at something so silly is making me want to participate too.

I turn my attention to the ridiculous display in front of me. Music starts up and the parents start parading their babies around. Most of the babies look like babies usually do — a little bewildered and curious about everything going on around them. A few babies cry despite their parents' best effort. But some, including Gabi, smile at everyone.

"She's a fucking winner," Wes whispers to me.

"Afro Puffs is giggling. She could win it." The baby is even cuter now that her dad is doing a little dance with her in his arms.

Eventually the little parade of infants ends, and the slightly older age group comes on. Once they're done, the group moves over to the padded floor, where the race will be.

"I'm already feeling richer," Wes says, adjusting his sunglasses.

"Feeling richer and being richer are two different things," I shoot back. "The race is going to settle some things."

The race is simple — one person stands on one side, and another stands with the baby on the other. The first baby to reach the other side wins. Except they're babies, so who knows which way they'll go. Race Car Driver Baby is squirmy and cranky, so maybe he'll be fast.

"Ready, set, go!"

Instead of taking off like little bullets, the babies look around in confusion. The adults near the finish line start waving toys and calling for the babies. Some pick up on what they're supposed to be doing and start crawling over to the other side. The cheering builds, mixed with groans as some babies start crawling toward the crowd and other ones just sit there.

Race Car Driver Baby sits on his butt for a second, but starts to slowly crawl toward his dad. *So* slowly.

"C'mon," I murmur. "Go faster."

"Dino Suit's smoking him," Wes says, nudging me with his elbow.

Like he heard him, Dino Suit abruptly stops and sits on his butt for no reason.

Wes groans as I cheer for Race Car Driver Baby, who closes the final gap and wins it.

"Suck it," I say with a laugh.

"A win's a win," he says with a sigh. "But I could still win it with the pageant part."

The judges are still tabulating the scores for the pageant. What do those score cards even look like?

Regardless, Afro Puffs wins it all, and everyone around me groans. I put my hand out for Wes and he sighs, putting cash in my hand.

"Now *I* feel rich," I say, tucking the cash into my hip pack.

"And to think, if you hadn't let loose and placed bets on babies, you'd be a hundred bucks poorer," he says. "Want some pie on a stick?"

"Sure."

The booth doesn't have a line and we each get a different pie on the stick — he gets pecan, I get chess pie. Despite myself, I moan after taking a bite. It's so indulgent but it's so damn good. I put my fingers to my lips so I don't do it again or embarrass myself.

"Sorry, it's just been a while since I've had chess pie," I say.

"I mean, it's good." Wes shrugs, biting into his pie. "Moan away."

Is he for real? I can't help but grin. "Or do you just want to hear me moan?"

He barks a laugh in surprise. "Rose. Are you flirting with me?"

My face gets hot immediately. "It was just a kneejerk reaction! It didn't mean anything."

"Sure, sure." His crooked smile makes me both annoyed and pleased that he's aiming that smile at me. "I'm going to mentally tuck that sound away for later."

Tuck it away for what? I can guess. And it makes me heat between my thighs. I shake my head and look away so I don't accidentally give him more fuel to tease me.

We arrive back at the booth, where Sabrina and Jasper are slinging drinks. The line has calmed down a lot.

"We ran out of your drinks to sample," Sabrina says, handing someone a moonshine margarita. "Let me give you the cards."

We go behind the booth and start counting things out, the cards that favored his on one side and mine on the other. At first it's about even, but then it pulls to be mostly his cards.

"Looks like I win," he says, running his thumb across his cards like a stack of playing cards. "They like the simplicity of it."

I sigh, because they're right. The comments on my card all say similar things — they weren't sure what it was supposed to be. Probably because there's so much going on.

"Fine, you win," I say, half-bowing. "What's your prize? A favor?"

"Yeah, just a favor." The wicked grin on his face sends a tingle down my spine. "I reserve the right to cash in on it anytime."

I might regret giving him this prize.

CHAPTER ELEVEN

WES

The hot air of the day sticks with us until night, so I lay on top of my blankets and stare at the ceiling instead of falling asleep. It's so hot that Murphy is choosing to sleep on the slightly cooler floor rather than snuggling up to me, and Dennis is sleeping on the windowsill. Even if the temperature was right, I tend to have a hard time winding down after busy days like today.

Plus, I have a lot to think about. Or I guess a lot I can't help but think about, like Rose.

It's getting harder and harder to fight off the lust that's plaguing me whenever I look in her direction now that we've toned our rivalry down a bit. It's the way she looks, of course, but it's also the way she moves, like she knows exactly what she wants to do and how to do it. Which then gets my brain going in directions it shouldn't in public.

But fucking her would be such a bad idea. We're roommates. We're coworkers. We have history. Plus, I don't know how that would pan out. Maybe if we just fucked once...

No, still a bad idea. We just made things between us less complicated, and here I am trying to fuck it up again.

I hear Rose shift on the other side of the ridiculously thin wall. How did I not notice that I could hear every single creak and sigh on the other side of the wall when my old roommate was here?

I sigh and press the heels of my hands to my eyes, then reach over to grab my phone. The emptiness in my thoughts is quickly filled with Rose. Does she have Instagram? I downloaded Instagram again after Nana showed us the video that Rose posted. I look side to side, as if someone can look over my shoulder, and do a quick search for her name.

She has an account, and her account is public, to my surprise. She hasn't posted in months, but she used to post frequently. Some of the posts are of drinks she made, complicated shit propped just so in dark, sophisticated bars. Then there are a few photos of her. Only one person is consistently there — a tall, glamourous looking Black woman named Jo. Her best friend, maybe?

Besides that, there are very noticeable gaps in time between the photos, like she's gone through and deleted a lot of them.

Once I start creeping, I can't stop. I scroll back, trying to gather as much information as I can on her indirectly. Everything is curated, the top moments of her life, but I do get some insight. She used to go to bars a lot and made a lot of drinks. And when she went out, she dressed up for the occasion.

Blood rushes south as I take in some of the outfits she wore back then. Short skirts with more demure tops, or vice versa. Her cleavage is so fucking perfect, and I want to bury my face between her tits. Deep red lipstick seems to be her favorite across the years.

I'm years and years back in her feed, driven by lust. But one photo stops me.

It's from Halloween and she's sitting on a plush velvet seat, lounging backward like she's a queen on her throne. Her costume — a generous term — is a black, barely there top, and shorts so tiny that they'd probably show half her ass if she were standing. A black witch hat sits on her head, which is the only indication of what she's dressed up as.

But it's that look on her face, like a cheeky little smile she fucking knows how sexy she is and how good she looks, that's getting me. That kind of confidence is my weakness.

Use your black girl magic for good, not evil <3, the caption says.

I take a breath and let it out slowly. *Fuck.*

Despite knowing that I need to stop lusting after her, my hand skims southward toward my cock, almost on reflex, but I stop.

Am I really going to do this? Jerk off to a fucking picture on Instagram?

I pause, my hand at my waistband of my boxers. My dick's already straining against the fabric and sometimes I jerk off to help myself go to sleep. But Rose is literally on the other side of the wall.

Fuck it, it's not like jerking off makes a ton of noise.

I shift so I can push my boxers down, but in the process, my phone starts to slip in my hand. And as I catch it, I double-tap and like the witch photo.

I suck in a breath so I don't yell *fuck* and quickly unlike it. But it's too late.

"Are you years deep in my Instagram?" Rose says from the other side of the wall, a laugh in her voice.

I run my hand over my face. I can't even respond because there's no good way to respond to this. I just have to fucking die here and have Waylon throw my body into the woods. Not even a funeral because then everyone would have to know why I died. From being a thirsty asshole.

"That picture is pretty hot," she continues, giggling. "I can see why you like it."

"It was an accident," I say, even though it'll bury me even deeper into the ground. Why can't I kick my soul out of my body like I'm shoving someone out of a moving car?

"An accident from four years ago," she adds.

Just fucking kill me.

I don't fall asleep for another three hours. And I don't jerk off either.

THE ONLY THING worse than facing Rose in the morning is hiding from her. I stroll downstairs in nothing but shorts since it's still ten thousand degrees out, even at this hour. I check the thermostat and it's turned to blasting. Maybe it just needs more time to get the rest of the house.

I find Murphy standing next to the back door and let him outside. Opening the door makes the temperature even worse, like opening the door to a sauna. He hates the heat anyway, so he does his business and I venture into the steamy yard to clean up. When he comes inside, he lays on the tile part of the floor, like he's already had the life sucked out of him.

Rose is in the bare minimum amount of clothing, a tank top and tiny little shorts. I pull my eyes away from her ass just in time for her to turn around.

"Sorry, I didn't start the coffee yet," I say. "Do you still want hot coffee even though it's boiling in here?"

"No, I'll have mercy on you and make us iced coffee," she says. Sweat drips down into her cleavage. "Is the AC even working?"

"Apparently not," I say. "It's fucking hot. Let me take a closer look."

I go further into the living room and put my hand to the vent. Shit. Nothing. I sigh.

"Not working?" she guesses.

"Nope," I say. "I'll call someone."

There's only one 'someone' who could possibly help — Randy the repairman. He's so well known as the repair guy that I don't think anyone knows his last name. The bad news is that he's by far the best and it's just him and his son, so there's usually a wait.

Better to get on his list now.

I call Randy and his son, Rob picks up.

"Hey, man," I say. Rob is a regular at the bar and we've been friends for a while. "Can you guys come out and take a look at our AC? It just died."

"Yeah, yours and half the town's. Don't know why." He sighs. "We can, but it'll probably be a while. Assuming everything goes well."

"It's fine. I know you guys will be able to fix it." I run my hand through my hair, which is damp with sweat already. "What time are you thinking?"

"Between three and six? I know that's a big window, but we'll text you when we're thirty minutes out," he says.

That's four hours from now, shit.

"We might have some cancellations though, if you don't mind sticking around in front of a fan at home?" he adds, mistaking my silence for irritation.

"Okay, that sounds good," I say.

"We'll see you then."

He hangs up. Rose is standing at the edge of the kitchen, ice water in hand.

"Bad news?" she asks.

"Kind of. We just need to wait like four hours, maybe more." I toss my phone onto the island. "But we can sit around and wait here if they have a cancellation."

"Shit." She sighs.

"You can borrow my car and go into town if you want to?" I grab the iced coffee from the counter.

"I was planning on hanging out at home since I'm kind of tired. And there aren't any good movies out so I can't go to the theater." She takes a long sip of her drink and presses the glass against the side of her face. "Plus I saw a fan in the garage so I was going to grab it, lay on the couch, and watch something. If you want to join me, I mean."

Even after embarrassing the shit out of myself last night, I'd rather do that than dick around in town for no reason. It's the kind of hot that takes the energy out of you.

"Okay, we can do that." I stretch and her eyes skim all over my body. "I'll get the fan."

I go to the garage and grab the fan, then come back to find her sprawled onto the couch. I put down the fan and turn it on full blast. Murphy immediately stands in front of it, closing his eyes.

"Come on, Murph." I pick up the fan and prop it up higher. "I know it's hot as fuck but come on."

He looks back at me and sighs before going to lay down further away. I turn the fan on so it's blowing back and forth across the couch, touching the dog too, then I go fill up the pets' bowls with cold water. Dennis lays down next to the bowls, and I lay down on the opposite side of the couch from Rose. She's flipping through Netflix.

"What do you want to watch?" she asks.

"Dunno, pick whatever." I shift so we aren't touching at all. Her thighs are going to be the death of me, looking like that. So thick and touchable.

"You're going to regret saying that." She smiles and finds something, pressing play before I can read the description.

"It's not a cheesy romcom, is it?" I ask. A blonde woman in a tiny bikini is walking on the beach toward a man and throws her arms around him. "Ah shit, or reality TV"

"Reality TV. And not even the legit shit on Bravo or anything. Bottom of the barrel stuff." She puts the remote on the coffee table, an adorable smile on her face. "Where all the deliciousness gathers."

"I never would have thought you'd be into this kind of thing," I say. The woman in the bikini is now fighting another woman in an equally small bikini, pulling her hair. "What even is this?"

"It's called the Real Deal of Miami," She sips her iced coffee and puts the cup against her cleavage.

"The 'real deal'? Isn't it Real Housewives?" I ask.

"No, it's a bootleg version of that without the marriage

part. It's basically just people causing a bunch of drama in their relationships and going to restaurants." She shrugs. "I don't have to use a single brain cell to enjoy it."

We sit back and watch. It's weirdly entrancing in its stupidity. It's all just drama — the people are good-looking and go out to bars every other night. Their 'jobs' are just flimsy glue to keep the show going.

"This is so stupid," I say when the first episode ends. "Why would Ainsley hook-up with Darryl when she knew that Braxlyn was into him?"

"You're invested?" she says with a grin that makes a dimple show in her cheek.

"I mean, it's the whole show." I stretch my arms into the air. Her eyes go to my biceps, then to where my shirt rode up. "Hooking up. Getting drunk. Having fun. Not that much to be invested in."

"A regular Wes Stryker evening?"

"Ehn," I say, rubbing the back of my neck. It's warm under my hand and it's not just the heat. "The rumors of my harem of women are overblown."

"I wasn't saying you had a whole *harem*." She laughs, curling her knees up to her chin. "I'm just saying you're popular."

"So popular that I've had women over every single night. It's a nonstop party." I laugh, but it trails off fast. When was the last time I hooked up with anyone? It's been before Rose arrived. And even before that it had been a while.

At least that makes all the pent-up lust in me make sense. I haven't had sex in almost a month, and it's been even longer since I've had anything good. No wonder I was about to jerk it to an Instagram photo.

"I think last night's incident shows that the walls are way too thin for either of us to hook-up." She shifts, her knees pressing together tighter. "Unless we want to make things extremely awkward."

The thought of hearing her being fucked ignites two fires within me — one that makes me pull a pillow across my lap to hide what's going on in my shorts and one that fills me with an alarming amount of jealousy.

Thankfully the show comes back and she goes quiet again, her attention drawn to everyone dancing at the club. I can't get back into it.

It doesn't help that this whole show devolves into hooking up every other second. It's more than tame enough for TV, but it stokes fires inside me that I wish I could put out. And like Rose said before, the show doesn't require a single brain cell to watch, which doesn't occupy my racing thoughts.

"What?" Rose asks. I blink — I've been staring blankly at her, but not really looking at her.

"Is that really my reputation still?" I ask. "That I have a harem of women at all times?"

She scoffs, pausing the show. Then, her expression turns a bit softer. "Does that bother you? I figured you'd be into it. You don't get that reputation by being. Y'know. Mediocre."

She pulls her knees closer to herself, like a shield. God, she's too fucking tempting when she looks at me like that.

"Are you saying that I have positive reviews?" I ask, unable to keep a smile off my face. "What have you heard, Rose?"

She narrows her eyes at me. "Do I need to inflate your ego more?"

I shrug one shoulder, then rest my arm along the back of the couch. "By saying you'd be inflating my ego, I assume the reviews are excellent."

"Mm." She shrugs too. "I don't know. I feel like you might be overrated. Seems a little too good to be true."

Those words have a taunting edge to them, the kind that makes me want to take the bait. Blood rushes south, my cock pressing up against the pillow I thankfully pulled across my lap. She looks me up and down, taking her time to soak in every inch of me.

"You want me to show you what everyone's talking about?" I ask her.

"If you feel the need to make a point, sure," she says, tilting her head to the side and letting her long braids spill over her shoulder. Her nipples are hard through her thin t-shirt, and all I want to do is flick my tongue across them.

Doing this would be really fucking stupid. Really hot, but *really* stupid. This is Rose, for fuck's sake. Putting aside the fact that we're roommates, we're barely friends.

But the way she's looking at me, a mix of anticipation and heat completely wipes my head clear of thought.

Fuck it.

I crawl over her and kiss her, pinning her to the couch. She melts underneath me, opening her thighs so I can fit in between them. The kiss alone is electric, the kind that makes me heat everywhere. I nip her bottom lip, then trail my lips down the side of her neck.

Her tiny intake of breath makes me even bolder. I rake my teeth along the spot I just kissed, letting myself skim my hands down her body. Finally exploring all her soft curves is like solving a puzzle. I can finally connect the fullness of her tits with the weight of them in my hand, and the softness of the skin under her tank top to how smooth she looks everywhere. The scent of her body wash under the slightest bit of sweat makes me want to keep my head buried in the space between her neck and shoulder.

I pull her tank top over her head, admire the flimsy excuse for a bra that she's wearing, before pulling that off too. Fuck, she's absolutely perfect — each breast is more than a handful for my big hands, and her deep brown nipples harden even more when I suck them into my mouth. I toy with how much I suck them, going from gentle to more harsh, and back again.

She loves it all, squirming and dragging her nails through my hair. When she brushes against me just enough to cause friction and it's like she's taken me down her throat. Holy shit.

Maybe it's because I've been so pent up and maybe it's because of the challenge she threw down in front of me, but I've never felt this close to the edge without being touched directly.

"Are you going to come before you make me come?" she asks, her voice breathy. She grinds against me again and I suck in a breath, dipping my head into the crook of her neck.

"I'm not. I always give before I get my own." I grab her hips and pin them down before I eat my own words, dipping one hand into her panties. She's soaking, her clit a hardened nub. Just the lightest glide of my fingers against it makes her arch and gasp. "Looks like you're close anyway."

"I'm not," she lies, digging her nails into my shoulders.

I keep my eyes locked on hers as I dip a finger inside of

her. The look on her face makes me smirk, as does the tight squeeze of her pussy around me.

"Your body's saying otherwise," I say, stroking up and making her cry out.

"Wait." She grabs my wrist and sits up. The subtle sway of her breasts is like a fucking hypnotist's pendant. "If you make me come before I make you come, then I'll believe the hype."

"Oh, that won't be a challenge." I prop myself up on my elbows and grin at her as she hops off the couch and shimmies her panties off.

"You sure about that?" she asks.

"Ride my fucking face, Rose," I say. "I'll let my actions speak for themselves."

She straddles my face backward like she was made to do it. I haven't come in my pants while eating pussy since high school, but looking at her pretty pink pussy inches away from me is making me feel like I'm back there again.

Her scent makes my mouth start to water, and when I taste her?

I know I've fucked up. Because no one has ever tasted this good on my tongue, and the idea of never doing this again is unfathomable.

She's almost suffocating me with her pussy, but I don't care. I lap and suck at her clit, sliding a finger inside of her. She momentarily moves to push my shorts down, my cock springing free. The little pleased sound she makes is a nice ego boost, and the way her small hand wraps around my length is even nicer.

"This isn't fair," she says, pulling away. "I can't use my whole mouth."

"Not my fault you're short," I say, momentarily lifting her off my face.

She shoots me a look over her shoulder that makes me want to see how she looks if I fuck her from behind, and scoots forward so she can take my tip into her mouth.

I groan, letting my head fall back. Her mouth is hot, wet, and perfect. I wish I could see how her pretty lips look wrapped around my cock, but feeling it is already overwhelming enough.

I have to prop myself up on the arm of the couch so I can reach her, then get back to work on her pussy before she actually beats me. First I slip a finger into her before lightly sucking her clit. The way she squeezes around my finger and squirms is enough to make my cock throb.

Trying to make her come while I'm trying not to come is going to make me lose my mind. The only way I can get through this is to try to make her come as quickly as possible so I can finally get some relief.

Thankfully I figure her out fast. She loves steady rhythms and a mix of my tongue and lips, so I give her both. The way she moans around my cock nearly undoes me — the sound, the vibration, the wetness of her mouth.

I feel my balls start to tighten so I crook my fingers inside her, putting steady pressure in a spot she likes. The way her thighs shake and her pussy almost crushes my fingers only makes me harder. She lets my cock out of her mouth with a pop so she can rest her head on my stomach. With a shudder and a moan, she trembles and comes.

Is there anything better than feeling a woman fall apart all over your face? Nope. And it's even better knowing I won. I keep going as she rides the waves, her wetness coating my face.

She collapses on top of me, her breath warm against the base of my still rock-hard cock. Just that little bit of warmth is almost unbearable, but I can still keep myself under control.

"I win," I say, my voice hoarse.

"Yeah," is all she says, her voice dazed.

Before I can ask her if she wants to finish me off too, someone knocks on the door. Murphy leaps to his feet and starts barking, running toward the front of the house.

She rolls off of me, nearly falling to the floor, and I hop up. My legs are like jelly and my dick is still uncomfortably hard. I grab my phone and see a missed call from Rob. Like a dumbass, my phone is still on silent. Rob called me a half hour ago and shot me a text, saying he's on the way.

"I can...um, I'll answer it?" Rose says, glancing at my cock.

"Please." I walk straight into the kitchen and open the freezer, putting my face into it. Hearing Rob's voice kills my boner, but it's not enough to kill the lust pumping through my veins.

What the fuck did we just do?

CHAPTER TWELVE

ROSE

Well, I fucked up.

I'll never be able to wipe the image of Wes's charming smirk before he gave me the best sexual experience of my life. It wasn't even the fact that I came absurdly hard — it was everything. The slow, methodical way he worked me up, the way he read my movements and changed how he touched me.

And I even liked the teasing. Both the verbal and the physical. That's the worst of it. When did his teasing flip from annoying to kind of...fun? After he called the truce, I'm guessing, but I didn't think I'd flip that fast.

I press my hands to my face as if that'll calm the heat radiating through my skin. We're supposed to be presenting our initial drink ideas to John David later today. How am I going to work with Wes if all I can think about is yesterday? Especially on a day as important as this?

I woke up super early today to practice my routine for the competition in Nashville (without tasting the drink, of course), in the hopes that it would keep my mind off things. It totally didn't, but I do feel a bit more confident in it.

"Hey, you good?" Wes asks through the bathroom door.

"Yes!" I say with a little too much pep. "Just a second."

I finish putting on makeup and take a deep breath before opening the door to face Wes. He looks completely normal, like he didn't just blow my mind yesterday off a stupid bet.

I'd mostly been joking about the whole harem that Wes allegedly has, but he's completely unfazed by yesterday. He'd really taken it as fulfilling a bet. My heart sinks before I can rationalize myself out of it. What was I expecting? We've barely become friends. Why would he make a big deal about some extremely casual sex? And why would I feel any kind of way about it?

"Be out in a bit," he says.

He gets ready in fifteen minutes, and we hop in his car to head to the bar. Usually most mornings we bicker about who chooses the music and why, but today he lets me put on something without even glancing down. He bites his cuticles and drums his fingers on the steering wheel, his eyes and attention on the road but clearly a lot going on in his head.

We reach the bar and head inside. It still smells like the cleaning supplies Sabrina and Jasper used last night.

"Alright," Wes says with a sigh. "What're we up to today? Tweaking the joint drink? Or working on our own?"

"Testing the joint drink and making sure the flavor is good with the recipe we made," I say.

"Okay, sounds good." He starts gathering the ingredients for the drink.

"You nervous about later?" I ask.

"Hm?" He glances at me like he'd forgotten I was there. "A bit, yeah."

"It'll be fine. We've done a lot of prep for this," I say. "And we can do a little bit more today."

"I know. But John David can be..." Wes vaguely gestures, but I know what he means.

"A hardass."

"Yeah." He sighs through his nose. "Especially to me."

"Still, we have the hard evidence that our idea could be profitable," I say.

"I guess." He sighs and starts pulling ingredients.

I've never seen him this low in confidence, and it tugs at my heart.

"I don't remember JD being this..." I try to think of a softer word. "...grumpy back in high school."

"He wasn't." Wes measures out the proper amount of moonshine and puts it into the shaker. "I don't know if something changed with him, but you know how I was back in high school. A total dickhead. Just floating through life and skirting by because of who I am. I had no idea how much of a leg up that gave me in getting away with shit. I feel shitty about it now."

I pause, studying his profile as he works. Is he really acknowledging this right now? Without prompting? It feels way too good to be true. The one lingering thread in my annoyance toward Wes is being snipped away.

"But reality hit me when I left the Jepsen bubble," he says, popping the top onto the shaker. "It's a long story, but I fucked up and ended up in jail for the night."

"No one wanted to bail you out?" I ask, leaning onto the bar.

"Trust me, I wasn't going to call my parents, or even Nana." He huffs a short laugh. "I called Ash, since he was down in Miami and making good money, and he basically told me to get fucked and accept responsibility for once."

I cover my laugh. Ash is like Wes, minus the light-hearted, goofy side — he was two years ahead of us in school and had a reputation for being kind of an asshole. Talented, honest, and weirdly charming, but an asshole.

"That sounds like Ash."

"Yeah." He shakes the drink up, then strains it. "He saved me in a different way, though. I started taking my life more seriously. Then after I dropped out and moved back home, I tried to show everyone that I'd changed."

"I'm assuming JD didn't see those changes?"

"Not really." Wes puts a tasting straw into the drink and tastes it. "No one does, besides Waylon and Ash. Ash isn't even here. I've been fighting uphill to get them to take me seriously."

"I'm sure they will," I say softly. "Even I can see you've matured."

He genuinely smiles at that. "Yeah?"

"Yeah. I mean, not a lot of guys can openly acknowledge their advantages in life, much less try to correct them." I lift a shoulder, then dip a tasting straw into the drink too. It's perfect — fruity and summery. "And you created this truce. You're not the same guy who caused chaos at the bonfire every year and got away with it."

"Thanks, Rose. That means a lot, actually," he says. He shifts, like he's uncomfortable with the compliment. "Speaking of, the bonfire's coming up soon. Do you want to go? I can guarantee there won't be chaos. At least from me."

Jepsen's bonfires are legendary, but going to one of those would mean being confronted with everyone I've been trying to avoid. I won't have work as an excuse to not chat about what I've been up to and where I've been like I do at work.

"I guarantee I'll make it fun for you," he says, picking up on my reluctance.

I *have* been a bit stir crazy lately. My socializing has been from work, which isn't enough.

"Okay, sure," I say.

"Great. I swear it'll be fun, or we can leave." He picks up the drink again and puts his tasting straw into it. "This is really good."

"We just have to convince JD that we're on the right track, which shouldn't be hard," I say.

We double check all of the ingredients and costs, then work on our own drinks without running into another incident like last time.

Eventually John David comes in with a cup of coffee, looking slightly annoyed. But I guess that's just his face.

"Hey," he says. "Let's get started."

He sits down without saying that much else, leaning back in the chair. Like his brothers, John David takes up a lot of space — tall, broad shouldered — but something about his eyes make him seem more imposing.

But I'm confident in what we've put together, so he can stare me down all he wants.

John David's expression doesn't change that much as we walk through everything — the market research, our joint drink ingredients, and the costs. Wes does a good job of explaining everything, and lets me take over on the spots I'm more familiar with, then JD finally tastes it.

"That's about it,' I say once we hit the last slide. "Any questions?"

John David sits there for a few moments, not speaking. For the first time today, my stomach starts to sink. Wes starts to fidget before John David lifts a shoulder.

"Not bad," he says. I blow out a breath and glance at Wes, who looks even more relieved. "Do you think you'll have enough time to prepare for the convention?"

We quickly go over our plans for the convention, and thankfully, John David doesn't have anything else to say about our work.

"Just have the report on what your plans are for the convention to me by early next week," John David says, checking his phone. "I'll talk to y'all later."

He leaves without another word and Wes relaxes against the bar.

"See, we did good," I say.

"We did." He gives me a high-five. "Maybe we can actually finish this thing to celebrate."

I slide the drink over to him and he takes a sip. A little tug of hope for him appears in my gut. Maybe he took a little step forward in JD's eyes. At least I hope he did. It's way easier to root for Wes than I thought it'd be.

CHAPTER THIRTEEN

ROSE

I take a step back and look at myself in the mirror. I'm in denim shorts and a t-shirt, my comfort outfit. I don't want to try too hard, especially since I'm not looking for that kind of attention at the bonfire tonight. Or hell, maybe it's exactly what I need. Except banging someone from high school in this small town, where everyone will know it in a matter of hours sounds like complicating my life even more for no damn reason.

It's my first time going out to socialize without having the chance to deflect with work at the bar, and the idea of it is making my stomach churn. I haven't been face-to-face with any of my old classmates who might know about the show yet (aside from Ted), and I don't want to explain it. Especially if Wes is nearby. I just want to pretend none of it ever happened.

I sigh and tap a little more lip gloss on before stepping out of the bathroom.

"I'm ready," I call down to Wes as I head down the steps. He's sitting next to the door, scrolling through his phone.

"Okay, cool." He glances up at me, his eyes skimming over my body in a way that makes me flush. How can he do that? Men check me out all the time, but they don't make me feel anything. "You look really good."

"Thanks." I grab my purse. "Let's head out."

He looks good too, even though he's not wearing anything different than usual. It's a rare, less humid night, so he's wearing jeans and a t-shirt. The t-shirt fits him perfectly, as do those jeans. They're well-worn, contouring to his ass in a way that's too perfect.

We hop in his car and head off, going deeper into the woods rather than closer in town until we reach a clearing. This area was going to be a more official offshoot of the national park, but it ended up just being a few clearings connected by some trails. This was the go-to make out spot for most people in our high school, myself included with the many misguided choices in guys I had.

The party is in full swing by the time we pull up to where all the cars are parked. Wes parks near the back and we walk over together. The few people lingering in the parking lot say hello to Wes from a distance, but don't acknowledge me. The closer we get to the action, the more my heart starts to pound for no good reason.

I take a deep breath. It'll be okay. It'll be fine.

When we walk into the clearing and people see Wes, they immediately light up. I forgot how popular he was and how I was just far away enough from popular to envy him. As much of an angsty teen front I put up, I wanted to be well-liked just as much as anyone.

"What's up?" Wes says to the small cluster of people who give us the warmest hellos. "You guys remember Rose, right?"

"Hi." I give them a shy wave and resist the urge to fiddle with my earrings.

"Yeah, hi!" Gigi, who was in some of my honors classes, bounds toward me first. She throws her arms around me in a hug even though we were moderate acquaintances at best. She smells like White Claw and Bath and Body Works body spritz, but the friendliness of it puts me at ease. "It's been so long! You're such a babe!"

I laugh, pulling at my braids. "That's a stretch but thank you."

"Take the compliment, Rose." Wes reaches into a huge cooler and starts digging around. "What do you want to drink? Beer? Hard seltzer?"

I lean around him to take a closer look. All shitty beers, but to be honest, I'm not looking for a craft beer experience at my hometown bonfire. I pick one and Wes unearths a bottle opener to crack it open for me.

Everyone else says hello and as they do, I slowly connect their adult selves to the ones I knew.

The bearded man in front of me with Craig, one of the more popular guys in our grade. We were neighbors growing up, so he was one of the few people in the popular crowd who I was friendly with. There's also Jessica, who was kind of a bitch back in the day, and Reagan, who was also an asshole. But both of them look a little less shiny and intimidating now.

Thankfully none of us were close enough to keep up with each other after high school, so I don't get questioned about why I'm back or what happened to all the stuff that I was going to do.

I slam a beer, then grab another one, happy to listen in to Wes commanding everyone's attention with ease.

This...isn't bad at all. I almost feel stupid for worrying about it the longer the conversation goes. It's not like I have a massive sign that says Huge Failure around my neck.

"There's Jasper and Sabrina," Wes says to me eventually. "Let's go say hi."

We dip out of the conversation, Wes gently guiding me with a hand on my shoulder. It's big and comforting, and with the heavy buzz I have going, something I want to lean into.

"Want another drink?" I ask. I'll be hungover tomorrow, but I'm also past the point of caring.

The corner of Wes's mouth creeps up. "You sure you should? Because you look drunk."

"I'm *so* not drunk," I say. "But I will be after another drink."

"I'm excited to see drunk Rose." He hands me another beer from a different cooler and grabs a bottle of water for himself.

"Drunk Rose is..." I take a long swig of the beer. "Drunk."

"Wow, revolutionary." He laughs. "I can't believe I never thought that a pixie-sized woman slamming some beers after eating a single slice of leftover pizza would be feeling all that liquor."

"Pixie sized?" I let out an ugly snort. "Wow. Wow."

"You're what, five feet tall?" He holds a hand up as if to measure me. "Pixie sized."

"Maybe you're just fucking enormous." I look up at him. He *is* big, both in his height and across his shoulders. The beers make me want to press myself against him just to see what it would feel like.

"Not the first time I've heard that," he says. I snort again despite myself and his grin widens. "You walked right into that."

"I know, I know. But —"

"Hey, Rosie," a voice I never wanted to hear again says from behind me. Wes's eyes narrow, looking at my very first boyfriend over my shoulder.

I take a breath and turn to look at him. To my satisfaction, he doesn't look great on several levels. He still has the cringe, semi-emo style we had back then and he's grown a beard, which looks patchy even in the low light.

"Hi." I start to turn back toward Wes, but Dylan comes around the side to talk to us. Wes sizes him up. Dylan was staunchly against the popular crowd in high school, particularly Wes. All of his rebellious talk was so edgy and cool to me back then, but now that I think about it as an adult, it was mostly shit that a teenager who hadn't experienced anything besides a neat little small town would say.

"You aren't going to give me a hug?" Dylan pouts.

"Why would I?" I scoff. "Don't you remember how things ended?"

They'd ended exactly how my latest relationship had — being cast aside for someone else. Seeing him again is like I've been kicked back into those feelings — feeling like I'd always be second best, no matter how hard I tried to be what they needed me to be. Like he'd gotten everything he needed from me — terrible sex, mostly — and tossed me away.

"Water under the bridge?" He lifts a shoulder.

"Fuck off, Dylan," Wes says with a surprising amount of heat. "Go bother someone else."

"Why are you here?" Dylan asks, raising an eyebrow. "And why are you suddenly defending her? You were a dick to her before."

"Because anyone with a pulse can tell she doesn't want you here." Wes nods off to the side. "So leave."

For a second I think Dylan is going to take a swing at Wes. It wouldn't be the first time he got into a fight. But Wes stands his ground. If I had to put bets on either of them, I would choose Wes — just his sheer height and size dwarf Dylan.

"Whatever, man," Dylan says, walking past Wes and purposefully bumping him. Wonderfully mature.

"You good?" Wes asks, looking over his shoulder to make sure Dylan is actually gone.

I blink. "You didn't have to do that."

"Sorry." He glares at Dylan's back as he walks away. "He was always a fucking dickhead and he still is. He comes into the bar every once in a while and gets plastered. Which wouldn't be bad if he wasn't fucking obnoxious. I should ban him."

"Don't apologize." Is the fluttering in my chest because of the beer or because of his help? Yeah, I'm capable of handling it, but to be honest, I would have let it go on longer to not make a scene. Wes picked up the vibe and shut it down. For me.

These drinks are making me feel too many things.

"C'mon, there's cornhole over there." He points his

water bottle to the far side of the clearing, closer to the second bonfire.

"You don't have to stick with me the whole night if you don't want to," I say. "I think I see Sabrina and Jasper."

"Then let's get them to come play cornhole with us," he says. He must pick up on my skepticism without even looking at me because he grins. "You wanted to have a good time, so I'm going to make sure that happens."

He says it so earnestly that my body flushes, like it can't process the idea fully without it coming out as heat.

"So, you're assuming you're the most fun person here?" I ask.

"I know I am. Plus, I want to beat you again," he replies before yelling, "Jas! Sabrina!" loudly enough to be heard over the music. I can't even get a good word in.

The two of them join us, hand in hand. Sabrina is definitely tipsy, leaning against Jasper. The way they look at each other with such affection pulls at my heart more than it should. How am I not 100% jaded by romance at this point?

"Cornhole?" Wes asks. "Sabrina and Rose on one team, us on the other?"

"Hell yeah. Sabrina is going to lose so hard." Jasper gently tugs on her long, dark braid and kisses her on the forehead.

"I'm going to win out of spite." Sabrina marches over to one of the boards.

We all follow and split up, me and Sabrina next to one board and Jasper and Wes on another.

"I'm a cornhole champion," Sabrina says in a way that absolutely does not inspire confidence. "Watch."

She picks up a bean bag and lobs it underhand, missing the other board completely.

"Was that a warmup?" I ask as Jasper laughs.

"Totally a warmup," Sabrina says.

Sabrina's "warm up" turns out to be her being drunk and uncoordinated. I'm not great at the game even when I'm sober, but it's more fun this way. I can't aim to save my life either, and the guys demolish us.

"Oof," Sabrina eventually says after tossing a beanbag way off to the side. "Woozy."

"You want some water?"

"Please." She presses the back of her hand to her cheek. "Ugh, I'm going to be so hungover tomorrow. And it's Jasper and I's anniversary and he had all these plans..."

"It'll be fine. I'm sure he'll take care of you."

"He will." She leans against me for a second, which is getting in the way of me going to get her water. She's way more gone than she was when we started.

"You good, babe?" Jasper asks, tossing aside his bean bag and jogging over to us.

"Went a little too hard," she says, going from leaning on me to leaning on Jasper.

Jasper wraps his arms around her, brushing some hair out of her face.

"I knew I should have given you more food before we left," Jasper says with a sigh.

"I just need water." Sabrina rests her forehead on Jasper's chest.

"I'll grab some. I need some anyway," I say, trying to ignore the stupid surge of jealousy inside of me. What's it like to find someone you can trust like that? Someone who looks at you like you're their favorite person and keeps you safe?

Every relationship I've been in has felt like the opposite — like I'm the one who's always doing more while not getting all that much in return.

Whatever. Finding that kind of relationship would require taking a chance on someone, and that's not something I'm willing to do at this point.

I find one of the many coolers peppered around the field and open it. As I rifle through the ice to find water, I feel someone standing above me.

"Sorry, just —" I look up and just barely hold back a quiet *fuck*. It's another one of my exes, Scott. What's going on tonight? "Uh, hi."

He looks more or less the same, but with some scruff on his jaw. What's also the same is the cold look in his eye.

"Hi." He just stands there. Instead of grabbing a second bottle of water for myself, I get another drink and stand up.

"It's all yours," I say, gesturing to the cooler.

"I'm shocked you bothered to come back," he says, a fake smile on his face. "Weren't you going to have some show with your famous boyfriend?"

"Why were you stalking your high school ex on Instagram?" I shoot back.

"Why not?" He smirks. "You were all high and mighty so it's nice to see that you're right back where you started."

I suck in a breath. I don't understand him. *He's* the one who flat out admitted that he used me for (terrible) sex, then moved on before he even had the balls to break up with me. Why is he kicking me down again?

"Hey, you good?" Wes swoops in, his hand on my back. It's warm and steadying.

"We were just catching up," Scott says. But it's a little too late. Scott escapes, slipping away.

"Are *you* good?" he asks, studying my face like I was physically harmed. "You looked like you saw a ghost."

"More like the ghosts of exes past." I squeeze the bridge of my nose and take a deep breath. "I just need a little space away from the party."

"Then let's go."

Wes guides me away from the cornhole area and over toward the woods. Someone put up some lanterns, so we aren't completely in the dark.

"I never knew you dated that much," Wes says.

"Well, 'dated' is a stretch. I guess you'd call it situationships these days." I sigh. "I lost my virginity to Dylan and he pretended that nothing happened when I called him out for being with another girl at lunch. And I went with Scott to prom. He dry-humped me in his parents' BMW, came on my dress, and drove me home. Same deal — started dating some other girl whose name I don't even remember the very next day and we had a horrible argument over it. But it really fucking hurt."

I swallow the tightness in my chest. Or at least I try to. I guess I managed to suppress those memories better than I thought until now.

"What assholes," he says.

"I know. And I learned nothing." I sit down on a log that looks like it was purposefully positioned as a bench and stretch my legs out in front of me. "I haven't thought about them for literally years but now that I'm reflecting on them, they're basically like the little guys you fight before the big boss. And the big boss is my most recent ex."

The alcohol has my tongue loose, but whatever. For once Wes isn't trying to flirt or joke around and I need to know I'm not crazy for feeling like I've been hit by the emotions bus.

"When did y'all break up?" he asks. He stretches his legs out too, mirroring me. His extend out way further than mine.

"About a month before I came here." I look out into the woods at nothing in particular. "It was really messy for a lot of reasons — we worked together and were together for six years. And we lived together, so I got kicked out after it all fell apart. Then I ended up back here."

Those few sentences make it sound like it was a simple process and not one that yanked me apart and scattered all the pieces all over the place.

"Wow." He runs a hand through his hair and lets it fall into his lap. "I'm sorry, Rose."

He infuses those few words with so much sincerity that it makes my eyes sting with tears. I don't think I've ever known anyone else who can do that. And he always has, even back when I didn't like him as much as I do now.

"Thanks," I say. "I feel kind of stupid for not seeing it sooner. He was the kind of guy who took everything so seriously. Which I get, but when it extends to taking yourself super seriously..."

"It's annoying?" He chuckles.

"Exactly." What early-twenties me thought was serious and mysterious was just a fragile ego wrapped up in pretentiousness.

"He sounds like a tool."

"I'm the one who dated him." I pull at the tab on my drink. "Which makes me a tool by extension."

"What? No. What kind of bullshit logic is that?" Wes says, his eyes surprisingly intense all of a sudden. "You aren't with the guy anymore. So that just means you have sense. And it's not like he laid out everything about himself on the first date. The ugly shit takes time to come to the surface."

I hold his gaze, drumming my fingers against my can. My logical side knows that he's right, but something in my heart still feels like it's all my fault for even being interested in Erik. How did I not see that he was using me for years? "I don't know."

"I'm totally right." The corner of his mouth quirks up. "You're definitely not a tool. I'd call you out on it if you were."

He says it with a surprising amount of warmth, the kind that feels like a verbal hug. How does he do that so easily? Make people feel like they're special? I hate myself for wanting that to be just for me for whatever reason. I'm definitely not catching feelings for him, but for someone like Wes — someone who everyone likes — to make me feel like I'm something?

It feels good. And not a lot has felt good lately.

"What a raving compliment," I say, trying to ignore the fluttering in my chest. "Anyway, now you know my bullshit with men, so it feels like you need to even the score."

"Even the score?" he echoes. "I don't really date. Or do situationships. Once or twice and that's it. Nothing serious."

Before we started this whole roommates/coworkers situation, I would have heard that, used it to confirm what I already felt, and moved on. But now it feels kind of weird, to be honest. I can't see him having a steady girlfriend, but the more I get to know him, the more I can see how he'd be a good boyfriend — he's keeping me comfortable and safe even though he doesn't have to do that at all. A lot of guys, like my exes, wouldn't have picked up on how I felt or done anything about it.

And he listened.

God, Wes Stryker. A good boyfriend to some girl out there. I must be drunk.

"But you already knew that," he adds after chugging the remains of his water bottle. "Everyone knows that."

"Does that bother you?" I frown. Wes is just naturally flirty — it's an extension of his goofiness and laidback attitude. But something in his tone feels off.

"You're asking some deep questions for someone who's allegedly drunk." He smiles, bumping me with his shoulder, but there's a bit of emptiness behind it.

"Sorry." My ex hated when I would dig in like that.

"It's fine." Unlike my ex, I can tell he really means it. "I just don't have an easy answer to that."

We sit in comfortable silence and I finish my drink. I yawn, covering my mouth, and he catches it.

"I swear I'm not usually this boring," I say, covering up another yawn.

"I'm kind of over this party anyway." He stands up and offers his hand. "Want to go home?"

I take it and he pulls me to my feet, making me stumble into his chest. He's so warm and smells like a mix of his soap and woodsmoke. He catches me and lingers just a bit longer than he needs to.

"Yeah, I do."

CHAPTER FOURTEEN

ROSE

"We got all the stuff?" Wes asks me as I come out of the house to his SUV. He takes the final bag from my hands.

"Yep." I take a deep breath. "I mean, the sales team has the rest, right?"

"Yeah." Wes tucks my bag into the trunk and shuts it, then gets into the car.

I get in too and take a deep breath even though we haven't even left.

The sales team for Stryker Liquors is already in Nashville, and will run the booth in the convention center. We're mostly going to network with businesses that could carry the drink, get feedback on the drink so far, and of course, I'll compete in the competition.

I know my drink and routine inside and out, and I've spent all my spare time practicing. But the idea of going and actually competing after being out of it so long is making my stomach turn.

At least the drive to Nashville is only about two hours

and the competition is later today, so I have slightly less time to worry about how my routine is going to go.

"You get sick on long car drives?" Wes asks as he pulls out.

"What? No."

"Then why do you look like you're about to puke?" he asks, glancing at me out of the corner of my eye. "You nervous?"

I sigh through my nose. "Yeah."

"About the competition?"

"Yeah. And I guess just seeing things how things go with the drink," I say.

"You practiced a bunch." He pulls out onto the main road. "Don't worry."

I roll my eyes. "Okay, but are you a judge?"

"No, but I know what a good drink tastes like, and that one is one," he says. I study him, trying to see if there's even a hint of sarcasm there. There isn't. He catches my skepticism. "Fine, don't believe me."

I sigh. "It's hard to believe anyone when I haven't competed in years and years."

The last competition I did was several years ago, when I'd only been dating Erik for about eight months. That was back before he started corralling me to do most of his work for him. It was all about the blog and propping him up.

I need to move on to the nationals more than I've ever needed anything in my life.

"You've competed with me. That's something, isn't it?"

"I've competed with you my whole life," I say, looking out the window. "I don't know my competition that well."

Wes nods, considering my words in silence as we pull

onto the interstate. I'm not particularly in the mood to talk and I keep going over every possibility — every possible spot where I could mess up, every area where I could do better.

"So what if you lose?" Wes asks out of the blue.

"What? What do you mean?" I ask. We pass by a sign for a Dunkin Donuts off the side of the highway. "Coffee."

He switches lanes. "What it says on the tin. What if you lose the competition? Not saying you will, but you seem super worked up about it."

I rest my head back against the headrest, my stomach churning. "It just means a lot to me to win. To show myself that I can do it."

To convince myself that I'm not crazy, too, but I don't add that. I *know* I was the brains behind the entire blog, at least for the last three years, but I can't shake Erik's little voice in the back of my head, telling me I'm wrong.

"That's a good reason. But if you're competing against yourself, then you don't need to kick your own ass about it." He pulls into the drive thru at Dunkin Donuts.

"It's more than that." And I don't really want to get into it. He picks up on that, thankfully. We order coffee and some donuts, then get back on the road.

We sit in silence for a while before he turns on music. It's a good mix, not something I would have thought he'd listen to. We make small talk the rest of the drive until we reach Nashville. Getting through downtown is a pain in the ass, as is getting to the parking spot we have reserved, but eventually we make it to the front desk.

"Last name?" the woman at the front desk asks. She looks like she'd rather be in prison than behind this desk.

"Stryker," Wes says. "Should be two rooms."

The woman behind the desk frowns and clicks around. "We have one room for Wesley Stryker."

"We had the reservation made for two rooms." Wes's brows furrow as he starts tapping around on his phone.

"There's one room." The woman behind the counter just stares blankly at Wes, like it's his problem.

Wes sighs through his nose and keeps scrolling, my stomach sinking deeper and deeper as he digs. Maybe sharing a room won't be *too* bad? It's not like we have to touch. I can keep it together with a bed's worth of distance.

"Look — two rooms." Wes shows her his phone.

The woman behind the desk squints, types something, then squints again. "You should have been notified that we're overbooked."

"We weren't." Wes drops his phone on the desk.

"Are there two beds, at least?" I ask.

"There's a king-sized bed." She looks between the two of us. "I dunno, she's kind of small. Just put some pillows down the middle or something."

Wes heaves a sigh and rakes his hand through his hair. "Are you sure there aren't any other rooms?"

"I'm sure. We're booked up for that liquor thing happening downstairs. Same with every other hotel nearby." She gestures vaguely around herself. "You want the room or not?"

Sharing one room with separate beds was horrifying enough, but sharing one bed after everything? It's like she just handed a lighter to someone standing a puddle of gasoline.

Wes looks at me, then up at the ceiling.

"Fine," he says. "Can we at least get a roller bed or something?"

"Out of those." The woman types away, then slaps an envelope with the key cards onto the desk. "Sorry."

"Whatever," Wes grumbles, taking the envelope.

We head to the elevator in silence. Or at least almost-silence because my heart is thumping so hard. What are we supposed to do? Keep our hands to ourselves?

Well, yeah. That's exactly what we should do. What happened on the couch was a one-time thing. Period. A bet, more or less. A very pleasurable bet, but still — nothing serious. Nothing meant to be repeated.

We reach the room and Wes opens the door.

"What a view," he says, gesturing at the lovely view of the brick wall of the building next to us.

"I mean, the service isn't much better." I try to ignore the huge bed in the middle. How are we going to share this? "The pillow barrier might be a good idea."

"Why?" Wes puts his backpack down and smirks at me. "Afraid you won't be able to keep your hands to yourself after the other day?"

My face burns, but I think I manage to keep it cool. "No, it's just that I don't want you to kick me in your sleep or something."

"Sure. Whatever. I'm sure we can keep our hands where they should be," Wes says. "What do you need to do before tonight?"

Remembering the competition kicks me back into reality.

"I need to run through my routine once or twice. Prepare some garnishes that take a while." I take a deep breath and let it out. "And then I need to get dressed and do my makeup and all that... But the email I got says I won't be able to go prep for a few hours."

I open my extra bag, which has all my gear and the bitters I made. I checked it obsessively before we left, but I look through it again to make sure that it's all there.

"Will practicing help you feel better?" he asks, his voice low. "If it does, you can practice on me."

I blink up at him. There's not a hint of sarcasm in his tone, which makes my heart bounce in my chest.

"Sure," I say. "Thank you."

I grab my outfit for the night and my makeup, then Wes grabs my bartending stuff, then we head downstairs to the convention hall. Since it's the first day, it's busy, with different brands of liquor at the respective booths. Some of them are much bigger than others.

I scan the crowd, hoping that people I know aren't here. I doubt it — the competition later is for the entire eastern half of the US, but why would they come? All of Erik's friends are so up their asses that anything that's outside of the tri-state area is considered the backwoods.

Eventually we reach the practice room, which is bustling with activity. It's still a bit early, so there aren't a lot of people here.

"Okay, hit me," Wes says, sitting down in a seat across from one of the small tables. I start to scan the room to look at my competition, but Wes waves his hand. "Don't look at them. Look at me."

Looking at him is also distracting, but less anxiety-inducing. He stretches out his long legs and relaxes like he's about to watch a movie.

"Can you time me?" I ask, straightening out my shaker.

"Yep." He pulls out his phone. "Start whenever."

I take a deep breath and start. Putting together the drink itself isn't complicated, but the extras I made add complexity — the bitters, the simple syrup. I explain each ingredient as I add it, and what I want each ingredient to do for the flavor, and some fun facts about the ingredients. Once I finish, I step back and he taps his phone, showing me the time.

"How was it?" I ask.

"Great. Smooth and natural." He stands up. "Let me taste it, though."

He picks up the glass and takes a sip, not taking his eyes off me. I scan his face as he swallows, biting the inside of my cheek. Finally, he nods, smiling before handing it back to me.

"That's really fucking good," he says. "I want to drink more of it, but I don't want to get too drunk."

"Good." I shake the tension out of my arms. "It doesn't taste too boozy?"

"Nope, it's just right." Wes squeezes my upper arm. His hands are big and warm, just the right amount of comfort.

"Okay." I let out a breath again and try to sink into his touch.

"Relax, Rose." Wes smiles at me in a way that makes it feel private and just for us. "Just run through it a few more times so it's practically habit and you're all set."

I nod and head back for another round. Each time my nerves are still there, but the muscle memory kicks in. Eventually my phone buzzes with my alarm, and I see good luck texts from my family and Jo.

"I should head over," I say to Wes.

"Alright." Wes stands up and starts gathering a few of my heavier bags. He does that a lot, I've realized, but I've never appreciated it more than I do today. My hands feel too shaky to carry a bag filled with liquor bottles.

We stop outside of the exhibition hall where the competition is being held. I check to see if there's red lipstick on my teeth, then tuck my phone into my bag.

"You look great," Wes says. "Don't worry about that."

"Thank you." I shake my arms out again. "Should I worry about everything else?"

"Nah." Wes smiles. "Break a leg or something."

"Thanks." I push my braids behind my ear. "See you later."

"See you."

He lets me walk ahead and into the room where the competition will be held. Since this is just the regional round, it's only judges. I hate the space — it's just a bunch of tables in a somewhat bright hall instead of a bar-type feel. I should have practiced in this kind of lighting.

All the competitors are split into groups based on our last names and are guided to seating areas in different spots of the room. We get to watch the others, which is sort of a relief. Even though my stressed-out state, I can tell I can do better than a lot of these people.

At least until my name is called and my nerves take over everything. I walk up with my gear and place it on the table, taking a few deep breaths. The judges smile at me, at least, which helps me unglue my mouth and start talking.

My routine goes by in a hyper-focused blur. My hands were shaking half the time, but the judges laughed at my jokes and didn't immediately spit the drink out.

"Thank you," One of the older judges says. "You can take your seat again until we dismiss everyone."

"Thanks." I gather all my gear and head back to sit down, sighing with relief.

But then I glance down the row and my heart seizes. What is Erik doing here? He catches my eye. It's like a dagger to the heart.

He couldn't have known I'd be here, right? I blocked him everywhere and don't keep in touch with any of his old friends (not that I wanted to).

I look across the room for the fastest way out, wishing I could mess with my phone or something to distract me. Why can't we leave yet? It's not like we'll tell everyone what's happening the second we step outside?

I look away, tidying my station. Can I just take a shot of this tequila without anyone judging me?

The wait is pure torture, and the second they open the doors to let people out, I try to bolt for it in as casual a way as possible. But I'm toward the back of the hall, and I can't get through fast enough. A big hand comes down on my shoulder and I shove it off of me. Of course, it's Erik.

"What do you want?" I ask, swallowing and looking him in the eye for the first time since he kicked me out. "Don't touch me."

"Can I not say hello?" he asks, his brows furrowing. "We're adults who can talk to each other after a breakup."

His condescending tone is like nails on a chalkboard.

"Can we, though?" I ask. "It's easy to say that when you're not the one who got the short end of the stick."

His eyebrows go up like I just spoke to him in tongues. "What do you mean the short end of the stick?"

"This is the same exact conversation we had when you

kicked me out." I start to walk away, but he easily keeps up with me. "You know exactly what I'm talking about."

"I know what you're talking about, but I don't agree." He huffs. "You can't take credit for something I did."

I nearly scream at him again – how can he just say that he did everything when I was the one to create the recipes *and* post and promote them? Him tweaking the amount of bitters or changing a sentence or two of my copy doesn't count as "his work". Am I just an AI or something to him? A tool?

"I thought we could be more mature about this, but I guess not," he says, mistaking my silence as a cold shoulder instead of pure, horrified shock and disbelief. He takes a few steps ahead of me."I hope you do some thinking about your behavior, Rose. It's not very attractive."

"What makes you think I'd ever want to do anything to attract you?" I spit back.

He looks back at me over his shoulder, looking me up and down. Then, he keeps walking, saying hello to a woman and air kissing her cheeks.

I hope you do some thinking about your behavior.

The words ring over and over again in my head, my blood boiling. And even worse, tears sting my eyes. I can't cry in the middle of this convention hall.

But I can't help it.

CHAPTER FIFTEEN

WES

I've been a dickhead to Rose countless times across our entire lives, but I've never, ever said anything to make her cry.

Whatever that guy said to her must have *really* fucked with her. My first instinct is to go fuck with *him* and choke him out using that stupid fucking tie he has on, but Rose comes first.

I push through the crowd toward her and grab her shoulder. She jumps, surprised.

"You good?" I ask, scanning her face. She's pulled it together to some extent, but her eyes are still red and puffy.

She nods and turns away from me. "Let's go to the convention hall while we wait for the results."

"No, sit down, Rose," I say, grasping her by both shoulders. "You're all over the place."

She lets me steer her over onto a bench, tucked away from the passing crowds. I squat down in front of her and run my hands up and down her forearms, trying to get her grounded again.

"You're holding your breath," I say softly. "Breathe."

She sucks in a breath and lets it out, then does it again.

"Fuck," she finally says, her hands shaking. She clutches her knees. "I can't believe him."

"Who hurt you?" I ask, resting my hands on top of hers.

"My ex. Not physically but it doesn't matter."

"The one you told me about at the bonfire?" I ask.

"Yeah. He always ripped off all my ideas and now I'm wondering if he did it again here." She looks up at the ceiling like she's trying not to cry and balls her hands into fists. "Fine, you can't technically copyright recipes, but he could at least *pretend* that he collaborated with me instead of just stealing all of the fucking credit and pretending that I can't even make a fucking Cosmo and —"

"Slow down." I cup her face, which is boiling hot. I've never touched her like this before, but it felt right. And she isn't moving away. "Slow down. So he stole your work and passed it off as his own?"

"Yeah." She takes a shuddering breath, a tear escaping. I wipe it away. "The abbreviated version is that I worked with him on his cocktail recipe blog for years and really blew it up — he got to a million followers on Instagram too. I did *everything*, right down to the recipes, and he just added a little flair at the end. I was so delusional thinking we were working *together*."

She takes another deep breath and I keep my mouth shut so she'll continue opening up.

"But yeah, I did all that for him. A TV producer came calling about a show. He didn't even acknowledge all the work I did behind the scenes, because he convinced me it was for 'brand consistency' while I was doing it. Anyway, he convinced me that he was going to include me as a part of the show as his co-host, which I blabbed about all over social media.

"But then, I caught him cheating on me with someone we used to work with. When I confronted him, he dumped me first and told me that he'd changed our contract for the show to cut me out of it. I was out of a job, a boyfriend, and a place to live in the span of an hour," she says.

"So that's why you came back to Jepsen," I say, letting my hands slide down to her shoulders. My thumb rests at the pulse at the base of her neck, which is still going wild.

"Yeah. Kind of hard to stay there when I mostly had my best friend, who lives in a studio apartment with her boyfriend. All my other friends couldn't let me crash at their places for one reason or another. I could have gotten a job at any old dive bar but I really, really had to get out of the city." Her voice cracks and she clears her throat. She sniffs and carefully dabs at her eyelashes with the backs of her fingers like she's trying not to break down.

I absently run my hands up and down her forearms, trying to keep my cool. Losing my shit wouldn't help at all.

I hate this. I fucking hate *him*. Her walls have fallen and crumbled into dust, but instead of seeing even more glimpses of the fun, smartass woman who's always kept me on my toes, I see a woman who's been fucked over by a smug asshole who should have been the guy she could trust with everything. A woman who's been hurt by a lot of shitheads.

But she's still here and she's still fucking *trying*. She could have just taken a job at any dive bar or quit the industry entirely. But she moved home, taking a little hit to her pride, because she knows that she's great at this. And she's trying to build herself back up, too.

And seeing that is something special.

"Come here." I pull her into a hug, right in the middle of the convention hall. She's obviously surprised at first, but she slowly puts her arms around me and rests her forehead against my chest. It's a simple hug, but feeling the tension roll out of her body the longer I hold her pleases some part of me that I didn't even know existed. Her hair smells nice, like coconut, and she fits just right against me.

"You showed up again even though you could have just quit. Doesn't that count for something?" I finally ask. "I think that's fucking amazing."

She swallows and shakes her head. "Don't you think it's dumb that I ended up in that situation? He hardly paid me. He convinced me that we were doing the same amount of work even though my work made the biggest impact on *his* brand."

"What does that have to do with not quitting?" I ask, raising an eyebrow. She looks at me, a look of familiar, but mild exasperation at me calling her out on her face. "I've done a *lot* of really stupid shit in the past. But if I lingered on that all the time, I wouldn't be able to move forward."

The uncomfortable sting of knowing that even if I've moved on, my family mostly hasn't, appears in my chest. Despite her encouragement, I can't shake the sting.

"I don't know," she finally mumbles. "It just hurts."

"Listen. Fuck that piece of shit and his stupid striped shirt and tie," I say, holding her small body tighter. She smells so good, like whatever she put on her braids mixed with her perfume. "Do you know what you've done, though? You've kicked ass and didn't let him push you down."

Finally, she cracks what's close to a smile, before it falls again. "We haven't even gotten the results of the competition part. What if I lose?"

"Doesn't matter." I pull back, letting my hands rest on hers on her knees. "You could have quit. But you did it anyway. You aren't going to let him win no matter what the results of the competition are."

She looks down at where my hands are resting on her legs but doesn't make any indication that she wants me to move them.

"I fucking hated his striped shirts. Especially the formal ones," she finally whispers.

"He looks like a mime going to junior prom."

She bursts out laughing so loudly that people turn and look. "Oh my god."

I grin too. Her genuine laughter could keep me going for months at a time. "Am I wrong?"

She shakes her head. "But that means I fucked a mime for years."

"But you aren't now." Thankfully. Now that I've seen this fucker, I hate the idea that he ever touched her. What a pretentious piece of shit.

"God, yes. It's just the whole package." She sniffs, straightening up. "Sorry for breaking down."

"Don't apologize for that." I stand up and offer my hand to help her up. "Anyone would. And like I said, you didn't quit. And you're going to make it to the next round. And even if you don't — which isn't possible — you still kicked ass. Okay?"

She squeezes my hand back. "Okay."

"Let's go eat and get a drink. We can get news on who's moving onto the next round later."

I hang onto her hand just a second longer than I have to. But she doesn't let go for another few moments either.

"What's around? I'm starving," she says.

"I know a spot, but you have to trust me," I say. Her eyebrows shoot up. "I swear."

"I feel like that's the start of many of the hot mess stories you have from high school," she says. "But your chaos is more contained now so...fine."

I can't help but grin like an idiot. That feels so good to hear from her. "Thanks, Rose. Come on."

I guide her through the convention hall and out onto the streets. I have to check the map to make sure we're going in the right direction, but soon we're off. It's a bit of a walk, but she doesn't seem to mind. Eventually we reach a nondescript red door with a burger etched into it.

"It's not a murder den," I say once I take her expression in.

"Are you sure? Because this seems like the beginning to a horror movie and the odds are definitely against me in that situation," she says.

"I promise." I open the door for her and she goes in, eyeing me skeptically.

The inside doesn't look much better either. We walk down a dingy hallway toward the restaurant, and when I open the door at the end of the hall, we're greeted with a huge pair of fake boobs right at eye level. I look up and lock eyes with a Dolly Parton-impersonating drag queen, who grins down at me.

"Come on in, darlin'," she says, waving us in and handing us bingo cards. "We're startin' another round of bingo soon, so get your order in."

I guide Rose toward a table near the raised stage where the Dolly Parton drag queen is strutting around, watching the crowd.

"Bingo? Really?" Rose says into my ear.

"Bingo's fucking great, and the burgers here are good." I shrug and lay out our cards. "I swear we'll have a good time."

She eyes me. "How often are you playing bingo?"

"When I'm feeling bold and go with Nana," I say. She snorts, and I can't help but let the corner of my mouth creep up. "You haven't been to Bingo at the rec center, clearly. I feel like we're moments away from a brawl at least four times in a night. There's a lot of drama for a room with an average age of sixty."

She blinks. "But Bingo is just...chance?"

"Tell that to Nana." I hand her a food menu. "Just roll with it. I promise. And pick a burger. They're all good."

Her eyes narrow but she takes the menu. A waiter takes our orders just in time for the next round to start. I spread out my cards and grab a pen.

"What's the drama at Bingo night?" I ask.

"B40!" Drag Dolly Parton calls out. "B40."

"Where do I even start?" I put a dot on B40 on my card. "You want to go iceberg style, where I start with the basic stuff and get to the juicier gossip under the surface, or do you want me to just start anywhere?"

"Start from the tip of the iceberg," she says, glancing up at Drag Dolly.

I think about where to start while Drag Dolly calls out a

few more numbers — there really is a lot of gossip and back-stabbing to go through.

"Remember Mrs. Rossman from middle school?" I ask.

"Our social studies teacher?" Rose asks, coloring a dot for G9. "Yeah."

"She's in a love triangle with Mr. Greer from gym class and that lunch lady who was always stingy with the tater tots," I say.

"Oh, that's barely hot goss," she says with a snort. "Everyone could feel the tension."

"Really?"

"Yeah, for sure," she says. "Second lunch period? The drama was palpable. And apparently still so hot that it's going like ten years later."

I grin and scan my card for another number. "So I guess I need to go deeper."

"Way deeper."

I tap the end of my pen on the table a few times. "Then what about Kenny down at the cafe and the war with his neighbor over the hedges?"

"I haven't heard that one yet."

I tell her all about Kenny fighting with his neighbor over the height of their hedges, and all the other small town shit that Nana tells me when we go to Bingo. Rose's mood lifts as we talk and lifts even more when we get our burgers.

"This is crazy good," she says in between bites. I wish I didn't know how she moans when she loves food, because now that's all I can think about. "How'd you find this place?"

"By accident." I put a dot down on a number after Drag Dolly calls it. "Waylon was going through his second breakup with Catherine so we took him to Nashville for a guys weekend. We were wasted as fuck and stumbled in here, then decided to stay. The drag queens gave him a pep talk and put us in a cab when we got too far gone."

"That's super sweet," she says. "I would have loved a pep talk from a drag queen when things fell apart with Erik. I got one from Jo, which was great, but any outside help in an amazing outfit would have been welcome. Actually, weirdly enough we were at a drag brunch the day I met Erik. I wish one of them had somehow told me not to go for it."

"They're drag queens, not psychics."

"I know, I know," she says. "Still. Whatever, I'm done with dating forever."

"Forever?" I raise an eyebrow.

"G95! G95!" Drag Dolly calls out. "G 9 to 5, honey."

"Oo, I'm one off." Rose places a dot down on her board. "Yeah, I'm just over it. Over all the serious bullshit that comes with relationships. Love is dead."

"Jesus." I take a sip of my beer. "That's kind of intense."

She looks at me and raises an eyebrow. "Is it? I got fucked over by Erik, and by most of my exes. Why would I try again if I have a bad picker?"

I eat a few fries to give myself time to think. Waylon's the exact same way now after everything imploded with Catherine, and I understand him on that front. It's still depressing, though.

"I guess I get it," I say. "I'm sure getting fucked over like that would put me off too."

"Thank you!" she says. "Jo doesn't get it. I love Jo to pieces and she's basically my sister, but just because she found love doesn't mean it's for everyone. She and her boyfriend are basically made for each other."

Her tone has a wistfulness to it. It doesn't seem like jealousy, though. I feel like she's less committed to this no dating thing than she's saying, but I don't want to call her on it.

"Then what are your plans for the future?" I ask. "Single forever?"

She blows out a heavy breath. "I guess so. I mean, I have friends. I'll definitely try to get laid."

I need to ignore that. I wish we didn't align on this one thing after everything. Getting along with her like this *and* knowing what she tastes like is testing my patience.

"175," Drag Dolly calls out.

"Bingo!" Rose throws her hand up in the air. "Yes!"

"Told you it was exciting," I say.

Rose grins and lets Drag Dolly wrap a hot pink feather boa around her shoulders. We get two drinks on our tab for free for winning that round, and we stick around for a few more. Eventually we finish our food, and the crowd starts to file out.

"You want to go back?" I ask.

"Yeah, let's do it."

We walk through the streets, the crowds thinning as we reach the hotel, and head up to our floor.

When we open the door, the big bed we'll have to share stares back at us.

CHAPTER SIXTEEN

ROSE

I feel gently buzzed by the time we get back to the hotel, but seeing that bed in the middle of the room sobers me up, fast.

Tonight has been genuinely fun — more fun than I've had in years. With Wes.

Wes. The hot-but-irritating guy who's been making it his mission to one-up me since we were literally in diapers. The guy who was sweeter and more supportive than anyone else has ever been in my entire life after one of my most embarrassing moments.

And the guy who made me come so hard that I still get shivers from the memory. Who I have to share a bed with.

My body flushes with warmth, but I walk inside like nothing is wrong.

"I call dibs on the bathroom," I say, going into my bag to grab my pajamas.

Wes grunts in response as I go get ready for bed. I brush my teeth and wash my face, then go back out. I'm in my least sexy pajamas — a huge t-shirt that goes down to my knees and short-shorts.

I *will* resist Wes tonight. No matter what. I can't let him being super nice for...ok, for a while now, but extra nice tonight let me lose my mind.

I replace the cotton pillowcase with my satin one, then crawl into bed and plug in my phone with a sigh. Hotel beds make me feel like I'm wrapped in a cloud, and I can pass out just as well away from home as I can in my own bed. Well, when I'm not sharing a bed with someone like Wes.

Wes comes out of the bathroom a few minutes later, wearing nothing but a snug pair of black boxer briefs. All the breath leaves my lungs in a rush. Why does he have to look like he was handcrafted to be hot specifically to me? And to a bunch of other people, but the way he looks hits a particularly annoying part of my brain, one that I wish didn't exist.

And when he turns to the side so I can see the curve of his ass?

I sink lower under the covers and take a subtle, but deep breath. *Control*. I can have self control.

"Okay," Wes says, throwing back the covers and sliding in next to me. "Just a heads up, when I wake up with a boner — "

"*When?*"

"Pretend it's just a morning thing." He scrolls around his phone as if we aren't talking about his dick.

"As opposed to what?" I let my phone fall onto the comforter below me.

"As opposed to the effect of sleeping next to you all night." One side of his lips quirks up.

I roll my eyes, even though I'm fully throbbing between my thighs. "I'll keep that in mind."

I try to read a book on my phone, but all I can think of is what he said. The idea of waking up with his body pressed against mine, his cock hard, is driving me insane. All of the thoughts that I had the day of our little...competition...come rushing back. The feeling of his tongue on me. His gorgeous cock. It legitimately feels unfair that he's gifted down there too.

Reading this book isn't helping either — I'm right at the smutty part, and reading that right next to the guy who I'm actively trying to not fling myself at? Not the best idea I've ever had. I end up staring blankly at the screen, wanting to read on, but knowing the further I get, the wetter I'll become.

"Have you read a single page of that book?" he asks.

"Have you been watching me this whole time?" I shoot back.

"Maybe I was reading over your shoulder." He grins and cranes his neck to see my phone. "Something about choking on someone's cock like a good girl?"

"Oh my god." I slide even further under the covers, my whole body heating with embarrassment and arousal. Hearing him say those words is making me literally ache between my thighs.

"What?" Wes turns on his side to face me and rests his head on his fist. The position makes the muscles in his arms pop. "Nothing wrong with that. If the repair guys hadn't come, wouldn't you have done the same thing?"

Hell yes, I would have. The short time I was able to suck his cock has replayed in my head ever since. He has a sexy voice, but hearing his moans was something else entirely. I bite my lip, shifting and pressing my thighs together.

This was *not* supposed to happen. I was supposed to resist him. All that pre-emptive masturbating before this trip was useless. If anything, it's made me crave his touch more.

"Tell me, Rose," Wes says, putting a finger under my chin and turning my face toward him. "What do you want to do? You want to suck my cock like a good girl?"

I let out a slow breath. Fuck it. I can't stand a chance when he's looking at me like he wants to fuck me into oblivion. What's the point in me resisting?

"Yes," I say.

He grins, pushing back the covers. "Strip and come here."

I do as he says, then crawl between his knees. He palms his cock through his underwear, taking me in. When I go to pull at his briefs, he steps back.

"You're not going to take it without asking, are you?" He brushes my braids over my shoulder and I narrow my eyes at him. His eyes light up in amusement. "Ask for it."

"Please," I say, staring at the bulge right in front of me. I've never hated giving blowjobs, but I've never been this eager before.

"Please what?" He finally shoves his boxers down, his cock springing free.

"Please let me suck your cock." My whole body flushes with heat. Usually the guys I sleep with don't say much at all — they just grunt or tell me to flip over — so I never said much either. I like this way too much.

"Very nice." He guides my head down and I take his tip into my mouth.

I start with what I did last time, teasing his tip and sucking on the underside of it. He sucks in a breath, his hand resting on my head but not forcing me to move. Little by little, I take more of him into my mouth, feeding off every twitch of his hips and soft moan. Eventually he starts thrusting into my mouth, just a little bit.

"You don't suck cock like a good girl," he says, his hips pressing forward until his cock hits the back of my throat. My eyes water, but I love the way he's looking at me, so I stay still. "You do it like a girl who likes to be a bit bad."

He keeps my head down as he leans forward, reaching over me. His fingers brush over my opening, which is just enough of a touch to make me moan. I want him inside of me.

"So fucking wet," he says, sitting back and sucking on his fingers. "Come here."

He gently nudges me off, pulling me up the bed like I hardly weigh anything, and hovers over me. We lock eyes for a moment before he bends down and kisses me, sliding an arm under my body so we're pressed together. His kisses make me feel dizzy in the best way, like I'm on a roller-coaster.

"Fuck," I hiss when he sinks one finger inside me.

"So damn tight, too." He strokes his fingers just right, making my toes curl and back arch. "You going to squeeze my cock the way you're squeezing my fingers?"

I nod because he's taken the air out of my lungs. He finds the spot on my neck that makes me lose it every time and sucks on it as he finger fucks me, making my legs quiver and shake.

"Please. My nipples," I manage to choke out. I'm already

so close, but I can't make it on his fingers alone. He could keep me here for ever, right on the edge, until my brain is permanently wiped.

"Since you asked nicely. And since these tits have been the star of every fantasy I've had for the past month." He dives right in and sucks my left nipple. I cry out so loud that I put my hand over my mouth, and he pulls it away. "Don't cover your mouth. I need to hear you fucking scream for me."

I dig my fingers into his hair as he sucks my nipples, working each one in tandem with his fingers. His hand speeds up and I rocket along right with it, coming hard and crying out. It's the kind of climax that rolls on and on, washing over every part of me.

I finally come down and he smiles, satisfied.

"You're going to do that again on my cock," he says, standing up. "Understand?"

"Can't," I say. I'm a puddle on the bed. "Not more than once in a row."

"It wasn't a question. It's just a fact." He digs around in his back and comes back with a condom. "Now spread your legs for me. I'm going to fuck you into this mattress until you're falling to pieces and hoarse from moaning so much."

I watch him roll on the condom, nice and slow, like he's doing it to tease me. He grabs me by the ankle and drags me toward him, pressing my knees back toward my chest. I suck in a breath when he puts his tip against me and starts to press inside.

His cock feels huge inside of me, stretching me as he works his way in. He's gentle even though I'm so soaked that he could slide right in.

"Deep," I say softly, holding my legs back. He braces his hands over me, rolling his hips and closing his eyes.

"So fucking deep. Do you know how much I've wanted to be inside you?" He leans down and nips the side of my neck.

He's reduced me to just feeling. Snarky comebacks that I would shoot back to him in any other circumstance fail me as he thrusts, his own breathing picking up. Every glide of his cock against my g-spot makes tears come to my eyes, it feels so good.

I look up at Wes, whose look of pure pleasure is different than anything I've ever seen from him. His eyes are closed, his brows furrowed and his lips parted. It's so hot that I clench around him. He grabs my leg and stops.

"Fuck, Rose, warn me before you do that," he says, his voice rough.

"Do what?" I squeeze him again and his eyes flutter closed. "That?"

"You're a fucking brat," he says with a laugh, pulling out of me. "Come here."

He once again flips me around like a doll, positioning me on my hands and knees. We're facing a mirror, our bodies framed in it. His eyes roam over our reflection as he grips my ass, giving it a hard squeeze. I shake it back and forth, pulling a smile from him.

"I know, baby," he says. My eyes nearly cross when he slides into me hard and fast. "You need this cock, don't you?"

God, yes. Instead of speaking, I just moan. I want to bury my face into the comforter but watching him fuck me isn't something I want to miss.

He fucks me harder this time, pounding into me at a

relentless pace. His grip tightens so much on my hips that I know I'll have bruises later. I don't even care. I've never been this out of my mind while being fucked before. I'm so damn loud right now, but the louder I am, the harder he fucks me. I could exist in this space forever.

"Let me see that pretty face while you come for me," he says breathlessly.

He reaches around and rubs my clit. The jolt is so intense that I nearly faceplant into the bed. I try to keep my eyes locked on our reflection as he touches me just right, the combo of his cock and his hand pushes me to the edge. Seeing him clearly trying to hold it together before he makes me come sends me right over.

He was right. I come on his cock so hard that he has to hold me down as to not slip out, my voice hoarse as I cry out. He lets out the most delicious grunts as he chases his own finish, finally folding over my body and going limp.

He uses what seems like the last bit of strength to pull us up the bed and put us on our sides. It takes us a while to catch our breaths and for reality to sink in.

I just fucked Wes Stryker. This is so bad. This is so messy.

But still, I want to do it again and again.

CHAPTER SEVENTEEN

ROSE

"Look at you, Miss Champion," my cousin Natasha says as she pulls up to Wes's place in her well-loved Honda Civic.

I roll my eyes and open the door, sliding inside. "I'm not the champ - I just ranked high enough to go onto the national championship."

I'd gotten an email about it because we left before they finished calculating the scores. Since it's just a regional competition, there wasn't a whole award ceremony.

"Well that's just the first stepping stone to being a champ." She pulls off when I buckle my seatbelt. "I'm manifesting."

I sigh. If I get into manifesting with her, we'll end up in the same annoying spiral we always end up in. She seems to sense it too, because she turns up whatever K-Pop playlist she has playing.

"Nice place, by the way," she says. "And congrats on not murdering Wes yet."

I snort, casually resting an elbow on the edge of the door

even though I feel like bursting into flames. I still can't believe what happened in Nashville. Ok, my body believes it — I still feel a tinge of soreness between my legs from what we got up to the second night after we spent the day on the convention floor, speaking with possible vendors for the drink. And also from what we got up to the last night we were there. And also the morning after.

Good lord.

In the span of two nights, he managed to do what every other guy I've been with hasn't. Again. And again. If I thought what we did on the couch the day the AC broke was a good trailer, the movie blew it out of the water.

But on any other level? I can't believe I did that. I was weak. And what can this possibly lead to? We're friends — I can accept that and actually like hanging out with him now — but when did I start sleeping with friends? I'm usually the friend telling my other friends not to make things complicated this way.

And we're coworkers *and* roommates? When did I get so messy?

"What?" Natasha glances over at me, her eyes wide. "What was that?"

"What was what?"

"That heavy ass sigh." She rolls to a stop at a light. "What happened with Wes? Is his dead body in the house? It's hot outside. You can't just let him sit in there!"

I run a hand down my face, trying not to laugh. "Tash. No."

"Did you two..." She makes a gesture that has to be referring to sex.

"Why is that what you leapt to after *murder*?" I ask, raising an eyebrow.

"Because they're both passionate. And I've seen that man, so I wouldn't blame you." She turns. "So I'm guessing yes, you did."

I sigh again.

"I knew it!" she says, speeding along to my parents' house. "There was such a *thing* between you two at the distillery event. Everyone on social media saw it too."

"Natasha. Please." I close my eyes. "I can't right now."

"What do you need to be able to talk about it?" She glances from side to side. "Because we can stop somewhere.""

I stare up at the ceiling of the car, which somehow has a coffee stain on it. I *should* talk to someone about it. I haven't had the chance to call Jo about it yet, and as much as I love Natasha, Jo has enough distance from Jepsen and its whole ecosystem to give a more objective opinion.

But if I don't talk about this, then I'm going to implode.

"I just need to pick what we're watching while you do my hair. And a donut."

"Done and done." She pulls over to one of the newer bakeries in town, and we quickly get some donuts. Before I know it, we're at my parents' house, a chair set up in front of the TV. I flop down and pick up the remote, going to the free streaming service where the Real Deal of Miami is streaming.

"Oh my god, are you going to make me watch hours of this shit?" Natasha asks, grabbing the bundles of hair from my bag. "I got you a donut."

"A deal's a deal." I press play on the latest season. We're

going to be here for a long, long time so I won't subject her to this for the whole time. I'm not that mean.

"Fine. The price I pay for hot goss." She starts trimming the ends off my current braids and taking them down. "Tell me everything you don't feel weird telling me about."

I tell her everything aside from the nitty gritty details.

"Wow," Natasha finally says. "So basically you guys had a first date and he fucked your brains out."

"It wasn't a date." I start undoing the other side of my hair so I won't be here for a thousand years. "He was just taking me out to distract me from Erik."

"And he distracted you by taking you on a date."

"A date implies feelings. And yeah, we're friends, but nothing more. I can't date Wes," I say.

"Why not?" Natasha leans forward and grabs the scissors again. "He sounds like he's not a pain in the ass anymore."

"Because I'm never dating again?" I wish we had a mirror so I could see her face. "This whole situation was kicked off because I was running from a man who fucked me over. And Wes is Wes. He's the town flirt."

Natasha makes a sound of acknowledgment, but doesn't speak for a few moments. My fingers are already tired just from taking down a few braids.

"But you didn't say you don't have feelings for him. You just said you were never dating again," she points out.

"I definitely do not have feelings for him. I like him as a friend."

"But you don't sleep with friends," she once again points out accurately. "So what is it?"

I turn and glare at her. But she just smiles.

"It's friends with benefits, probably." I can't imagine him

not wanting to hook up again when it was that good for both of us. We share a wall for fuck's sake. "And yes, I know I'm being a little messy."

"A *little*?" she asks. "He's your roommate, former rival, coworker, and friend."

"Natasha."

"I'm just calling it the way I'm seeing it." She shrugs. "Anyway, he sounds super sweet to me so maybe this could be a thing down the line. That would make it a lot less messy."

Just the idea of ever being part of "a thing" again makes the donut in my stomach turn. Being a part of something feels like stepping into a room with no windows, blinding me to what's actually going on. I do trust Wes on a lot of levels, but the kind of trust I'd need to give a boyfriend is way beyond that. Way beyond anything I think I could give anyone again.

Besides, I don't see him like that anyway and I doubt he sees me that way either.

"That's because you don't have the full history of Wes Stryker," I say, shaking my hands out.

"I don't." She rubs my scalp where she's undone a section of braids. "But based on what you're saying, he's grown up into a half decent guy."

I don't know how to respond to that without starting up more conversations I'm not ready to have. We watch (or rather I watch) the Real Deal of Miami, take a break when I go to wash my hair, and wrap up my new braids several hours later with some episodes of Lucifer. I change into my clothes for work and Natasha drives me to the bar.

"Thanks for the ride and for the hair." I give her an air kiss on the cheek.

"No prob." She squeezes my shoulder. "And don't do anything I wouldn't do."

I raise an eyebrow. "That's kind of ominous."

"Just be safe, dumbass." She waves me away. "Now go to work."

I hop out and take a deep breath, blowing it out as I cross into the bar. Some music is playing, so Wes has to be here. My heart leaps into my throat despite myself. We somehow managed to not talk about what happened the entire time we drove back to Jepsen, mostly because we were talking about the competition and what I'm going to do for the next round.

But at the same time, we can't really hash out what went down between us when Jasper or Sabrina will be in to work any minute.

I spot Wes in the back, grabbing a box from a high shelf. I hate that I feel a pulse between my thighs just looking at his shoulders in his t-shirt.

"Hey," he says when he notices me, flashing me a smile. "Your hair looks nice."

"Oh, thanks." I put my hand on my head like I'd suddenly forgotten about my new braids. Natasha never pulls my hair too tight, but they're so fresh that I still feel the gentle tension across my scalp. "Need help with anything?"

"Not unless you grow a foot taller. I've got it." He puts the box down, then grabs another.

"I can use a ladder." I rest a hand on my hip.

"You know how that ended last time." He turns toward me fully, his eyes skimming up and down my body.

My nipples tighten into peaks. I remember all too well. It

was a shock to the system, feeling his hands on my body. He seems to sense that I'm remembering, because he approaches me, boxing me in against the wall. His body heat radiates against me, the clean woodsy scent of his body wash overwhelming me.

"You still want to do this?" I blurt. "It wasn't just a Nashville thing?"

"What, you didn't think I was done with you, did you?" he asks, his fingers under my chin. He grins, then kisses my neck just lightly enough to send chills up and down my body. "We've just gotten started."

"Have we?" I ask, tilting my head back so he can get to that perfect spot on my neck. His lips brushing against it is like pressing a button to weaken my knees.

His hands span my waist and he pushes me back against the wall. We're half-hidden behind the metal cabinet in here.

"Wish you were wearing a skirt." He easily scoops me up and holds me, my arms going around his neck. "I could just push it up and see what you're wearing underneath."

"What if I wasn't wearing anything underneath?" I let my head tilt back and he rakes his teeth along my neck again, just enough to make me bite back a moan.

"Can I hold you to that?" he asks, sliding his leg between mine. All I want to do is grind against him but some shred of self control is still inside of me. "Because now that's all I'm going to think about."

The door to the outside shuts and the sound of Jasper and Sabrina's voices comes through. I tense, but Wes slowly sets me down and straightens my shirt, his fingers skirting against my skin.

"Seriously, Rose," he says, his eyes still filled with heat

even though we're a reasonable distance apart now. "A skirt. Nothing underneath. Consider that the favor that you owe me from the bet."

"When?" I ask, resting a hand on the cabinet to keep myself steady. Wes's dark eyes are literally making me lose control of my limbs.

"Surprise me." He winks — actually winks without it being weird, and steps out of the room.

I sag against the wall and let out a shaky breath. Okay, I'm in over my head.

CHAPTER EIGHTEEN

WES

My dad has had the same office toward the edge of town for my entire life, and the inside is more or less the same as it was when I was a kid - aggressively 90s, with newer carpet that still has that weird squiggle design, florescent lighting, and outdated furniture. It's such a sharp contrast from home, where Mom updates the furniture and decor more often than anyone probably should.

Dad's even had the same receptionist as he's had for ages, Mrs. Ridley. She also looks stuck in time, with the same dyed big hair and old school makeup. She's perfectly fine as a person — which is surprising given how unbearable Dad can be — but seeing her makes my stomach churn. I've had my ass handed to me by my dad way too many times in his office.

"You here to see your father?" Mrs. Ridley asks.

"Yep." I tuck my hands into my pockets. "He's here, right? I'm here to give him a report on the convention."

"Yes, he is. Have a seat." She gestures to the wildly uncomfortable couches to her left.

I sit down. Is Dad actually busy or does he just want to make me wait? The latter seems like something he'd do. Especially now. I wish Rose were here, and not just because she doesn't have all the baggage with my dad that I do. She's just...steadying in a way I can't pinpoint. Knowing that she's never bullshitting me - because she's never, ever bullshitted me — is comforting in a weird way.

I rake my fingers through my hair, then put it back into place. I don't feel things after hooking up with anyone, but I can't deny sleeping with Rose changed things. We haven't had the chance to do anything more, so maybe the charm will wear off and things will go back to normal.

I'm guessing it'll happen that way — usually my feelings for women fade fast instead of intensifying the more I'm exposed to her. Yeah, what we've done has been the best I've ever had, but it's the best I've had up until now. Who knows what'll happen to me in the future?

I sigh through my nose. It's fine. I don't need to worry about the feelings if they'll fade soon, right?

"Wesley," Dad says, startling me. "Come on."

I get up and follow Dad back to his office. It smells like him, the cologne he's worn since I was a kid filling my nose. It's not a scent I enjoy. His office looks like an unironic version of Ron Burgundy's office from *Anchorman*, complete with the bourbon and crystal glasses on a shelf.

I sit down in the small chair across from him and sling my bag across my lap to get out my laptop.

"I heard there was a good response from the convention," Dad says, easing himself into his massive leather seat. "You got the information?"

"Yeah, on my laptop. I emailed it over too. To you and

John David," I say. Still, I open my laptop because Dad doesn't actually check his email himself.

I put the laptop on his desk and tilt it for us both to be able to see it. Dad puts on his glasses and leans forward.

"Here's the list of vendors who are interested in distributing the canned cocktails," I say, showing him the spreadsheet.

"Any of them jump out at you?" Dad asks, squinting at the screen.

"Publix Liquor stores. Said they were interested in possibly carrying it in some select liquor stores. The representative and I had a nice conversation on the second day," I say. "I sent the contact information to John David already, and I think he said they set up a meeting."

Dad, for the first time in my life, looks genuinely impressed. With me. The rush it gives me is so heady that I nearly forget what I'm supposed to be doing.

"And these, which are highlighted," I add, clearing my throat.

Dad squints at the spreadsheet, even after I zoom in, and comments on which vendors to listen to and which ones to ignore. He also likes the responses to all the sample drinks, even without knowing which one is Rose's and which one is mine.

Dad eventually checks his phone, which is usually my cue to leave. This time, though I sit there for a moment until he actually speaks.

"Not bad," he says to me, poking at his phone. "Just deliver it."

He puts the phone up to his ear and I guess I'm dismissed. I put my laptop into my bag and head out, my head buzzing with a mix of emotions. Relief, because that's finally over. Exhilaration, because I managed to get the one thing I've wanted out of my father from him on a random afternoon. Then something else — dread.

How am I dreading this when I'm moments from finally getting what I've wanted from Dad my whole life?

I drive home in a haze, trying to wrap my head around everything and not getting anywhere. When I head inside, I hear music playing in the kitchen and follow the sound. Rose is in the kitchen, still in a short denim skirt and a tank top that's skintight, making a bowl of cereal. The flare of lust that comes up in me is so intense that it wipes away my thoughts.

But then she turns and looks at me, smiling in a way that has my heart flipping upside down. Back when we were teenagers, I always saw her smiling like this at friends and always thought she was cute. Having that smile directed straight at me is still a shock to the system, like a flash of bright light.

"So," Rose says. "How'd it go?"

All the feelings that have been swirling in my head the whole drive are on the tip of my tongue, but I shove them down. It feels too raw right now, and borderline nonsensical, to spill my guts to her. I should be happy.

"Good. He was actually pleased." I put my hand out for Murphy to sniff, petting his sides when he reaches me.

"For real? That's great!" She looks genuinely excited for me in a way she wouldn't have been even weeks ago. "What does he want next? Just to have us keep tweaking the recipes?"

"Uh, he kind of didn't really say." I run my hand through

my hair. "I'm guessing JD will follow-up with us at some point in the next few days."

"Did he say anything about the drink he liked more?" she asks.

"Nope, we just went over the orders for our joint drinks and the two other ones," I say.

"Hm, ok." She takes a bite of her cereal. "I guess we'll see when he decides. I don't know how much more I could tweak mine. We don't have that much longer to go."

That pit in my stomach deepens even more at the thought of this ending. When it's over, will she move out? I guess it depends on whether she wins the competition between us. And even if she doesn't, she'll get a cash prize if she wins the next round of the cocktail competition out in LA. So she'll be leaving no matter what.

"What's wrong?" Rose asks, tilting her head to the side. "I figured you'd be excited."

How did she pick up on that? Since she asked directly, I don't want to brush her off.

"I just feel conflicted, I guess." I lean against the counter. "Dreading something, but I'm not sure what."

"Hm." She puts her cereal bowl down. "Dreading something with your dad, or just in general?"

"With my dad." I pause, trying to sort out the feelings. "I don't want to disappoint him after getting that praise."

"A fear of failure, basically."

"Yeah." I run both hands through my hair. "I hate this."

"You're human, Wes." she says. She drains the rest of her cereal milk. "And you'll fuck up. But you can succeed again."

It's a simple idea, but she's right. It's not like one good deed can flip everything around. It's a long, ongoing process.

Especially with an asshole like dad. Hell, JD is his favorite and Dad can barely give him praise.

"Yeah," is all I can manage to say.

I take a deep breath and let it out my nose, thankful she has her back to me at the sink while I pull it together. I stare at her ass instead, trying to shove the feelings out of my head. I need to focus on what I should be focusing on — what we actually are.

"You're staring at my ass so hard," she says. I raise an eyebrow when she turns to look at me. "The reflection in the glass. Also, I just know you."

I laugh. "Can you blame me? That skirt looks fucking good."

"What's underneath is even better." She hikes up her skirt. Nothing is underneath.

I grin and box her in against the counter from behind. God, she smells so nice.

"Just like I said." I dip a finger into her from behind and she sucks in a breath. "Good girl."

She loves being finger-fucked, so I turn her around and lift her onto the counter so it's easier to stroke her where she likes it. Her head falls back, so I take the opportunity to kiss the side of her neck. I have the strong urge to mark her, but I push that thought out of my mind.

Instead, I kiss my way up to her lips. The kiss is hungry, more intense than I was anticipating. She slides her fingers in the hair at the nape of my neck and holds me closer to her. Her pussy flutters around my fingers, the wetness soaking my hand.

I get lost in it until I feel like someone is staring at us. I open one eye and find Dennis just far enough from Rose for her to not feel his presence.

"Dennis. Read the room," I say.

"What?" Rose glances over and bursts out laughing. "Oh my god."

He slow-blinks back at me and starts to climb into Rose's lap.

"Let's go to your room," she says, scooping up Dennis and sliding off the counter. "So we don't get interrupted again."

She drops Dennis off on his favorite perch on our way upstairs. Once she's in my room, I pick her up and gently toss her on the bed, making her squeal.

"You love doing that, don't you?" she asks, pulling her tank top off. It's one of the ones with the bra built in, so suddenly she's naked in my bed.

I take her in for a few moments. The heat in her brown eyes makes my cock twitch. And her lips around my cock are even better than any fantasy I've had about them. Every other inch of her is perfect too, from her soft, warm brown skin, to her dark nipples on her full, pert breasts to the softness of her lower stomach.

God, she's so fucking gorgeous. I can't believe that she's even real.

"What?" I ask, realizing I hadn't answered her question. "Yeah, I do."

I reach behind my neck and strip off my shirt, then shove my shorts to the floor. I'm too desperate for her to tease this time. She gasps when I open her legs and dive right in to eat her pussy. I love the way she tastes, the way her soft thighs squeeze my head. I even love the way her nails scratch at my scalp almost a little too hard.

The way she comes is my favorite. It radiates from her head to toe, her back arching as she cries out.

I barely give her a minute to recover before I'm rolling on a condom and sliding into her. The quiet *yes* she lets out when I bury my face into the crook of her neck encourages me to fuck her hard and fast.

Am I getting the tension out? Maybe. But she feels too good to slow down.

I turn her onto her side and slide back into her again. I must be hitting her sweet spots because she clenches around me and clutches the blankets. With a few rubs of her clit, she's coming again, and I'm not far after. The release is so intense that my vision blurs and I grunt, filling the condom.

I'm spent, and so is Rose. By the time I dispose of the condom and come back, Rose is sprawled out on her stomach. I climb into bed next to her, but not too close.

I want to pull her closer. I want to linger in this warm feeling, the happiness of having gotten her off. The happiness of being with her, period. It feels so much easier than it has with anyone else.

The realization hits me like a train.

I don't know if it's platonic for me anymore — if it ever was, honestly — and I don't know how to fix it.

CHAPTER NINETEEN

WES

"Fuck you, man," Jasper says after I send his character flying off the screen in Smash Bros.

"Sucks to suck," I say, putting my controller down and stretching.

"I'm just hungry." Jasper sits back and digs his phone out of his pocket. "Once Waylon gets back from the store, I'll go back to kicking your ass."

Every once in a while, Jasper, Waylon, and Waylon's best friend Jeremiah and I hang out at Waylon's place to play video games and shoot the shit. As much as I don't want to admit it, I need it — I need a distraction after yesterday. I can't get Rose out of my head no matter how much I try. The game worked for a bit, but now that I'm not actively playing she's there again.

"Yeah, right." I pet Duke, who's sprawled out on the ottoman in front of us. Murphy gets jealous right away and lifts his head from the floor to put his head in the way of my other hand.

We sit in silence for a bit, with Jasper texting Sabrina, probably. I always knew they had a thing going on — I put money on it and won — but I'm still a little surprised that they're going as strong as they are. It's been a year and they're still almost annoyingly obsessed with each other.

But Jasper used to be my wingman, the guy who was always down to pick up women with me. And now he's all in with Sabrina like they're already fucking married.

I glance over at him. The look on his face fills me with something strange — something that isn't quite curiosity alone.

"When'd you decide to say fuck it and go for Sabrina?" I ask.

"Hm?" Jasper looks up at me, confused. "Why?"

"Just wondering." I turn my full attention to Murphy, who rests his head on my knee. "You liked her for a while, from what I saw."

"Dunno. Everything was just building and building inside, then last year at the bonfire, we had a thing." He leans back into the couch. I can guess what the 'thing' is. "And we got stuck overnight at the bar that night when the tree fell on our cars and had to talk about it. My feelings for her were real, so telling Santiago I was into her wasn't as terrifying. He can't justifiably kick my ass if I'm going to be a good boyfriend. So far, no complaints."

I nod. I wish he'd given me advice I could apply to this situation with Rose without actually telling him about it directly. It's not like I have to deal with an overprotective brother breathing down my neck. I just have Rose and all the history between us, which might be coming back to kick my ass.

"Why are you asking?" Jasper asks, grabbing his beer and taking a swig. "You trying to go for Rose?"

"What? No," I blurt, more reflexively than anything. Because he's spot on. Jesus, am I that obvious?

"What's happening?" Waylon asks as he comes in, grocery bags in his arms. Jeremiah comes in behind him, loaded with bags too. Murphy and Duke hop up to greet them, tails wagging.

"Wes is into Rose," Jasper says. He doesn't even have a teasing lilt in his voice, which is somehow worse than him ragging on me about it. If they ragged on me about it, it would mean it wasn't serious.

"I'm..." I can't even say I'm not into her without feeling like I'm a damn liar.

"Yeah, doesn't everyone know?" Waylon says, gently nudging Duke aside so he can go into the kitchen.

I glare at him, but he just shrugs good-naturedly. At least he's not rubbing that in my face. I guess I must really seem hung up on her.

"Rose as in your roommate?" Jeremiah asks, eyebrows going up. He has another six pack with him, which he holds up so he doesn't whack one of the dogs in the face. "Bad move."

Jasper and I get up to help them in the kitchen. Or more accurately, Jasper's coming to hang out while Waylon and I do most of the work. We're grilling tonight, and Waylon and I are the only ones who know how to cook something that tastes decent.

"Agreed," Waylon says, grabbing a beer and cracking it open.

"Go heat up the grill," I say to him, nudging Murphy and

Duke out of the kitchen. "And take the dogs so we can prep without them stealing something."

Waylon shoots me a look, then whistles for the dogs to follow him. They trot outside behind him, and I shut the door.

"But seriously, Rose?" Jeremiah asks, cracking open a beer. "Y'all have always been at each other's throats and now you're into her?"

I whip out a chef's knife, wishing I hadn't even opened this topic. Letting all my feelings for her stew in my head sucked a little less.

"Maybe it's just physical?" I say, even though the words don't even feel true as I say them. "We don't have any problems there."

"Maybe you're just hypnotized," Jeremiah says, leaning against the sink and taking a sip of his beer. "It's so good that you can't stop thinking about her."

"I mean, it is good. Extremely good." So good that I don't want to give them any details — another red flag. I don't give them every single detail about a woman but saying more about how a hookup was usually comes naturally. I want to keep whatever we have to just us.

As if there even *is* an us.

"You could hook up with someone else to shake her out of your system," Waylon says as he comes back in, leaving the dogs outside. Murphy presses his nose against the glass and gives sad eyes to the package of ground beef in my hands.

"How'd that work out for you?" I ask. Waylon's monogamous as fuck, but he tried casual hookups after Catherine cheated on him. He had some run-ins with some truly insane women.

"The hell? You're the one that suggested I try that after everything with Catherine," he points out.

"Okay, fine, true." I wash my hands. "But how was I supposed to know you were a magnet for the most batshit women?"

"Catherine didn't tip you off?" Waylon scoffs, picking up a knife and a cutting board.

"No one would have known she was the way she was, man," Jeremiah says, using some of his locs to tie the others back. "You were blindsided."

"The point is that you could go back to your old ways," Waylon says, clearly done with the attention on him. "Get her off your mind."

"I say you tell her," Jasper says. "Better than just leaping on to someone else if your feelings are that strong."

I grunt in response and start forming the beef into patties. Finding a woman to distract me would be as easy as scrolling through my phone and shooting off a text. But the idea of doing that feels disloyal, even if it technically isn't. And more importantly, it doesn't sound appealing. At all.

I want Rose, period. I've never experienced this kind of need before — it's consuming and obsessive. I want all of her to myself.

But telling her how I feel? Just the idea is making my stomach churn.

The others take my silence as a sign to move on. Jasper starts talking about football, which leads to Jeremiah and Waylon arguing about their fantasy league for the upcoming season. It's months away, so I don't give a fuck yet. I just listen and keep prepping the food.

Eventually we migrate outside to grill. Waylon takes over, and Jasper, Jeremiah and I drink and occupy the dogs with a ball.

The sliding glass door opens, but on my side of the house. It's Rose. Murphy rushes her, tail whipping back and forth, and she puts her hands up so he doesn't tackle her. She's dressed to go out, in a short skirt and a tank top. The skirt sends my mind to dirty places that I shouldn't be going to right now.

"Hey," she says, looking up at me with a little smile. "Sorry, didn't mean to interrupt guys' night. I just wanted to give you a heads up that I'll be out pretty late with Natasha. We're going to a party over at Crescent Hill."

A party? I look over her outfit again and tamp down all the irrational things I want to say. She's going to get hit on. There's no way she won't. What if she hooks up with someone else? I fucking hate him, whoever this completely hypothetical man is.

I take a deep breath and let it out of my nose. How can I be so possessive over a woman who isn't even mine?

Instead, I just nod and say, "Okay, cool."

"See you later, then," she says. "Bye, guys."

The others say goodbye too, and we all sit there in silence for a disturbingly long time — until we hear Natasha's car pull up, then away.

"Dude." Jasper snorts. "You looked like you went through a whole journey through grief just then."

I grab a tennis ball that the dogs abandoned and throw it hard across the yard, just to get some tension out. Duke and

Murphy make a run for it, but Murphy breezes right past it, looking around in confusion.

"Fine, you're right," I say. "How do I tell her how I feel?"

"What? You just do?" Jeremiah asks, looking at me like I'm the crazy one.

"Says the guy who's been with the same woman for ages," I say, looking to Jasper.

"Same advice," Jasper says before polishing off his burger. "Just tell her straight up how you feel and what you want."

"There isn't another way?" I sit down at the table again.

"Gotta rip off the Band-Aid, man," Jeremiah says with a shrug.

I try to gather my thoughts, putting my hand out for Duke to give me the ball again.

"She's skittish," I say, taking the ball from Duke. He sits, his eyes laser focused on the ball. "Her ex was a shitbag so she's not exactly jumping to be in a relationship. Assuming she's even into me. Telling her head-on after we've just been fuck buddies for a bit seems like a good way to get turned down fast."

The idea of rejection scares the shit out of me. I've been turned down by women for casual hookups — what guy hasn't? — But I've never even had feelings for anyone like this and haven't been rejected.

Fuck, now I get it. The idea of putting all the soft parts of myself out there and her turning me down sounds like a fucking nightmare.

"You don't have to just blurt out all your feelings for her at once," Jasper says. I guess he picked up on my mood. "Just do nice shit for her until you think she catches on, then tell her. It'll be less of a shock."

"What if she doesn't? Sometimes women just don't get it." Jeremiah laughs. "I took Hope on four dates before she realized that they *were* dates."

"Sounds like your game was just weak," I say.

Jeremiah just laughs more. "For real though. It might work, but you might have to just tell her, straight up."

"Nah, I like the idea of easing her into the idea. Our birthdays are back-to-back. Maybe I could do something for hers?" I sink back into the couch. I don't know how to be this guy, the one who's trying this hard. "But there's also the problem of her leaving."

"That's a big problem," Jasper says. "When?"

"Whenever she gets enough money to. If my dad likes her drink more, it'll be in about three weeks. If Dad likes my drink more, we'll buy more time." I cross my arms over my chest. Other guys live like this all the time? Just overwhelmed with feelings?

I don't want to think of her leaving. I don't want to think about waking up in the morning and going downstairs to make coffee just for myself. I don't want to think about evenings with women who I barely know, who don't want to know me beyond the bedroom.

But I don't want to go backward and go to the safe shit. I want to take the dive with her. But I don't know if she'd want to go with me.

"You think you could do long distance?" Waylon asks, getting up and grabbing more chips.

"I don't even know if we could start with just dating in person." Even more questions pop up in my head. I know how dating works but at the same time, I have no idea how to be a boyfriend. Then again, Jasper was just like me and now he and Sabrina are happy.

"You'd regret it though, right?" Jeremiah asks. "Not going for her, then having her move away."

"Yeah," I say readily.

"Then there you go." Jeremiah shrugs. "You need to tell her how you feel and you have three weeks to do it."

"Fuck." I slam back my beer. Even though the idea of telling her how I feel is terrifying, the idea of losing her feels even worse.

Now I just have to create the perfect plan to slowly let her know that I'm into her to the point where she picks up on it. Then I have to spill my guts to the woman who hated mine a month ago and hope she doesn't crush my heart into a thousand pieces.

Shit.

CHAPTER TWENTY

ROSE

I can sense when my parents are up to some shenanigans before I even get out of bed the morning of my birthday. Usually I get a text from Natasha right after midnight, and a text inordinately early from my parents, but my phone just has messages from Jo and a few other friends.

I yawn, stretching and rolling out of bed. Wes is downstairs cooking something that smells heavenly, like cinnamon buns. He has to know today is my birthday, since he and Waylon's birthday is three days from now. Is he making those for me? Or is he making them because we both have the day off and he has time to do it?

I brush my teeth, then wander downstairs. I hear low voices in the kitchen, like Wes isn't alone. And when I round the corner, I find my parents and Natasha there.

"Happy birthday!" they all say, immediately smothering me with hugs.

"Oh my god." I smile into my mom's shirt. Even Murphy

butts his nose in between all of us. "It's Wednesday. Why are you all here?"

"For breakfast, obviously. Dinner would have been too predictable." Mom smooths my edges a little bit. "And Wes says he makes great cinnamon rolls, so why not? We can take a morning off."

"Thank you." I bite my bottom lip, trying not to get too choked up. Coming back to Jepsen was never my thing, but I did miss my family. I never realized just how much until now. Growing up my birthdays were like this, and I took them for granted.

"Coffee's ready too," he says as he hands me my favorite mug. The coffee looks just right.

He gives me that grin of his as I take a sip, which is way too much before coffee and even more overwhelming in front of my family. I want to lean into him and feel the softness of his shirt against my cheek.

"Good?" he asks.

"Very."

He grabs the foil-covered sheet tray of cinnamon rolls and takes them to the table, his smile softening as he passes me.

Wes pulls the foil off the cinnamon rolls once I sit down. The scent of warm, buttery cinnamon rolls that must have taken ages for him to make. They have a beautiful glaze on them, with sprinkles across the top. I know he hates waking up early — did he just not go to sleep? Or did he wake up to do this for me?

"Wait, candle," Natasha says, digging into her purse. She pulls out a little pack of sparkly candles, and pokes a few into my cinnamon roll. Wes lights each one.

"Can we skip the awkward singing of happy birthday?" I ask, glancing to my dad. His voice is like nails on a chalkboard.

"Is that a thinly veiled attempt to get me not to sing?" Dad asks.

"Yes," Natasha, my mom, and I all say.

Thankfully, Dad doesn't put up a fuss. I blow out the candles and he just serves me a cinnamon bun and then serves everyone else.

"Oh my god," I say, barely managing to not moan the way I want to when I take a bite of my cinnamon bun. Wes's eyes brighten. "These are ridiculous. Why didn't you tell me that you made these?"

"Because I'd be making cinnamon rolls every other day and they're more of a birthday type of thing," he says, amusement making his dimples deep.

I take another bite, the sweetness melting on my tongue. "But now I know you can make these so I'll never stop asking for them."

"Maybe I'll make an exception, then," he says with a warm, lazy smile.

My face gets hot, but luckily Mom launches into a story about some stuff going on with the kids at the summer art camp where she's teaching, which leads to an easy, comfortable conversation. It's the perfect start to the day. Eventually everyone has to go to work or class, so Wes and I walk my family back to my dad's car. Everyone gives me another hug and tells me happy birthday before heading out.

"Thanks for playing host," I say. "I hope my parents weren't too pushy in getting you to host."

"Nah, they're cool." He heads inside. "And to be honest, those cinnamon rolls are a flex, aren't they?"

"Oh, shut up," I say lightly as I follow him.

"They are! I could tell how much you wanted to moan the moment they hit your tongue." He grins. "You would have moaned if we were alone."

How can he make my whole body heat up just by lowering the tone of his voice? It's like he found the frequency that hits me just right.

"Whatever, you clearly know they're good. No need to gas you up anymore." I pick up my coffee again. Dennis is still on the cat tree across the room, but I hope he hasn't dunked a paw in while we were outside.

"Have any plans for the rest of the day?" Wes asks, wandering into the kitchen.

"Mm, not really," I say. "I was going to go to the pool at the rec center but it's probably crawling with kids. The next best option is the lake, but I kind of hate the lake."

"You want to go to a pool?" Wes asks, looking at me over his shoulder. "I can take you to a pool that isn't overrun with children."

"Oh?" I rest my hands on the counter. "Where's this magical pool?"

"It's a lot more fun if it's a surprise." He grins and opens the fridge, moving some things around. "We just have to swing by the store to get some food."

"Sure, let's do it," I say readily. Wes's eyebrows go up for a second, like he wasn't expecting me to say yes so readily. "What? A private pool and snacks sound more relaxing than kids screaming all around me on my birthday."

Wes tilts his head to the side for a second before he shrugs.

"Ok, then let's go."

We both go upstairs to grab our stuff and change into swimsuits. Hanging out with a shirtless, sun-kissed Wes Stryker on my birthday seems like a win for me.

We hop into the car, Murphy in the back seat, and drive through town. After a quick stop to grab food, we keep driving through town until we go out to the highway.

"Where are we going?" I ask as town gets further and further behind us.

"My parents have a cabin," he says. "It's about thirty minutes away. It doesn't sound far away enough to be a vacation home, but it feels different once you're in."

"A cabin with a pool?"

"A bourgie cabin, yeah." He smiles. "It's super private. Cool views."

We reach the cabin twenty minutes later. It's much smaller than his parents' house, but still beautiful, perched up high on a mountain. Inside has much more of a rustic, cabin vibe, with wood beams across the ceiling and paintings of landscapes on the walls. The big floor to ceiling windows in the back are the big draw, though. There's the promised pool, with views of the valley below.

"This is amazing," I say, walking out onto the back patio. "Do you guys come here often?"

"Nope, which is a shame." He follows me outside and puts our snacks on the table. "Someone comes to keep it up, though."

He reaches behind his head and yanks his t-shirt off,

tossing it to the side. I barely have the chance to take in his muscular back before he dives right into the pool.

"You coming or are you just going to admire me from the sidelines?" he asks with a grin, pushing his wet hair out of his face.

I pull off my thin swimsuit coverup and toss it onto the seat along with his t-shirt. His eyes rake up and down my body, brazenly.

"I should ask you the same thing." I dip my toe in the water — it's freezing.

"I'm happy to just admire you from here." He swims up toward the edge of the pool. "Not even going to deny it."

Standing over him, having him look up at me like I'm a goddess, gives me a rush. It makes me want to sit on his face.

"Just admire me?" I ask, playing with the ties on either side of my bikini bottoms.

"I thought I'd have the self control to at least swim a little while," he says. "But I don't know why I ever thought that when you look this good."

I bite my lip to hide my smile, crouching to sit down in front of him. The water is still shockingly cold, but his hands on my knees warm me up instantly.

"Did you know that the closest neighbors we have are three miles in either direction?" he asks, parting my knees. "And we're on the highest peak?"

"Are we?"

"Yep." He slowly pulls the tie on one side of my bikini bottoms, than the other, taking his time like he was unwrapping a gift. "Which is perfect because I'm planning to make you scream so loud that people'll hear it for miles."

"Planning to?" I lift my hips, smirking down at him. "Sounds like you're not sure if you can."

I love the determined gleam in his eyes when I rile him up likes this, even though I know he can blow my mind in seconds.

"Have I told you that you're a brat?" He barks a laugh as he tugs my bikini bottoms out from under me.

"Would this be as fun if I wasn't?"

The smile he shoots me could melt me faster than the sun. "Nope."

He looks at my pussy like it's the only thing that exists, his eyes heavy-lidded. I let out a soft breath when he parts my lips and lightly plays with my clit using his thumb. His curls are soft when I slide my fingers through them, breathing out softly as he circles my clit with his tongue. My back arches off the cool tile when he lightly sucks it into his mouth.

I clench around nothing, spreading my legs wider in the hopes that he'll go faster. But he takes his sweet time, tasting me, savoring me. Every once in a while, we lock eyes. It *should* feel too intimate. I don't think I've ever looked a man in the eye when he was going down on me. But it makes this so much better.

"After that first time I ate your pussy?" Wes asks, circling my center with his fingers. "I got addicted to your taste. And to this sound."

He slides two fingers into me and I moan, my knees squeezing his shoulders.

"And to this one." He crooks his fingers up *just* right, pulling a gasp from me. "And I love how fucking wet you get when you come on my face."

I nearly yank his hair out when he devours me, making me come so quickly that I barely have time to wrap my head around it.

"That was fast," I say when I finally catch my breath.

"Because I know I can make you come as many times as I want you to." He hops out of the pool. The water makes his swim trunks hang low on his hips. "C'mon."

He extends his hand to me and helps me up. Then, he guides me over to one of the lounge chairs next to the pool and undoes my bikini top, leaving me naked. I've never been butt naked outside, but then again, he did just go down on me a few feet away. No need to be shy about this.

He pulls a condom from his swim trunks and says, "Get on your hands and knees. Hold onto the back of the chair.

I do as he says, arching my back so I'm fully exposed to him. He climbs onto the seat behind me, jiggling my ass and giving it a squeeze. He's taking his sweet time rolling on the condom, then slides in inch by inch. His strokes are slow too, so I squirm, trying to get him to speed up.

"Be a good girl and stay still," he says, pulling out, then going in like he has all day.

"Who said I wanted to be a good girl?" I push back against him hard, making him suck in a breath.

He pulls out all the way and I whimper, looking back at him. Seeing his wicked grin as he strokes his cock — the condom slick from being inside of me — makes me clench from being so empty.

"Well?" I ask, shaking my hips.

"I'm just waiting for you to say you want to be a good girl. Because only good girls get fucked," he says.

I laugh and push backward, like he'll slip it in. But he spanks me instead and I gasp, glaring at him.

"I said what I said, Rose." He smacks my other ass cheek hard, then squeezes it. The burn — the good kind — makes me suck in a breath. "Stay still while I fuck you, then you'll get a reward."

"Fine." I put my hands on the back of the chair again and stay still.

"That's it," he says, fucking me slow, but so hard that I cry out. "That's my good girl."

His good girl. I like that more than I should. But before I can think about it any harder, he builds up a hard, steady rhythm that takes my breath away.

He reaches around and strokes my clit, making me climax and cry out just as loudly as he said I would. It's one of the orgasms that takes me out of my body for a moment, and he doesn't let me catch a break before pleasuring me more.

"Hold on, let me lower us," he says, reaching around with the other hand and grabbing the handle that makes the chair lay flat. He stays inside me as he puts us down.

Being flat on my stomach unlocks new angles of pleasure that I didn't know I could feel. The weight of Wes on top of me, the sun heating our skin, is pure bliss. He fucks me slowly — which I don't mind this time because I'm so stimulated that I could cry.

He braces himself on his elbows next to me, kissing the side of my neck as he comes with a sharp inhale. His cock pulses inside me several times before he finally relaxes, his body softening but not squishing me in the process.

I let him catch his breath before he rolls us onto our

sides. We lay there, my head tucked under his chin and his arm thrown around my waist. Eventually he sits up and runs a hand through his hair.

"You want macaroni and cheese? I can make some," he says,

"Did you read my mind?" I ask. My smile probably looks goofy with how huge it is, but I can't help it. Cinnamon rolls, now macaroni and cheese? "That's my favorite."

"Believe it or not, I pay attention to the type of shit you like." He smiles and gets up, going to grab his shorts.

"You aren't going to cook naked for me?" I pout and his grin widens.

"Trust me, cooking hot cheese naked is a bad idea. I know from experience." He pulls on his swim trunks.

I burst out laughing. "What? Have you burned your dick with hot cheese before?"

"Unfortunately, yes, and no, I'm not going to explain more. Go lay down while I cook." He slaps my ass again as he passes, chuckling.

I take a quick dip into the pool, then hop out and put my bikini back on to lay down again. The sun on my damp skin feels perfect. Just as I'm about to drift off to sleep, my phone rings. I'm almost pissed off until I see it's a Facetime from Jo.

"Happy birthday!" she says the moment I answer. It looks like she's in her apartment, probably working from home.

"Thank you." I can't help but grin, even though I miss her so much it hurts. We always went all out for each others' birthdays — big parties, dinners, even trips. I wonder what we'd be doing if I were back there.

"Where are you?" She squints at me.

"The pool." I glance over my shoulder. Wes is inside, his back to me at the stove. "Wes's family's pool at their fancy cabin."

"Just the two of you?"

"Yeah." I play with the ends of my braids. "I had breakfast with my family, and he made cinnamon buns for us. Then he brought me here."

"Girl."

"What?" I ask with a sigh.

"That's going above and beyond. That's boyfriend level shit," she says.

"It's not—"

"It *so* is," she says, rolling her eyes. "And so sweet."

"It is super sweet." I bite my bottom lip. I trust Jo with my life, and she always has a good read on situations. But... "Is it boyfriend material though?"

Jo levels me with her 'cut the bullshit' stare. "Rose. He sounds super sweet and he's doing nice things for you. Nicer than Erik, for sure, and not a tool. That's boyfriend shit."

"It's just one day. My birthday. We go hard for each other every year," I point out. "He can do the same."

"But thoughtful plus banging plus attraction..."

"Means friends with benefits and that's it." That's *it.* I have to draw the line somewhere.

"Why are you trying to avoid having feelings for this guy?" Jo asks, genuine confusion on her face. "It's okay to like someone. Especially someone who's supportive and bangs you into oblivion regularly."

"Because I told myself I wouldn't fall for anyone."

"But it sounds like you have. Or you are, at least."

"No, I'm not," I say, a little bit snippier than I intended to. I swallow. "Sorry. That was a little much."

"No, I'm sorry," she says with a sigh. "It's your birthday and I'm jumping down your throat about all this."

"It's okay," I say, curling my legs underneath myself. "I wish you were here."

"Same." She shifts around on her bed. "The weather here is absolute ass and work is so dumb."

She vents about the weather up in New York and her job, which is sending her all over the place in the next few weeks, including Atlanta and Miami. Then she updates me on all of the other things going on, like her upstairs neighbors who practice the same 2 songs over and over again, and her neighbor who seems like they might have 5 cats despite the no-pet policy.

"Ugh, I need to run," Jo says. "I have a stupid call."

"Okay, love you and miss you," I say, swallowing the lump in my throat.

"Love you too and miss you so much." She blows me a kiss. "Bye."

I end the call and tears abruptly spill onto my cheeks. I don't think I want to move back to New York, but I wish I could have Jo here. I've been reconnecting with Natasha and I'm making friends with Sabrina, Jasper, and some of the regulars at the bar. But something about the time Jo and I met, and just how well we clicked created a lifelong bond.

I hear the sliding glass door open, and I sniff, pulling myself back together. It was just a little cry, so my sunglasses should cover the evidence.

"Another birthday phone call?" Wes asks.

"Yeah. It was Jo," I say. "It was really nice to catch up.

Usually we go all out on each other's birthdays so this year's the first lowkey one I've had in a while."

"Here." He hands me a big bowl of mac and cheese.

"Thank you." It smells like heaven and tastes just as good too.

He stretches out on the seat next to me, digging into his mac and cheese too. At some point he slipped on this swim trunks again, and they're low on his hips.

"What do you mean by all out?" he asks. "Like skydiving and shit?"

"God, no. I hate heights." I shudder. He grins, opening his mouth to make a joke, but I hold up my hand. "Cutting you off before you make a short joke."

"Damn it." His grin widens.

"You're so easy to pin down." I stir my mac and cheese, forcing myself to slow down so I don't inhale it all. "Anyway, all out as in big parties and ridiculous gifts. Like I got her a painting from one of her favorite artists once — which wasn't cheap — and she took me to a three Michelin star restaurant. When we were more broke, we just spent the whole day together and splurged on what we could."

"That sounds awesome," he says.

"It was."

We sit in comfortable almost-silence. I hit a level of relaxation that I almost never hit — the kind where I can just sink into the moment and enjoy it. Of course, my brain doesn't want to let me have it for too long. My attention drifts to Wes, who's finished his food and stretched out, his hands resting on his stomach.

"Can I ask you something?"

"You just did," he says. I shoot him a look over my sunglasses and he chuckles. "Yeah."

I bite my bottom lip and shield my eyes from the sun. "This has been really nice. Why'd you bring me here?"

"Relax, Rose," he says, adjusting his sunglasses so I can't see his eyes. "Am I not allowed to do something nice for you? As a friend on your damn birthday? It's lunch and I need to eat too."

Is he *allowed* to? Of course. But is it confusing the hell out of me? Absolutely. It's not that I don't trust he's sincere – he might be a smart ass, but he's not the type to do something fake like this. It's just that I don't get *why*, as much as I appreciate all of this. We're friends, yeah, but none of my friends (besides Jo) have ever done anything like this for my birthday. Particularly the ridiculously good outdoor sex.

I steal a glance at him, my heart fluttering in my chest so hard that it makes everything else inside me ache. When did I start falling for Wes? These dumb feelings for him that I keep trying to shove back into the cabinet keep trying to fall out with a loud clang, like a pot I hastily shoved in there.

Even classifying them as 'feelings for him' is dangerous. We have great sex and we get along really, really well now. Being with him is genuinely fun. But that doesn't automatically make a relationship. Besides, since when did Wes do relationships? And since when did I magically forget the fact that I'm amazing at choosing guys who'll fuck me over? Charmers, just like him?

But the more we spend time together, the more I realize that Wes isn't like the others. He isn't like anyone I've ever met at all.

CHAPTER TWENTY-ONE

WES

To be honest, if I wasn't a twin, my birthday would be kind of boring. Sharing it with Waylon gives us an excuse to have a big party, which is even better now that we have our own place. When we were younger, it was an excuse to get completely wasted, but now that we're older, it's just nice to have people over who understand that they need to get the fuck out by one AM.

People wish me a happy birthday as I wander through the house. It's early, but still somewhat packed. Waylon's side of the house is a bit bigger, so the party is mostly over there, with everyone spilling out into the backyard. Some others float in and out of my side, resting on couches and hanging out. A cluster of people are circled around Murphy, petting him, with Rose included.

With her birthday being so close to ours, it became a triple birthday party. A few of her friends from high school who still live in town are here too, along with Natasha.

I check my phone, then glance across the yard at Rose

again. She's smiling and laughing at something, completely carefree in a way that makes me smile too.

"Is your plan in action?" Jasper asks, sidling up to me with a drink.

"Should be." I check my phone. The last message I have from Jo is that she landed in Nashville, so she's about an hour and a half away.

Rose didn't hear me coming, but I heard her crying after speaking with Jo when we were up at the cabin. It fucking broke me. I can't imagine dealing with all the shit she'd been served up, then being separated from my best friend. So on a whim, I messaged Jo to see if she'd be down for a surprise visit some time. Today just happened to line up with her travel down to Atlanta for work.

"You think it's too much?" I eventually ask, running my hand through my hair. "Inviting her best friend in for a surprise?"

"Nah, it's super nice. Definitely 'I'm willing to go the extra mile for you' type of stuff, which is prime boyfriend material," Jasper says. "I bet you could tell her how you feel tonight if you want to."

"Yeah, and ruin my birthday if she shoots me down?" I take a swig of my drink. "I'll pass."

My gaze drifts to Rose yet again. She's wearing a yellow dress that's driving me crazy. She lifts her eyes to meet mine and smiles back too. And of course, my smile broadens without me even realizing it while my cock throbs at the sight of her cleavage.

Usually when I sleep with someone, my desire for them goes down — like eating a meal and being full. But with her,

I'm still ravenous. Every time, the chemistry gets deeper and the connection just solidifies.

I can't believe I called her *my* good girl while we were at the cabin the other day. But fuck, these feelings are too much. It's either the feeling of being with her, or the worry about whether she's getting the fucking message that I'm into her. Or worrying about whether she's over that whole 'never going to date again' thing.

So, mostly worrying.

"It'll be fine," Jasper says, leaning against the porch rail.

"Easy for you to say." I pull at my hair again.

Rose breaks away from the pack and starts toward us, an empty cup in her hand. She looks adorably tipsy, her walk loose and smile lazy.

"Want me to make you another drink?" I ask, grabbing her cup.

"Please."

She follows me into my kitchen, which is mostly cleared out besides a few people. Rose leans her hip against the counter.

"So, what can I get you?" I scan the rows and rows of bottles we have set up. "Want a surprise?"

"Always." She rests her forearms on the counter, which gives me an amazing view of her cleavage. The neckline of her dress frames it just right.

"Hm." I eye some bottles and grab some mezcal. She likes margaritas, so I'll make one with mezcal. "I'll keep it simple."

A new song comes on and she starts shaking her hips a bit. I want to lift the back of her dress and see what's underneath.

"Better watch out," I say, eyeing her. "You're distracting me."

"Maybe I'm doing it on purpose." She gives me a cute little grin. "Maybe I want to have more fun."

I put a top on a shaker and start shaking it. "You aren't having fun now?"

"I am!" she says, much more seriously than she probably has to. "This is a really great time. Thank you."

The softness in her tone wiggles its way into my heart. It's a strange feeling but I want to let it in all the way.

"Why are you thanking me?" I say, pouring her drink. "It's my birthday."

"Because it's a threeway birthday party," she says. I press my lips together to not blurt out the joke I desperately want to make. "Don't even."

"I didn't say a word." I slide her drink to her, then I pour myself the other half of the drink and raise my glass. "To birthdays?"

"That's boring." She looks up at me for a moment, then at the ceiling. "Let's make a wish. A secret wish."

She closes her eyes, like she's thinking deeply about it. My answer comes to my head right away. I feel fucking dorky for wishing for her, but I'll take every scrap of help the universe will send me.

"Okay," she says, opening her eyes. She taps her glass against mine, then takes a sip. "Birthday wish, made."

She's standing close to me, our bodies wedged between the narrow space between the island and the other counter. She hops up to sit on the counter, right as Dennis does. He strolls toward her, tail up.

"What'd you wish for?" she asks, putting her hand out for Dennis to bump his cheek against.

My face heats up despite myself. "If you say it, it won't come true."

"Dang, taking it seriously." She looks up at me, glancing at my lips.

"I take things seriously sometimes." I rest a hand next to her thighs.

If shit wasn't so complicated, I'd lean in and kiss her. Soft and slow, no ulterior motives. We hold each other's gazes for a few more beats. Her warm brown eyes almost make me lose myself and throw away all of my good sense.

But thankfully, Dennis decides to be an asshole and smacks a plastic cup off the counter. Then, I hear Rose gasp.

"Rosie!" a Black woman with a vaguely British accent says.

Rose leaps off the counter and flings herself at Jo. Jo is tall and slender, a contrast from Rose's petite height and curves. But the way they hug, squealing and looking over each other like they can't believe they're seeing each other makes me feel like I made the right choice.

"What are you doing here?" Rose asks.

Jo locks eyes with me. She very obviously sizes me up, and for the first time in my life, I care about what a woman's best friend thinks. Then again, I have to get points for arranging this whole thing, right?

"Wes invited me. I'm going to Atlanta for a work thing the day after tomorrow, so it's easy to get there from Nashville," Jo says.

Rose looks at me like she can't believe it, but in the best way possible. "Wes, are you for real?"

"Yeah." I run my fingers through my hair. My face is probably bright red and I can't get it to go away. "You had mentioned you missed her, so —"

She cuts me off with a hug so intense that I nearly fall backward. We've never hugged like this, but she fits against me so perfectly, her head tucked under my chin. Her warmth is comforting, and her softness is addictive. It's like she's been made to be in my arms.

I meet Jo's gaze over Rose's shoulder. Jo's eyebrow lifts, a small smirk on her lips. I've only known her in person for the past minute and a half but I can tell she's pleased. I give Rose a kiss on the temple — the most neutral kiss I can give her — and she lets me go.

"Thank you," Rose says, her eyes damp.

"Don't worry about it," I say.

"I will absolutely worry about it," she says, her voice low.

"Nope, have a drink," I say, handing her drink back. "And go have fun."

"Okay." She smiles up at me, then tugs me down by the shirt. Her lips press against my cheek. "But wait, hold this while I go to the bathroom."

Dennis chirps from where he's sitting on the counter, like he's annoyed that he won't have the chance to spill her drink. Rose gives him a scratch on the chin as she passes.

"So, mission accomplished," Jo says once Rose is out of earshot, leaning a hip against the counter.

"I guess so." I grab a cup and hand her Rose's to keep safe. "Can I get you a drink?"

"Sure. Just make whatever," Jo says. "Isn't that your specialty?"

"You know about that?" I scan the liquor we have, then I look at her. "You like gin?"

"Yeah, it's nice when it's used well."

"I always use it well." I grab some other ingredients and start making it, keeping an eye on Dennis even though he's on the ground again. "But going back, you know about my specialty drink?"

"You know Rosie and I are best friends, right? I know a whole lot about you," she says. "Funny how all her rants to me were bitching about you at first, then got kind of neutral, now she tells me how fun it is to be with you."

A sprout of hope comes up inside of me.

"Really?" I ask, finding a stirrer for her drink.

"Yeah. Obviously, you want more with her but haven't told her for whatever reason." Jo's brows furrow and she sizes me up again. "Why?"

I can see why she and Rose are friends — Jo's straight to the point in a way I can appreciate. I can't even deny what she said because it's true. Then again, arranging for her best friend to come to her birthday party from out of state seems like a "more than friends" gesture. Or at least and "overwhelming crush" gesture.

"She's really against relationships, right? She's told me multiple times that she doesn't want anything serious with anyone." I glance over my shoulder to make sure no one's listening in on this.

"She says she is. But how she's acting is saying something different. How she talks about you." Jo's tone is soft. "It's been a while since she's talked about anyone like that."

"Not even about her ex?" I ask despite my better judgment. I stir the cocktail I've made.

"God, no. Erik can get fucked," she says, her tone sharp. "And he was always kind of a douche, but she was happy, though. I mostly kept my mouth shut. But you're different. She used to not like you at all, and now she can't stop talking about all the things she does like about you."

I strain her drink into a cup and hand it to her.

"Still doesn't change the fact that she doesn't want a relationship," I say.

Jo tastes the drink and nods in approval. "But I'm telling you that she's into you. And that she likes you enough that you might as well shoot your shot."

I scoff. Easy for her to say when she's not the one who could get fucking wrecked.

"Does it matter, though?" I pour myself a shot, because this conversation is quickly turning into one that calls for that. "She's still going to leave as soon as she gets the money she needs to start over somewhere else. And if my dad chooses her drink, then she'll be gone next week. Trying to start something with her now when she wants to leave feels like a bad move."

Jo bites the inside of her cheek, mulling it over. But before she can speak again, Rose comes back.

"Thank you," she says to me when I hand her drink back. "Did you interrogate him yet?"

"No," Jo says, looking at me with a knowing glance. "We kept it civil."

"Then let's go outside — I want you to meet the dogs." Rose nods her head toward the back, gesturing for me to come too.

I follow her, trying to keep my thoughts on her right now

— her smile and how thrilled she is. Because that's all I can stand to think about.

CHAPTER TWENTY-TWO

ROSE

I still can't believe Jo is here. And I still can't believe Wes is the one who asked her to come.

I watch him talk to Jo, Jasper, and Sabrina, but I can't take in a single word. All I can think about is what he did. It was the exact thing that I needed, and he gave it to me without me even asking.

My heart is growing more and more, and looking at him just makes me want to smile.

This is so bad.

I pull my eyes away from him and focus on Jo, who was already looking at me. She raises an eyebrow in question, but for once, I don't want to answer it. Because I know what she's going to drill me about.

Eventually Wes gets dragged into another conversation, and Jo and I are sitting on a blanket in the yard with Murphy, who's stretched out napping.

"So, Wes," Jo says with a grin. "He looks even better in person."

"I know."

"And you two seem to have a little..." She wiggles her fingers. "Thing. A mutual thing. Beyond the sex, of course."

"He doesn't have feelings for me," I say. My face gets hot. I've kept way more details close to the vest when it comes to sex with Wes. And that feels more significant than it should be.

"Rosie," Jo says, glancing past my head. "A guy who's just your friend wouldn't ask me to come here for your birthday."

My heart is pounding so hard that it drowns out the bass of the music. He *knows* I miss Jo. And he doesn't even use Instagram all that much. It's not like he ran into her and suggested she come down. He had to go out of his way to make this happen. It's the thoughtful, sweet thing that none of the men I've been with have ever even thought of. But Wes did it.

"He's got it bad, Rose," Jo continues. "And just looking at the way you two are together, I know you're into him too."

My hackles go up. "I'm not."

Jo rolls her eyes. "You can't just magically tell yourself to stop feeling a feeling, love."

"I don't," I say softly.

"What's so bad about the idea of being into him?" she asks.

"Because." I search for the right words. "Because remember when I first got into Erik? He wooed me and I fell for it so fucking easily. Now Wes is nice to me for a while and fucks me well, and I fall all over again. For *Wes*."

Jo purses her lips, then bites the bottom one. "Do you

remember me asking you a lot of questions about that? Like asking why Erik was going so hard so fast?"

"Yeah." Because he had. He'd whipped out all the stops, treating me like a princess from day one.

"I didn't trust him," she says, leaning back on her hands. "But you looked happy, so I kept my mouth shut."

I snort. "Mostly shut. I could tell, but I appreciate that you didn't shit all over my parade while it was happening."

She gives me a gentle smile, but it fades. "My point is that Wes isn't the same. You two barely could stand each other at first and the idea of even living with him made you want to throw up. Now you're looking at him with heart eyes. You can't tell me whatever's going on with Wes is the same."

"You knew Erik, though. Longer than you've known Wes," I point out, even though I can see what a weak counterpoint that is to what she said.

Jo gives me a look, one that tells me she thinks I'm being a dumbass. But she can't be right about Wes being different or my feelings for him being real. I don't *want* her to be right. I tried so fucking hard to not be in this same position again, drawn to a man who can wreck me just as easily as he can make me smile. But to what end? I fucked myself over anyway.

I glance past Jo's shoulder, where I can hear Wes's laughter over the music. The sound of it makes my heart flutter, then clench.

"It doesn't matter, does it?" I say. "If his dad chooses my drink, then I get five grand and a fast track out of here. And I have the next round of the competition out in LA anyway, so

I'll be able to find a roommate and a new job while I'm out there. And that'll be it."

"You're not going to try," she says, her voice flat.

I shake my head. "It's better if I don't. I think."

Jo stares at me for a few beats, then sighs through her nose. "Whatever you want to do, Rosie. Just think about it."

"Rose!" Wes calls over the crowd. "Come here — I want to show you something."

"Think about it," Jo says again.

The rest of the night goes by in a flash, with the last stragglers heading out around one. Soon it's just Wes, Waylon, Jo, and I tidying up.

"This is the benefit of being closer to thirty than twenty," I say. "The party's over and it's not like five in the morning."

"Yeah, seriously," Waylon says with a yawn. "I'm going to bed."

"We'll head out, then," Wes says, clapping his hand on his brother's shoulder. "Night."

"Wait, where are you sleeping?" I ask Jo as we walk over to Wes's side of the house.

"I'm crashing on the couch because I know how you sleep," Jo says with a snort.

"As if you don't snore when you're drunk," I add.

"Wow, rude." Jo bumps me with her hip.

Wes already has some blankets and sheets for Jo, and we're all too exhausted for any other pleasantries. Wes follows me up the stairs and when I glance back, he's staring right at my ass.

"Creep," I tease.

"Do you honestly think I'd look anywhere but your ass?" He grins up at me.

"Well, probably not." I stop in front of our doors and lean against the wall, letting myself eye him. He looks so good, especially like this. Relaxed, hair a bit rumpled, softly smiling at me. "Good night. Thank you for adding me to the party. And thank you for asking Jo to come."

"It's no problem." He pulls me into a hug, a full one. I could bury myself against his chest forever, and take in his clean, woodsy scent under his soft shirt. We linger here for a few beats longer than we should. "Good night."

"Good night." I let go and slip into my room.

The booze in my system settles over me and I pass out, hard. I wake up the next morning with only a mild hangover, thankfully. My mouth is dry and I have that general sense of *ick* but my headache isn't too bad. Nothing a greasy breakfast wouldn't fix.

I go downstairs and find Jo still face down, asleep in the least elegant way possible. Dennis is laying on her back, licking his paws like he's the one who took her down. She stirs, then groans.

"Fucking hell," she says, covering her face with a pillow. "Why did my body just decide to stop processing alcohol?"

"Age." I brush her hair out of her face. "Want to sleep in my room? It's dark and there are pain meds."

"Ugh, please." She moves and Dennis leaps off her back.

"Wait, let me get you a drink." I head into the kitchen and find Wes in there, looking a bit hungover too. "Morning."

"Hey. Morning." He smiles at me over his shoulder. "You guys hungry?"

"Jo's going to sleep it off a bit more, but I'm hungry." I grab a bottle of Gatorade from the fridge. "Be right back."

I give Jo the Gatorade, scoop up Dennis like a baby, and walk into the kitchen. Wes is grating cheese into a bowl.

"Grating cheese instead of just using the pre-shredded stuff?" I hold Dennis with one arm and hop up on the kitchen island. "While hungover? I didn't know you were a superhero."

"It's grating cheese, not playing chess." He taps the block of cheese against the grater and puts the grater in the sink.

"What are you making?" I ask.

"The best hangover cure ever to exist." He takes the bowl of cheese and folds it into another bowl with batter. "You'll love it."

I love watching him cook and put things together. Something about seeing him in his element, moving with confidence, gets me a little hot. Even through the hangover.

I know better than to ask him what he's making right now, so I just wait.

"I can't believe your first instinct when you're hungover is to actually cook something," I say, scratching Dennis under his chin as he purrs.

"Because moving around helps and there isn't a single restaurant in town that can make this."

He starts cutting out biscuits with the flair of someone who's done it countless times before, and slides them into the oven. Dennis meows in annoyance and I put him down. I need to make coffee anyway.

I make a French press while Wes continues cooking, the scent of sausage and potato making my stomach growl. After I make coffee, I hand him a mug and watch him finish the food. He carefully slices three cheesy biscuits in half, then layers on a sausage, some scrambled egg, and a bit of hash brown cut into a circle with a cookie cutter.

He plates it carefully before presenting it to me like a gift.

He watches me take a bite, waiting for my reaction. It's *so* good. Cheesy, salty, and the potato on the biscuit? It's like it was made to cure my hangovers.

"This is the best thing I've ever tasted," I say, holding my hand over my full mouth.

"Yeah?" The delight on his face is so boyish and pure that it makes my heart skip. "I told you. Eat all of that, drink that coffee, and you'll be good to go."

We eat in silence, me sitting on the counter and him leaning against the counter next to me. Dennis winds his way around our ankles and Murphy stares at a polite distance, his tongue out. Wes slams two biscuits in the time I eat one.

When I finish, I legitimately feel like I've healed.

"Thank you," I say when he takes my plate and puts it in the sink.

"No problem." He grabs his coffee cup.

I hop off the counter and start helping him clean up. He's a surprisingly tidy cook, though, and finishes faster than I can help. I top off our coffee and sit on the kitchen island again, letting my legs swing. He rests a hand on one side of my leg, stepping between my thighs. His hand creeps up my shirt, cupping a breast.

Jo's probably out for the count, so we could get away with fooling around. He kisses the side of my neck and I let my thighs fall open further for him to step closer. His lips travel from my neck to my mouth. The kiss starts slow, but quickly gets heated, his other hand wandering over the rest of my body while the hand up my shirt tweaks my nipple. It's like an electric shot between my nipple and clit.

This feels almost too good to be true. A hot, funny guy making me breakfast, then getting me off?

"Wes?" I ask, putting a hand on his chest. "Why are you doing all this for me?"

"Doing what?" He stops, pulling his hand from my shirt and resting it next to my leg.

"You know what I'm talking about," I say. The big stuff, like the day of my birthday and the meal he cooked me. The birthday party. Calling Jo. Then all the little moments in between where he helps me out or makes me laugh.

He sighs. His dark brown eyes are so much more serious than I've ever seen them. I wait a few beats for him to gather himself and speak.

"I can't wiggle out of this, can I?" he says with a sigh.

"Wouldn't it be better if you didn't?"

"Because I'm falling in love with you," he says softly, but with confidence. "And I've never felt like this toward anyone and don't have a fucking clue on how to say it. It's a lot easier to show it."

My heart twists into a knot. I'm not shocked at all. Not in the slightest. Him saying it was just putting words on what I've been seeing for weeks. The guy who drove me insane growing up doesn't exist anymore — now the sweet, funny, thoughtful version of him is here.

I've been falling for him for a while too, and the realization is like ice water down my back. How did I end up doing the exact opposite from what I planned? What about the version of me who was gung-ho about making a name for myself — without anyone else? I still want to succeed and take back what I should have had before.

I can't do both.

"I can't," I whisper. "I'm leaving town. You're staying here."

I can't bring myself to give him the bullshit lie that I can't do or want a relationship. Because god, I do. I want mornings like this with breakfast, goofing off after shifts, and hanging out on the couch with Murphy while watching stupid TV shows. I want to laugh at his dumb jokes and see his pleasure that he made me laugh. And I don't even have words to describe our sexual chemistry.

It feels like it could work.

And I hate that I do, because it makes leaving so much harder. I need to win this competition so I can get back on my feet and start something new on my own terms. No one to accuse me that I did anything but work my way up to get there. Just me.

Wes gives me space again, his expression resigned. "I figured."

"I need to do this," I add. "I can't just let myself stop now when I'm close to getting back to where I was."

"I know, Rose. And I don't want to discourage you from your dreams." Wes just sighs through his nose, his eyes completely lacking the light that I've grown to love. Murphy noses Wes's hand and he pets him. "I'm taking Murphy out for a walk."

"Okay," I say softly.

I watch him go, Murphy trotting alongside him, and feel my stomach drop through the floor.

CHAPTER TWENTY-THREE

WES

I feel like my dad makes us wait to drum up our anxiety. I sit next to Rose in the lobby of the Stryker Liquor offices, jiggling my leg. Rose doesn't even stop me. She's calm — or at least she looks calm.

I haven't been able to look at her directly since the other morning when she shot me down. It sucked every bit as much as I knew it would, especially because I know it's just because she's leaving and not because she doesn't feel the same way. I didn't think getting shut down could feel worse, but that made it feel like a knife to the chest.

At least she spent most of the day with Jo, puttering around town. I stayed on Waylon's side of the house to watch Duke, even though he usually does just fine most days. Just... I needed space.

Maybe the timing is just right for this drink competition to wrap up. I can't avoid her forever.

"Wes, Rose," Mrs. Ridley says. "Mr. Stryker is ready to see you now."

We head back to Dad's office, where the door is propped open. Dad is behind his desk, and JD is sitting in one of the three chairs, his arms crossed over his chest. They're both a little more dressed up than usual in button-down shirts, with Dad wearing a tie too. Somehow that makes this feel so much more significant. Dad gestures for us to sit down and we take our seats.

I rest my fist on my knee so I don't start jiggling it again. But the way JD's eyes skim over me tell me he's caught me. I glare at him — why wouldn't I be nervous?

"So, the drinks," Dad says, putting a few sample cans on the table. He glances at the nondescript labels, which just have a single letter on them. "This one is the one y'all did together. It's good. Solid. It's clear you worked hard on it. Well done."

I let a breath out, sinking down in my chair just a little. At least that's out of the way.

"Now as for these drinks." Dad slides the sample cans across the desk. "They're both good. Something that I think'll sell. But we're going with drink B."

The cans are unmarked aside from the letter, and he slides it across the table for us to taste. Of course he'd do that to up the drama. I gesture for Rose to take a sip first and she picks up the can. She tentatively takes a sip and lights up. My stomach sinks to the floor.

"It's mine," she says, handing me the drink.

I take a sip too and yep, it's hers. Creamy, citrusy, with a little kick of something different. When I imagined this exact scenario, I always assumed I'd feel pissed off, but right now I just feel numb. I can't even think of what I'm losing when it comes to my career — the only thing swirling in my head is Rose leaving as soon as she can. Just like she said she would.

I exchange a look with JD, who's inscrutable as always. I'll be under his command for longer again. Who knows if it'll be enough for him to loosen up his reins.

"Congratulations, young lady," Dad says, an almost-smile on his face. "Your drink will be in stores in a few months."

"Thank you." Rose beams. "I'm so excited."

"And the five grand." Dad reaches into his desk and pulls out a huge checkbook. He signs a check for Rose with flourish and hands it to her.

"Thank you," she says again.

"We'll give you more details when the drink's all canned up and ready to go. The supply chain and marketing will take over from here," Dad says, pushing back from his desk and standing. "I have another meeting soon, so talk to y'all soon."

Rose, JD, and I head out of the office. Rose is tapping away on her phone, and glances back at me.

"Sorry, just a second. Just calling my mom," she says.

I stop to give her space, and JD stops next to me, his hands in his pockets.

"If it makes you feel better," JD says, his voice low. "I wanted to go with your drink. But Dad and some of the other executives voted the other way."

"You're trying to make me feel better?" I blurt. He's never once tried to make me feel better. Not in my entire life.

"Yes." His brows furrow, like he doesn't get why I'm asking that.

I sigh, letting my shoulders sag. Shit, he's trying. Better than him ripping me a new butthole for something the way he usually does. "Thanks."

Rose wanders away, her voice excited. I still don't feel much of anything. My life will go back to how it was before she got here — working shifts at the bar, hanging out with friends, rinse and repeat. I thought I was happy back then, but the thought of going back to that feels hollow.

Eventually Rose comes back, her eyes bright until she looks at me. Then, she looks a bit reserved.

"I'm ready to head out if you are," she says.

"Cool, let's go." I nod goodbye to JD, who disappears into his office.

Rose and I are quiet until we get into the car. Then, she sighs, folding her hands on her lap.

"Congrats," I finally say, because I can't say much more than that without feelings fighting their way to the surface.

"Thank you." She fiddles with a loose thread on her jean shorts.

The silence between us is miserably awkward the entire drive home, and I hate it. It's nothing like things were before. When we get home, Murphy greets us, oblivious to the energy in the air, and turns his ass toward us for scratches. I give them to him and keep walking into the kitchen. I don't know what I'm doing, and she doesn't either.

"I'm probably going to move my flight to LA up a little bit so I can meet with potential roommates and stuff," Rose says, playing with her earring. "Before the competition."

"Will someone be with you?" I ask, frowning. "To be safe, I mean. And so you don't get ripped off."

"Yes, Jo is going out there," she says. "And trust me, I've

looked at enough sketchy Brooklyn apartments to know when I'm walking into a potential murder den."

"Why are you walking into the murder dens if you know what you're walking into?" I ask, unable to not smile, just a little.

She can't seem to hold one back either, but she smothers it. "I'll be fine, Wes. You don't need to be concerned about me anymore."

"What do you mean?" I take the stuffed toy that Murphy brings me.

Rose pauses, resting against the back of the couch. "Because we're...nothing."

What a fucking punch to the gut. *Nothing.* I recover, though.

"Not even friends?" I raise an eyebrow and toss the stuffed animal, not taking my eyes off her.

"Of course we're friends." She runs her hand down her braids, tension across her forehead. "I mean, we're not more than that."

"Rose." I stare at her. My logical side is telling me to not let those butterflies pop up in my stomach at the sight of her, but that side loses. It could never win. "First of all, I'd give a shit if we were friends. And no, I can't magically turn off my feelings. I'll worry about you for as long as I know you."

She looks back at me, not even glancing down when Murphy tries to give her the stuffed animal next. I can't read her, but also, I don't know if I want to.

"Thank you, Wes," she says softly. "I'll probably be moved out by next month. I can pay next month's rent too if you need some more time to find someone else."

"Thanks." I swallow.

"I'm going to take a nap or something." She finally takes the stuffed toy from Murphy and lightly tosses it before wandering up the stairs.

Murphy doesn't even follow — he just looks at her back, then at me, tilting his head to the side.

"I don't know either, buddy," I say.

CHAPTER TWENTY-FOUR

ROSE

I had a vision in my head of LA — nice weather, influencers, traffic — but somehow it seems muted. Everything has felt muted, a blur, for the past few days.

After winning the five grand, I moved the ticket I'd gotten to go to the cocktail competition in LA up to the soonest flight. I need an entire country's worth of space between me and Wes right now. Seeing him is too raw. Replaying every moment from the time he said he was falling in love with me to when he said goodbye.

It's so much worse than I ever thought it'd be. Especially since I'm sitting here in traffic, staring out at the hazy, gray city. I'm itching to get my hands on the liquor I need for the competition so I can take my mind off something. Running through my routine in my head doesn't work. Reading a book doesn't work. Instagram doesn't distract me - it makes things so much worse. I started following people from town and seeing all of them again makes me miss them. Miss Jepsen.

I snort and look back out the window. Missing Jepsen? Really?

Eventually my cab driver drops me off at my hotel. It's nothing fancy, but it has a bed and Jo is there, waiting. I need the moral support and she needs to use up more vacation time. I'm sure it's just an excuse for her to make sure I don't end up wallowing or getting murdered by potential roommates, but I appreciate it anyway.

"Come here," Jo says the second she sees me.

I let her hug me, because she would have done that anyway. But this hug feels different — a healing hug.

"It's fine. It's great." I force a smile. "Can we just pretend nothing is happening besides the competition and apartment hunting? Because that's what I want to focus on."

"Okay." She squeezes my shoulders, then goes to a big box on the desk in the corner. "I got all the liquor you need to practice."

"Thank you." I go over to the bottles and take a look. "I'll probably practice tonight. Ready to check out a few apartments?"

"Ready as ever."

We get into a cab, which takes us to the first apartment. I won't be able to find an apartment on my own on my budget, so I'm meeting with possible roommates. Despite the chunk of change I got and the amount of money I've been scraping together, I don't have the money to live here for all that long paying this kind of rent.

I get that gross pit in my stomach, thinking about money. I could stay in Jepsen a bit longer, keep racking up tips especially since the summer is ending and the last bump of tourism is still coming. But then I'd have to live with Wes. See him everyday. Deal with everything we could be.

Shit.

At least these first potential roommates give me the creeps right away, so we go to the next ones. They're all influencers — moderately annoying but nice enough. The rent is lower there, but not close to many things. The third and fourth are also mid, but better. I tell them I'll get back to them in the next few days.

Jo and I hop back into a cab, heading back to the hotel.

"You're really sure you want to move across the country with no job lined up?" Jo asks.

"I've already sent out a few resumés and I have a few days after the competition to search too. And I can network." I shrug. "It shouldn't be too hard to find at least a basic bartending shift, even if it sucks. Plus I have my savings if I live super lean."

"You're really antsy to leave, then," she says — just a comment, not a judgment.

"I guess I am." I sigh. Am I being stupid? Maybe. But I've figured shit out in the past and I can do it again, right?

We get back to the hotel and I channel my antsiness into preparing for the competition. I do several rounds of practicing my drink in the hotel room, with Jo watching. She gets antsy after the fourth time and I stop.

"Do you want to go out or something?" I ask with a sigh.

"Yes, because I feel like you'd do your routine until you empty those bottles." Jo hops up. "C'mon, let's go to a bourgie bar and have someone else make us drinks. Maybe you can make some connections and get inspiration."

"Okay, I guess." Being outside might be ok.

"Good, I found a place that's supposed to be amazing," she says, pushing me toward the bathroom to shower.

Back in our early twenties, we used to love getting dolled up, blasting music in the bathroom, spending too much time waffling between outfits. Now I just do the most basic shower and slap on the bare minimum of makeup and an outfit to fit the dress code. Jo looks me up and down, clearly wondering why the hell I just gave up on myself, but doesn't say it out loud.

The bar isn't far, but it takes our cab twenty minutes to get there. It's exactly the kind of place I like — atmospheric without being too pretentious. Not too loud. The bar is sparsely seated, so we sit down at the end.

"What'll you two have?" the bartender asks. She's probably around our age, with the kind of haircut that looks right in between DIY and done by a pro.

I take a glance at the small menu of cocktails. "Anything as long as it doesn't have moonshine or bourbon."

"Moonshine?" The bartender raises her pierced eyebrow and smiles. "Not a whole lot of people around here ask about that. And what about you?"

"I'll take the same," Jo says.

The bartender disappears down the bar and starts making our drinks.

"So you're not even *drinking* moonshine or bourbon?" Jo asks, drumming her deep red nails on the bar.

"I've just been drinking it a lot." It doesn't matter that the flavor of it will always remind me of Wes - I've still just had too much of it.

"Sure."

"Jo, come on. Just say it."

"You miss Wes," she says.

My eyes sting with tears but I blink them back under control. "I've been gone less than twenty-four hours."

"Yeah, but you *miss* him. Since you shot him down." Jo rests her head on her fist and studies me. She doesn't have an ounce of mocking in her tone. She's just being real. I didn't give her all that many details even when we were hanging out in person the day it happened because it was too raw, and she knew it was.

But now it's all out there and I've had at least a week to process it. All bets are off.

"I don't think I shot him down." I glance at the bartender, wishing our drinks were ready. "I just...implied that we were going in two different directions."

"But he knows about how you feel?"

"Yes." I thank the bartender when she slides us our drinks. It's just okay — too heavy on the sweetness, so it's syrupy on my tongue.

"And long distance was out of the question?" Jo takes a sip, her nose wrinkling just a little at the taste.

"Starting a relationship off as long distance feels like a bad move. And it's not like he'll leave Jepsen. His whole family business is there. And I'm not staying there. I feel like giving it all up for a guy is completely against everything I've been aspiring to," I say.

"But what if your aspirations aren't actually yours?" Jo asks. "What if they're just a reaction to everything that happened with Erik? Then you wouldn't really be giving up anything."

"What do you mean?" I swirl my drink around. It's growing on me a little bit, but I still don't love it.

"I mean, think about it. You had beef with some of the stuff going on in Erik's world while you were in it, right?" she says. I nod — it was a bit pretentious. "And yeah, there's a lot of clout and fame going on, but is that really the thing that drove you?"

I take another chip and pop it into my mouth, mulling it over. I do love making drinks, the ritual of going out, sharing drink recipes that surprise people. But the constant pissing contests, pretentiousness (which okay, I participated in before I got a grip), and schmoozing was exhausting. And the higher up Eric and I got, the less time we spent on creating recipes and doing the fun part.

"So? It just comes with the territory, right?" I ask.

"True." Jo shrugs. "But do you think you'd be happy? Because I've seen you unhappy when you claim otherwise."

"I don't know. But I want to find out, at least, before I give up and go home."

"Don't think of it as giving up — just think of it as resetting." Jo raises her glass.

"Miss Optimism." I snort and raise my glass, tapping hers to do it.

"But for real, would going back to Jepsen be that bad? You can see your family more and to be honest, it's a super cute town. Not too crazy, but there's enough stuff to keep you occupied. All you need is me," Jo says with a small smile.

"But what about Wes?" I ask. "I can't go back to him now."

"What? Why not?" Jo frowns.

"Because I already burned that bridge." I rest my elbow on the bar. "I told him I chose this over him, basically. He's probably already moved on."

Even the thought of that makes me seethe with jealousy even though he's not mine.

"Well, maybe he hasn't," Jo says. "I'm rooting for both of you. But if you decide to go through with this, I'll support you.

"How diplomatic." I sigh. "Thanks, Jo."

"You'll sort it out, Rosie. You always do." She rests her head on my shoulder for a moment, and I rest my head on hers.

"I hope so."

CHAPTER TWENTY-FIVE

WES

"Murphy?" I call out into my empty house. "Murph. Buddy, where are you?"

I walk upstairs and check in the bathroom — no matter what I try to do, he drinks out of the toilet — and my bedroom. But I find him curled up in a ball on Rose's bed. Or the guest room bed. Whatever it is now.

"C'mon, buddy." I walk into the bedroom and pet him. Murphy looks up at me with the saddest eyes I've ever seen. "You can't look at me like that."

He keeps looking at me with the saddest puppy eyes I've ever seen. Like a little asshole. But he misses her, so I can't be too annoyed.

I miss her too. Way too much. She technically isn't moved all the way out, but she's in LA, looking at apartments and prepping for the competition. One foot is out the door and I doubt she'd ever change her mind.

I sit down next to Murphy, then lay down on my side. The sheets still smell like her, the blankets still smell like her.

Murphy gets up, turns in a circle, and throws his ass onto my side with a heavy sigh.

"Yeah, I know," I mumble.

I stare at the ceiling, trying to not to think about anything except the tiny hairline crack across it that I hope isn't a bigger problem. But Rose keeps drifting back into my thoughts.

At least my phone saves me — it buzzes in my pocket, momentarily startling Murphy before he goes back to sleep. It's JD.

"Yeah?" I say.

"Come down to the bar. I need to speak with you," he says.

"About what?"

He sighs. "Can you be here in fifteen minutes? It's too much to discuss on the phone."

I grunt a yes and hang up. What is that supposed to mean? JD barely says ten words in a day but he can't tell me something over the phone?

Since I don't want to face a double amount of bullshit, I peel myself off the bed and head into town with Murphy. JD is sitting at a high-top table with his laptop, for once not frowning at the screen. Bubba is with him again, and he gets up to greet me and Murphy.

"Hey, buddy." I pat Bubba on the butt when he turns it toward me and sit across from JD. "What's up, JD?"

"Did Rose leave?" he asks, looking at his screen and tugging at his beard.

"Not officially, but we'll need a new bartender soon to fill her place," I say, glancing down at Bubba under the table. He rests his head on my foot. "I can put out an ad if you need me to."

"Please do." He closes his laptop. "Because I'm making you manager."

I stare at him for a few beats because the words just slide right through my brain. But eventually I absorb them, even if I can't believe them.

"What?" I finally ask.

JD looks at me like I'm dumb, but if I'm not imagining it, he's amused too. "I'm promoting you to manager."

"Of the bar?"

"No, of the restaurant," he deadpans. "Of the bar, yes. You'd be taking over the last few responsibilities I have. I'm too overwhelmed to do everything for the company and manage the bar. And admittedly, you do everything important."

I scan his face to see if he's joking, but I don't think JD's ever told a genuine joke in his life. I don't think he's capable.

"You're serious?" I ask, still too numb in disbelief to say anything.

"I'm always serious, yes."

"Holy shit." I rake both of my hands through my hair as the realization of what this means sinks in. "Wait, but I lost. We're going with Rose's drink."

"I know you did. But it was a test," he says. "Just to see if you'd step up. And grow up. You did, and I know you can handle everything here."

It might be because I'm exhausted and kind of miserable, but hearing those words from JD of all people hits different. First the compliment after I lost, then this?

"Have you been body-snatched?" I finally ask.

The briefest quirk of JD's mouth is the only sign that he's heard me. "No."

"Did Dad approve of this?"

"He didn't have to." He closes his laptop. "Do you want this job or not? Because you've been asking me questions and haven't said you actually want it."

"I do," I say quickly. "I'm just shocked, obviously. Ever since the incident in college, you've treated me like I'm an idiotic child."

JD leans down to grab his bag, which Murphy has put his face all the way into. "Because you were."

"Thanks," I say with a scoff.

"But you aren't now. And haven't been for a while." He nudges Murphy away. "You've actually changed and have been showing it for a while."

"Thanks," I say again, but softly. "I've actually tried."

"I can tell." He slides his laptop into his bag and closes it. "It's not an easy thing. Was it because of Rose?"

"Um...I mean." I reach down and pet Murphy so I have something to do with my hands. I'm used to JD being direct, but I'm still caught off-guard. "What do you mean?"

Did he know we were sleeping together? We never hang out socially, but word in Jepsen travels fast.

JD's eyes narrow. "What do you mean by that?"

"We can't go back and forth asking each other what we mean," I say, as if that'll distract him.

"I mean did Rose act as a positive influence on you," he says, a touch of exasperation in his tone. "You two had a rivalry and as Dad suspected, it pushed you both to create something great."

My shoulders relax. So he doesn't know. He'd bring it up if he did.

"Yeah, I guess," I say. "She's a great bartender and she's creative. We got close."

"You were sleeping together," he says in that plain way of his.

Well, never mind, then.

"I mean..." So much for us being subtle. But what's the point in lying to him if he called it out and I'm never sleeping with Rose again? "Yeah. We were. Sorry."

He hums in acknowledgement, then looks up at the ceiling. "To be honest, I assumed that something's been going on for a while. Romantic feelings."

"Jesus, if you could see it then everyone in the fucking state could." I run a hand down my cheek. My stubble isn't quite a beard yet but it's been a few days since I've shaved.

"So you were?" His eyebrows go up in genuine surprise. "You were dating? Beyond one night?"

"Yes." I can't believe I'm talking JD of all people about my love life. "But now it's not an issue. Though apparently it wasn't ever an issue if we got the job done."

"I guess not." JD pushes his hair out of his face, contemplative. "It's a shame that it didn't work out."

"Since when are you invested in who I date?"

"Since you started looking like you've died inside," he says. I can't keep the shock off my face, so he adds, "I'm not oblivious. I just usually don't give a fuck."

I have to laugh at that. "I didn't know I looked that bad."

"You do." JD shrugs and reaches down to pet Bubba. "It's...odd. You're usually not the sad one of us."

I've never thought JD hated me deep down or anything,

but he's never been particularly concerned about me beyond being up my ass about work. The fact that he is makes me feel way too good, filling a spot I didn't realize was empty. But at the same time, I must *really* look like shit for him to give me comforting words.

"I'll get over it," I say, clearing my throat. "It's fine."

JD once again pauses, but this time, he gets a faraway look in his eyes. "You sure about that?"

"What is that supposed to mean?" I hop up. "You want a drink?"

"Sure, surprise me," he says. "I mean that can you be sure you'll be over her?"

I grab a bottle of Bubba Bourbon and a few mixers, plus some maple syrup. "I don't know? How am I supposed to see the future? I just know it sucks now."

"But you've never had a serious girlfriend," he says, getting up and approaching the bar. The dogs follow. "But you caught feelings for Rose. That has to mean something big. Not something you can get over easily.

"Sounds like some romantic nonsense to me." I start mixing up a twist on an Old Fashioned. "Besides, what do you know about this? No offense. You're basically married to the business."

JD swallows. "It's not like I've never felt anything for anyone before."

I wrack my brain trying to think of any woman JD has dated beyond an awkward blind date that Mom set him up on. Maybe in college or something. I've always known that JD and I aren't close whatsoever, but now I'm realizing just how little I know about my oldest brother beyond work and sharing a bathroom when we were growing up.

"I know, but you're usually not in your feelings either." I slide one of the drinks across the bar to him.

He raises his glass and we tap them together. Bourbon's not my favorite, but this drink is pretty damn good.

"The point still stands," he says, taking a sip of his drink. "Don't think you can get over feelings when they're strong. It's not always as easy as it seems."

I look my brother in the eye. He might be a fortress, but I can tell he's speaking from experience. What happened to him? Who managed to get past his sky-high walls to get to his heart?

I doubt he'll tell me, so I keep my mouth shut and actually think of what he's saying. I've never had to get over anyone before. Even in the rare situations where a woman has turned me down, I've been able to find another — getting over someone by getting under someone else.

But the idea of sleeping with anyone else makes me physically ache for the first time in my life. And the idea of Rose doing the same?

No, fuck that. I'm not even thinking about that.

"Okay, so I shouldn't get over it," I say, resting my hand on the bar and swirling my drink with the other. "But the problem is her. She's moving across the country and doesn't want to do long distance."

JD takes a sip of his drink. "But does she have feelings for you?"

"Yes."

"Then just talk to her again once she's had the chance to finish her competition," he says. "I wish I'd tried again. The worst she can say is no again."

"Oh yeah, like that's easy." I slam the rest of my drink.

"It's either that or wonder what might have been for the rest of your life. Up to you."

"Well, shit." When he puts it that way, what choice do I have? I'd hate myself if I didn't at least see how she felt about long distance. Or fuck it, I'd move to LA for her. We'd figure *something* out. I don't even have to work for the family business anymore, not that I'm telling JD that right now. "I'll try again, then."

"Good." JD finishes his drink. "Nice drink, by the way. We should can that too."

"Let's see how everything works with Rose's drink first." I try to contain my smile.

"I've gotta go," JD says. "I have to check-in on everyone at the distillery."

"Ok. Thanks, JD," I say. "For talking to me about it."

JD's ears go red. "Don't get used to it."

I grin. "What, you don't want anyone to know you're a big ass softie deep down?"

He shoots me a glare, which makes me laugh. For once, the smallest smile appears on his face in return.

"Some people know. Just not that many." He pats me on the shoulder. "Just think about what I said. Sleep on it."

I let out a breath. "I will."

I think about it for a solid five minutes before buying a flight to LA for tomorrow.

CHAPTER TWENTY-SIX

ROSE

I got lucky with the first round of the competition in Nashville — the time between arriving and competing was much shorter.

But the final round has a bit more fanfare around it, which means schmoozing at a reception before we go to the competition. Since I need to make some connections, I dragged Jo along with me for social support.

"Wine?" Jo asks, picking up two glasses from the table around the front

"I need to be sharp for later," I say, grabbing a small plate to load up on snacks instead.

"Putting a bunch of bartenders and people who love cocktails in a room before a competition feels like a dick move." She swills her wine. "Anyway, I've got my eye out for Erik. Who should we schmooze?"

"I don't know." I scan the room.

I can't tell just from a glance, but I know that there are people in the liquor industry, as well as bar and brewery owners. Any one of them could help me out with finding a job here. I'm not shy, but something is paralyzing me.

Bless Jo for knowing me so well. She wanders closer to the end of the food table, where people are looking for conversation. One of my competitors chats with us — she's from Dallas and she's sweet. But still, my eyes wander around the room.

I spot one of the junior producers from Erik's show near the door, the one who had reached out to us in the first place. My stomach plummets to the floor. She has to be here for him.

"What? Did you see him?" Jo stands in front of me like she's trying to hide me. I'm short but I'm not *that* short.

"No, just one of the producers from his show. Sonya, I think her name is." I step out from behind Jo and of course, Sonya spots me immediately.

She waves and I wave back, wishing I could down some wine. Instead, I just take a deep breath and let it out.

"Hey, Rose, right?" Sonya asks. She's beautifully put together in a sleek pantsuit that seems like it should be too much for the occasion, but isn't. Her dark hair is slicked back into a ponytail

"Yeah, Sonya?" I ask. She nods. "Good to see you again. This is my best friend, Jo."

"Good to see you too, and nice to meet you, Jo." Sonya shakes Jo's hand. "So are you here for the competition? I saw your name on the list."

"Yeah. I'm a bit nervous and wish it were happening right now," I admit.

"Don't be nervous." She squeezes my shoulder. Even though we barely know each other, the gesture doesn't feel overly familiar. "You're super talented. I'm surprised you didn't guest post more on Erik's blog, at least officially. I loved that drink you put together at one of the meetings we had."

I bite the inside of my cheek hard enough for it to hurt. "We collaborated a lot on the drinks and posts, so there's more of me on the blog than you think."

"And your Instagram," Sonya adds, pulling out her phone. "You've been working with Stryker Liquors? I like the social media posts I've been seeing with you. And the things you've cross-posted. Very cool."

"Thank you." My face heats up. It's nothing fancy or high effort, especially in comparison to what I used to do for Erik, but I still think they've turned out well.

"Speaking of, we've been playing around with the idea for a cocktail show that's super approachable and fun. It's not a show on the network, but our YouTube channel is growing fast. We've even created a studio out here to make it even more official," she says. "Maybe we could discuss a concept that you could star in."

"Oh, for real?" I blurt.

Thankfully, Sonya just smiles. "Of course. I really loved you in the meetings and I was upset that my boss reworked the deal to cut you out of it.

"Thank you," I say. I'd liked her a lot too out of everyone there.

I should feel elated — isn't this what I wanted? To have a show, which could lead to opening a bar and having a brand? The idea still sounds nice, but it's not hitting as hard as I figured it would when I was daydreaming about it.

It's probably just my nerves getting the better of me.

Sonya leans forward after glancing around. "To be honest, it's not going too well with Erik. But you didn't hear that from me."

That gets a smile from me. "Really?"

"I don't know for sure. Might just be a rumor mill." She digs through her bag. "I've gotta run to another meeting, but let's meet for coffee. Are you in LA for a while?

"Yes. For a few more days. I'm looking for roommates and a job," I say.

"You're moving out here? Even better." She pulls out her phone. "I'm actually heading out of town the day after tomorrow, so maybe we can exchange numbers and connect if you aren't free then? Maybe this job is a perfect fit."

"Sure."

I text myself from her phone so she has my number, and include my email address.

"And here's my card," she says, handing me a little embossed square of paper. "Good luck!"

Sonya waves and weaves through the crowd toward the door. Jo barely contains herself, squeezing my arm.

"Oh my god, Rosie, that's amazing!" she says, barely keeping her voice low. "Imagine if you got a show and Erik lost his."

"That would be crazy," I say, putting a cracker into my mouth.

Jo's brows furrow. "I figured you'd be doing backflips at that kind of news."

"I think I'm just nervous about the competition," I say, tucking the card into my bag. "I'm sure it'll feel better after the competition."

"YOU'VE GOT THIS, ROSIE," Jo says, massaging my shoulders like I'm about to go into a boxing match and not a cocktail-making competition. "Just breathe and don't look around."

My stomach is somewhere in my throat, and I'm sweating under my boobs. I've practiced this routine so many times that I could do it in my sleep, but doing it in front of judges — with Erik in the room — makes me feel like I'm going to forget it all. Shit, what if I do?

"You've got all the muscle memory in the world on your side," she adds. "And you look hot."

"Thanks." I laugh, rubbing my sweaty hands on my skirt. "I just need to go to the bathroom again."

"Okay, I'll be out here."

I weave my way through the groups of people clustered outside of the event hall, keeping my eyes down in case Erik is around. The bathroom is bustling with women who are either getting ready to compete or supporting someone who is. I quickly do my business, then check over my makeup as I wash my hands.

I look fine. It's going to be fine. A five-minute routine, then I've done everything I can do. I can think about everything else later.

I head back out, then I'm immediately ushered into the hall to wait to do my routine. Unlike before, we all have to sit through everyone else's routines. I hate that my last name isn't at the beginning of the alphabet. Then again, it could be worse. At least I don't have to be seated next to Erik, whose last name starts with a Q. And I don't have to get psyched out by seeing him go, probably using a drink recipe I created.

I watch everyone else go, my stomach twisting in knots the entire time. Everyone is *good*. Their presentations are smooth and they're using ingredients together in a unique, novel way. Does mine measure up?

"Rose Nicholls," the moderator calls. "You're up next. Please set up your station."

I stand on shaky legs and set up, visualizing my set up. Once I'm ready, I shove down my nerves and start my routine. The judges watch intently as I run through the drink I created. Wes's words of encouragement from the first round — that it's all muscle memory from here – help me a lot. I relax a little, letting autopilot take over without losing focus.

Once I'm done, a middle-aged judge sitting at the end smiles at me. Is it an approving smile? A polite smile? I can't tell. I just have to wait for them to judge everyone.

"Thank you, Ms. Nicholls. You can clear your station and be seated," he says.

I pack up my things and head back to the crowd. Erik and I lock eyes for a moment, but I brush him off. I don't want to give him any ammo against me.

There are fewer competitors this time, so Erik goes two people after me. I bite back a laugh, thinking of what Wes said about Erik looking like a mime going to prom. He *still* does. I barely manage to snuff the laughter out and watch him do his routine.

He adjusts his hair in the front, his nervous tic, and begins. As I suspected, he's doing a riff off an original drink I made for the blog. My blood simmers. What can I do at this point? He presents it well, which kind of sums up this whole situation — he can't create anything original, but he does a damn good job of selling it.

He finishes up and heads back over to where we're all seated, locking eyes with me and smirking. Fucking asshole.

One of the judges gets up and tells us we're dismissed while they calculate the results. I head outside and manage to get out before Erik can catch up to me just to piss me off.

I find Jo in the crowd and she pulls me into a hug.

"You did so great!" she says. "I know you'll win."

"Thanks for the vote of confidence, but did you see everyone else?" I glance around. "They were good. But as long as I beat Erik, I don't care."

I smell Erik's cologne before I see him.

"You think you can beat me?" Erik asks.

"Fuck off, Erik," Jo says before I can say it myself.

"Nice job using my drink," I add. "You added a lot of flair to that presentation."

Erik was more of a passive aggressive, stew-in-his-anger kind of guy, not a immediate spark one, so the irritation in his face makes my heart race. It's like someone flipped a switch inside him to set off a bomb. He's not a huge guy but he's more than big enough to intimidate me. And he wouldn't make a scene here, would he?

"Rose, it's not your damn drink," he says. "Get over it."

I shrink back on reflex, straight into a big, warm chest. Just from the way his hands grip my shoulders, I know it's Wes, and I sag in relief. I don't know why he's here, or when he arrived, but I just feel *safe.*

"Back the fuck up," Wes says, putting his hand out to put distance between me and Erik. "If you want to start shit, I'm more than happy to finish it."

CHAPTER TWENTY-SEVEN

WES

I've done a lot of dumb shit, but flying to LA to win Rose back might be the dumbest. Or at least the most impulsive. I shouldn't add to the dumbassery by punching her piece of shit ex like he deserves.

They spoke for about five seconds before he looked like he was about to do something awful, and I had to step in. Fuck this mime-looking piece of shit. He's never going to breathe the same air as my girl again.

"Who are you?" Erik asks.

"Doesn't matter." I step into his space and he takes a step back. He's long and lanky, just a few inches shorter than me, but I have a lot more muscle. "You don't have any business with her, so you can fucking leave. Or I could make you leave."

The one upside to being kind of a dickhead when I was younger is knowing that the other guy should always take a swing first — then anything else can just be self-defense.

"We *do* have business," he says, stepping into my space. I grin. I could kick this guy's ass in my sleep.

"Do you?" I glance at Rose over my shoulder. "Do you have business with this guy, Rose?"

"No."

"There you go." I say. "Get the fuck out of her face."

"I still don't know who you are, but you don't know anything about this." He steps around me and grabs Rose's wrist, yanking her forward. "Let's talk in private."

I shove him off of her, crowding his space until I slam him against the nearest wall. His eyes widen in shock. Is he really surprised that I'd be fucking furious that he's touching my girl? Especially against her will?

He better consider his next choices carefully, or I'll do more than push him against a wall.

"Don't fucking touch her, or I can make this a whole lot more painful for you," I say in a low voice, inches away from him. "I suggest you walk away so I don't kick your fucking ass once state over."

He looks me in the eye for a moment, and I clench my fist, ready to defend myself. But he just scoffs and pushes past me, walking away. The crowd watching disperses, pretending that nothing happened, thankfully. I take a few breaths and finally turn around to face Rose again.

She looks achingly beautiful, especially after this short time apart. Once I'm over the jolt of seeing her again, I actually take in her expression. In my worst daydreams, I imagined her being pissed off at me coming, or worse, completely not interested.

But she's smiling, her eyes warm.

"Hi," she says softly.

"Hey." I can't help but smile too, gently taking her wrist. "Did he hurt you?"

"No. It just hurt for a second," she says. She holds her hand up when I suck in a breath. "I'm fine, Wes. I swear."

I kiss the inside of her wrist anyway.

"Sorry I missed you competing," I say. "I should have been here."

"Wes, I didn't even know you'd come at all." Her brows furrow a bit. "Wait, why are you here?"

"To support you. And tell you that I want to find a way to make this work." I gesture between the two of us.

Rose blinks a few times in a row. "But you might have to leave Jepsen."

"I don't care," I say, tilting her head back. "I'll figure it out because I love you. I love your ambition and tenacity and the fact that you always keep me on my toes. I'd regret not giving us a shot for the rest of my life."

"Wes." Rose steps into my arms and rests her forehead on my chest. I wrap my arms around her and rest my chin on top of her head. Feeling her in my arms calms me down a little bit. She fits just right.

"What are you thinking, baby?" I ask.

"That this feels too good to be true and I'm scared," she says in a small voice that I can barely hear.

"Why is it too good to be true?" I ask, running my hand up and down her back.

"Because I love you and I didn't think I ever would love anyone again. Especially not you."

I burst out laughing, even though my heart is growing a thousand sizes from hearing her say she loves me too. "Especially not me?"

"No." She looks up at me. "You drove me nuts back in the day. I thought you'd be just as reckless and immature but you've shown me that you've grown. But you're still kind and a good friend and funny, and —."

"Hold on, hold on." I squeeze her shoulders and grin. "Did you say I was actually funny? Can you say that again?"

"Oh my god, stop," she says with a laugh. "You know what I mean."

"I know." I hold her again.

"I'm sorry I ran," she says into my shirt. "I was so stupid."

"Nah, you were scared. Which makes sense to me. And is it really running if you were coming here anyway?" I kiss her forehead. She's just tall enough to make forehead kisses easy, so I know exactly what I'm going to be giving her everyday. "But we're good now, right?"

"Very good." She smiles up at me. "And I want to go back to Jepsen."

"For real?" I ask, frowning. "You're sure? Because I'll figure out how to be wherever you are. I don't want you to give up anything just for me."

"No, I'm not giving anything up. I want to be in Jepsen. It feels like home again," she says. "And I think I was trying to get out of there for the wrong reasons. I know that making drinks makes me happy, and I still want to own a bar someday. But doing it all the way across the country and trying to do it all on my own just to prove a point to some asshole who doesn't matter to me anymore doesn't make sense."

My heart flips in my chest again and I squeeze her tight. For once, I'm at a loss for words. Rose will be back with me. We'll be able to be together. Work together.

"But have you gotten a new bartender yet?" she asks. "And what about—"

"Doesn't matter. JD promoted me to manager, so if I say you stay, you stay."

"Really?" Her face lights up. "Congrats."

"Thanks. I have a lot of ideas to make the bar even better. Hell, maybe if this drink thing works out we can start another bar or something," I say. "Whatever you want, we'll do. Okay?"

She smiles so hard that dimples appear in her cheeks. "Okay."

I lean down and kiss her like it's the first time. In some ways it is, I guess. Is it a bit much for being in public? Maybe. But I don't fucking care. I just care that we're here, and she's in my arms.

"We've calculated the scores for the championship," someone says over a loudspeaker. "Please go to Hall B for the results. Hall B."

Rose swallows and takes my hand so we can walk over together. Jo finds us as well — thankfully she gave us a little space during that whole situation. She hugs Rose before Rose heads over to where the competitors are seated, so Jo and I find a spot to sit together.

"Nice work," Jo says, crossing one leg over the other.

"Thanks. I wouldn't have been able to pull it off if you didn't answer my texts," I reply.

"I know Rose well. I could feel her misery even before I got here." Jo snorts. "I'm just glad she's happy. But if you hurt her, I'll —"

"Rip my balls off and throw them into an incinerator?"

She blinks. "Specific, but it works."

"I won't. I promise." I'd rather rip my own balls off than make her feel anything less than amazing.

"Okay," a man in a suit says as he adjusts the mic at the podium. "We'd like to thank all of our competitors this year. It was a very tough decision, as all the cocktails and presentations were incredible."

I shift in my seat. Even if Rose isn't going to use the prize money or the clout from this to build a life out here, I still want her to win.

"In third place is Blanche Lyons, from Dallas, Texas," the man says.

The crowd cheers, and a blonde woman jobs up the steps. A woman standing next to the podium hands her a small trophy.

"It's fine," I say to Jo, even though she didn't react. "She could still be second or first."

"And in second place is Dylan Wu, of Miami, Florida," the announcer says.

A section of the crowd goes nuts for Dylan, who strides up on stage and accepts a slightly larger trophy. My stomach twists in knots. If it's her shitbag ex who wins, I'm going to lose it.

"And our grand prize winner is..." The announcer pauses for a moment. "Rosalie Villegas, of Oklahoma City."

My shoulders sag and my stomach sinks, even as Rosalie's family and friends cheer. I lean forward to lock eyes with Rose, who gives me a small smile and a thumbs up.

"It's okay," she mouths.

Once Rosalie gets her huge trophy, the crowd starts to disperse. I see Rose's ex stalk off by himself, the asshole.

"That kind of sucks," Rose says when she reaches us.

"You seem very okay with this," Jo says, her eyes flicking to mine.

"I am. Because I know that in the big scheme of things, it doesn't matter." She laces her fingers in mine. "I still made a great drink and I still get to go to home to a great job and a great boyfriend."

"Boyfriend, huh?" I grin and put a hand around her waist.

"Of course." Rose leans into my touch.

I'm going to marry her someday, not that she knows that yet. But I know it for a fact already.

But instead of saying that, I just kiss her on the forehead again. She'll know soon enough.

CHAPTER TWENTY-EIGHT

ROSE

LA is a lot more fun with Wes *and* Jo. We spend the next few days exploring as tourists, which is a hell of a lot better than trying to find an apartment and a job at the last minute. I don't know what I was thinking.

We go to Disneyland and drive up the coast, taking every opportunity to be tourists. In just a few short days, we've all gotten a lot of sun and we have to part ways — with Wes and I heading back to Jepsen, and Jo going back to New York. It sucks to see her leave again, but she's already planning a visit.

But being back in Jepsen now that Wes and I are together feels just right.

"No, don't," I mumble as I feel Wes start to peel away from me in bed. We're squished into his, with both Murphy and Dennis in there too. Somehow Dennis is taking up the most space despite being the smallest.

"I need to make your coffee. We have that meeting with my dad and JD later, remember?"

"Shoot, right." His dad wants to meet with us today, presumably to talk to us about the drink again.

"Want me to bring it to you?" Wes kisses the back of my neck.

"Yes, please." I smile and roll over. "Thank you."

He leans down and kisses me on the forehead before leaving. He's in nothing but his boxers, so I admire the view as he walks away.

I roll over onto my stomach and grab my phone. I've been posting on Instagram more now that I'm kind of over the whole situation with Erik. Some of my followers comment, saying they're happy to see me posting my own stuff consistently again. Most of the social media duties for Stryker Liquors have been shifted back to their intern, though apparently they want to hire someone else to do it full time soon.

I scroll through, liking a few comments, before shifting over to my email. An email from Sonya is at the top.

My heart skips — with everything going on with Wes and the competition, I'd somehow completely forgotten that we were supposed to connect at some point.

"What is it?" Wes asks, coming back with two mugs of coffee.

"An email from this producer at the network where I was supposed to meet up with. She had an idea for a show on their YouTube channel and wanted to see if I'd want to star in it," I say, taking my mug.

"Really? That's great," he says, scooping up Dennis with one hand and getting back into bed. "What'd she say?"

I open the email and take a sip of my coffee. "Oh, it's long."

Hi Rose!

Sorry it took me a while to get back to you. Things have been a shit show — I'm sure you've heard Erik's show fell through because of creative differences (him being an ass, but you didn't hear that from me), so now we're trying to fill his slot.

"Holy shit, Erik's show fell through," I say.

"No shit?" Wes cranes his neck to look at my phone and I turn to show it to him. "That's amazing news."

I keep reading.

And that's where you come in. We think we could take that concept I mentioned to you in person to network TV. We'd make it big — we think you have the flair and the cocktail knowledge to make mixology accessible to a whole new group of people. The full concept is below.

The rest of the email details the concept — it would involve me going to a lot of bars in the LA area, trying drinks, talking to owners, things like that. Sort of like *Diners, Drive-Ins, and Dives*, but with a focus on unusual cocktails.

It sounds like something I'd watch. But being the person in it? It would have appealed to me not long ago, especially since I could rub it in Erik's face. But now I just want to leave Erik in my rearview mirror. He'll always be kind of miserable anyway, just because he's an asshole. Plus, this job wouldn't let me do what I love the most – coming up with drink ideas.

"This sounds cool and all, but I think I'm going to pass," I say after Wes finishes reading it.

Wes frowns. "Are you sure? Being on TV would be a huge boost for you. You'd make more than enough to open a bar. We could figure out how you could stay in LA for a while, then come back. Might be a pain, but I'm assuming you won't be filming for an entire year at once."

"Yeah, but I would be more of a TV personality and not someone who makes drinks all day. I love that part — the creativity. I want to be able to see regulars and make their favorite drinks. I want to create their favorite spot. Or maybe we can work on more drink ideas too, if we expand the canned drinks. There's more than one way for me to open a bar someday."

"That sounds perfect if you're sure." He kisses my temple.

"I think I'm sure. I'll email her back."

I email her back while we drink our coffee and cuddle in bed. Then, we take Murphy out for a walk before getting ready and heading into the Stryker Liquor offices.

The offices are kind of retro, and his dad's office looks like a parody of a fancy businessman's office. JD and Mr. Stryker are sitting and waiting. I'm not intimidated by them anymore, but I have no idea what this is about.

"So," Mr. Stryker says as we sit down. "I have an offer for you both."

Wes opens his mouth to say something, but closes it. It was probably a joke.

"We'd like to continue to expand our drink offerings," Mr. Stryker says. "We haven't been particularly organized about this in the past, but since we want to expand, we want to make an official position within the company to continue to churn out drink recipes for the canned drinks and for the bar and distillery. Is this something either of you are interested in?"

He leans back in his big leather seat. I glance at Wes,

who looks more relaxed than I've ever seen him around his dad.

"I think Rose would be perfect for it," Wes says.

"I was about to say the same thing." I study Wes's face. "You'd be great at it."

"So would you. And what's better experience for starting your own bar than developing drinks?" He shrugs, then looks to his dad and brother. "Rose should do it."

"It'll probably be part time at first," JD adds. "But eventually it'll be full time."

"So I can work at the bar and at the office?" I ask.

"Yeah, we can fix your schedule to do that," Wes says.

"I don't know what to say." I swallow.

"Just say yes." Mr. Stryker almost smiles, which feels like a massive victory.

This is the exact thing I wanted and it's falling right into my lap? I've been on a lucky streak so far — so why not?

"Then yes," I say.

EPILOGUE
WES

One year later

"Don't fuck this up for me," I say to Dennis, who's sitting on the corner of the kitchen counter. He meows in response, his tail twitching. "Thanks for the vote of confidence."

I open the oven and stick a knife into the cinnamon buns. It comes out clean, so I pull them out.

I hope the engagement ring I baked in here stood up well. Otherwise, I'll either poison us or ruin the proposal I've been agonizing over for weeks. The cinnamon rolls have a lot less stickiness in them than usual, just to make it easier to find the little plastic ring holder out at the right time, but I'm hoping the proposal will make up for the milder flavor.

I check the time. Today is Rose's birthday, so she's sleeping in. The plan is to propose to her with the cinnamon buns, have a celebratory fuck session, go to the rental cabin where we went for her birthday last year, and fool around some more. Then, we'll have a party up there with all our friends and family to celebrate.

Assuming she says yes. It's not like I'm springing this on her out of nowhere, but still — this is the biggest thing I've ever had to ask someone.

Murphy trots down the stairs and goes into the living room, which means Rose isn't far behind. I shoo Dennis away from stepping onto the cinnamon buns and shake some sprinkles on top. Rose shuffles downstairs, yawning. Her hair is still wrapped in its scarf and she's wearing one of my t-shirts, which reaches her knees. She's still the sexiest woman I've ever seen.

"Happy birthday, babe," I say.

"Are those cinnamon buns?" she asks with another yawn.

"Yep. And your coffee." I hand her mug to her and she gives me a sleepy smile. I kiss her softly on the lips.

"Thank you." She takes a sip of the coffee and gives me a little satisfied smile. "And the buns."

"The buns." I grip the edge of the counter so she doesn't notice my hands shaking. "Want me to plate up a roll?"

I put the ring toward the middle since she likes the middle roll.

"Yes please." She leans against the counter, doing a little dance.

I carefully use the spatula to take out the middle piece. Hopefully the small plastic ball isn't peeking out. When I slide it onto a little plate and pass it to her with a fork.

"Thank you." She takes the tiniest bit off the corner, to my dismay. I want her to dig in and run into the ring already. "Don't you want some?"

My stomach is churning, but I never turn down food. "Sure."

I give myself one roll and poke at it, watching Rose's every bite. Until she polishes it off and the ball holding the ring isn't there.

Fuck. I know that I put it in the middle one. Right?

I woke up ass early to make these, but surely I didn't fuck up that bad. Surely. Her ring isn't huge but it did set me back a healthy chunk of cash.

"What are we doing today?" she asks, slicing another roll in half.

I need to figure out where the fuck the ring went, but I can't tell her that.

"I'm going to go see if Waylon wants to walk the dog with us," I say. "And we can talk about it then."

"Mmkay." She digs into her other roll and starts looking at her phone.

I walk as calmly as I can to the door, then sprint the short distance to Waylon's. I burst into the back door.

"Waylon!" I yell.

Duke greets me with a bark, appearing around the corner. Waylon's always awake ass early, so I find him in the kitchen, putting together food for Duke and Sadie, the Pomeranian he's watching until the person who inherited her shows up in town. He feeds the dogs better than he feeds himself.

"What? What's wrong?" he asks, putting his spoon down.

"I lost the fucking ring. It's not in the cinnamon rolls," I say.

Waylon closes his eyes for a second. "What? How?"

"I don't fucking know!" I dig my hands through my hair.

Sadie senses my distress and stands on my foot, her front paws on my shin. "What do I do?"

"Hell if I know." Waylon goes back to making his dogs' breakfast. "Is it in another roll?"

"No, it's supposed to be smack in the middle because that's her favorite piece." I start to pace and Duke follows me, whimpering.

"Relax, Duke," Waylon says, turning to give Duke his slow feeder. Duke snaps to attention, licking his lips. I wait for Waylon to put the food down, then give Duke the release command. Sadie waits patiently and gets her food next.

"What do I do?" I ask again.

"We need to search the house, I guess." Waylon grabs a t-shirt and tugs it on. "Can you distract Rose?"

"I can."

We go into the house and find Rose where I left her.

"Happy birthday," Waylon says.

"Thank you." She smiles.

"Why don't you go take a hot bath while we prepare the next part of your birthday?" I ask. "It's a surprise."

"Yeah!" She finishes her bite and traipses upstairs. Murphy follows.

The moment we hear the water start running, we fly into action.

I hack up the cinnamon rolls, trying to see if the ring shifted somehow. Nope. Waylon digs through the cabinets and checks the floor. I tear apart the bedroom and search through the living room too. Nothing. Nowhere. *Fuck.*

"I don't know, Wes." Waylon rests his hand on his hips.

My stomach is completely in knots. I drag my hands through my hair a few times and take a breath.

"Fuck. This isn't how I wanted this day to go," I say.

"Babe?" Rose calls from upstairs. The tremor in her voice sets me on high alert and I rush toward her. "What's this?"

Rose is standing in the middle of the stairs, clutching the neck of her robe closed. And in her hand is a slightly chewed-plastic ball where I put her ring.

"Um...where did you find that?" I ask.

"Murphy was holding it in his mouth." She plucks the ring out of it, her fingers shaking. "Is this a ring?"

"Yeah." I clear my throat. Fuck it, I'll roll with it. I get on one knee. "Will you marry me, Rose?"

Rose stands at the top of the stairs, clutching the railing. For a second I think she's going to run back up the stairs, but instead she runs down and practically tackles me.

"Yes!" She leaps up, wrapping her legs around my middle and her arms around my neck. "Oh my god. I can't believe this. Why was in it in one of those little balls you get out of the machine with a quarter?"

"Because. It was a whole thing. It was supposed to be in the cinnamon rolls." I laugh, kissing her. She's shaking like a leaf. "And I guess Murphy got it."

"At least he didn't eat it." She studies the ring. It's simple, but sparkly. "It's so pretty."

"Put it on."

She hands it to me and I slide it onto her ring finger. It looks perfect.

"I love it." She admires the ring, still clinging onto me like a koala.

I kiss her, even though I'm smiling so hard that our lips hardly touch. Thank god this clusterfuck solved itself without disaster. I hike her up higher, my hands going under her ass.

Waylon coughs. I forgot he was even there. I put my hands back into safer spots without dropping her.

"I got the video of that," Waylon says. "Just the proposal, I mean."

"Send it to us." Rose buries her face into my neck, and I carry her across the room. "Did you know that I bet Sabrina that you'd propose today?"

"No shit?" I hadn't told Sabrina — or anyone but Waylon. How did she guess?

"Yeah. She said she saw you at the jewelry store." Rose unwraps her legs from my waist and puts her feet down. "Others probably know."

Fuck. I didn't think anyone had been paying attention to me that hard, but apparently not.

"Small town bullshit," I say with a sigh.

"But you love it."

"I do." I kiss her forehead. "And I love that you're here with me."

THANKS FOR READING! Want a sweet and steamy bonus epilogue featuring Wes and Rose a few years in the future? Sign up for my newsletter at https://BookHip.com/GPFTFPG and download it free! You'll also get updates on my upcoming books, looks behind the scenes, and some A+ memes.

ABOUT THE AUTHOR

Audrey Vaughn is a spicy small town romcom author who will show you all the memes and dog photos on her camera roll. She lives with her husband in Florida despite hating to sweat.

You can follow her on Instagram at @audreyvaughnbooks for some of these memes, plus updates on her upcoming books.

Printed in Dunstable, United Kingdom

65345499R00163